Second Growth

Town of Westwick

BOOKS BY WALLACE STEGNER
AVAILABLE IN BISON BOOK EDITIONS

All the Little Live Things (BB 709)
*Beyond the Hundredth Meridian: John Wesley Powell
and the Second Opening of the West* (BB 798)
The Big Rock Candy Mountain (BB 855)
Joe Hill (BB 728)
Mormon Country (BB 778)
The Spectator Bird (BB 705)
Wolf Willow (BB 708)
The Women on the Wall (BB 710)
Second Growth (BB 940)
The Sound of Mountain Water (BB 946)

WALLACE STEGNER

Second
Growth

University of Nebraska Press
Lincoln and London

First Bison Book printing: 1985
Most recent printing indicated by the first digit below:
1   2   3   4   5   6   7   8   9   10

A Note on Fictional Character

The making of fiction entails the creation of places and persons with all the seeming of reality, and these places and persons, no matter how a writer tries to invent them, must be made up piecemeal from sublimations of his own experience and his own acquaintance. There is no other material out of which fiction can be made.

In that sense, and in that sense only, the people and the village of this story are taken from life. The village I have tried to make is one that would exist anywhere in rural New England; though it is placed in northern New Hampshire, I hope it would have been just as much at home in Vermont or Maine, or even in western Massachusetts. The people are such people as this village seems to me likely to contain, and the cultural dynamism, the conflict on the frontier between two ways of life, which is its central situation, is one that has been reproduced in an endlessly changing pattern all over the United States. It should be, if I have been successful, as visible in Carmel-by-the-Sea or Taos or Charlevoix as on the fictitious Ammosaukee River. These people and their village took form in my mind not as portraits but as symbols. There are no portraits, personal or geographical, in the novel.

Library of Congress Cataloging in Publication Data
Stegner, Wallace Earle, 1909—
Second growth.
Reprint. Originally published:
Boston : H. Mifflin, 1947.
I. Title.
PS3537.T316S4   1985
813'.52   85-8540
ISBN 0-8032-9157-4 (pbk.)

Reprinted by arrangement with Wallace Stegner,
represented by Brandt & Brandt Literary Agents, Inc.

For Mary

Contents

Second Growth

1

God Wants You to Be a Good Girl

WHEN HELEN CAME DOWNSTAIRS in her raincape her mother was standing in the open front door, bending to peer up past the porch roof at the sky. 'Looks if the world was in a bag with the puckerstring pulled,' she said. When she spoke she whistled sharply around the loose edges of her plate.

'I wish it could ever manage not to rain on Friday nights,' Helen said.

Mrs. Barlow pushed the screen half open to see around the corner of the house. 'Car parked up to the school.'

Helen looked. The dark rainy shapes of church and manse cut off the square at the foot of the hill, but she could see over the roofs to the school, where the yellow eyes of a car glowed in the drizzle.

'That's probably Mattie getting her things,' she said.

'Seems if she might've done that when school let out.'

'When she left she didn't know but what she'd be back,' Helen said.

She went into the dining room and got the stamp and pad from a drawer. Her father sat under the fringed floor lamp in the wide-armed Morris chair he had had old Mr. Mills make him out of butternut wood. His feet in their elastic-sided slippers were up on the padded stool. They did not look like the feet of a paralytic. He read aloud from the paper without paying any attention to who was listening.

'Farm life curbs delinquency,' he said. 'The homespun

1

pleasures of the farm, such as animal pets, help reduce the problem of delinquency among rural juveniles, according to the essays submitted by the seventh grade pupils of the Berlin Mills school in a recent contest.'

As Helen passed him she saw his sagging, gray-bristled face, the tightening dewlap under his jaw as he lifted his chin, searching the columns of the Woodsville *Gazette* for things to read that nobody listened to. She supposed it gave a kind of purpose to his life.

'Good night, Pa,' she said.

He did not reply. Her mother moved aside in the doorway. 'It's Mattie, all right. I saw her come out with some things.' The whistle was so sharp on the last words that she exclaimed in irritation and shoved the plate against the roof of her mouth with her thumb.

'You sound as if you're tickled to death Mattie's leaving,' Helen said.

Her mother's face was placid. 'Well, ain't you? Now you've got yourself a job that fits your place in the village I can savor it a mite, can't I?'

Without answering, Helen went past her off the porch. Rain rattled on the papery cape, stung her face. The drive which came up the hill to her house and the church was dark and steep, and she felt her way until the blurred windows of the Richie house and one sputtering street light showed her the street flowing down into the square, with the terraced lawns of the inn wet and glistening above it. Going down along the hill under the inn she hurried, touched with an old obsessional fear that the whole hill, and her house, the church, the manse, and the inn with it, might suddenly slide down and obliterate the village. As soon as she crossed the square she could see on to the Grange Hall, where a drowned cone of light fell from above the door. With her cape held around her and her head down she ran for it.

The hall was deserted. In the entrance hall Helen set up her table, laid out stamp and pad, got the stained cash drawer from the cupboard. When she snapped on the lights the dance-floor inside the wide doors looked shabbier and emptier than it had in the half dark. The noise of her heels echoed. For a moment she stood looking around the big room with distaste. Against the walls the folding chairs looked brittle and paralytic; she found herself counting their stiff yellow backs as she sometimes counted the days, or the hours of an afternoon. At the far end, above the piano, the American flag looked as if a stir of wind would whip dust out of its folds.

She sat down and waited. The empty entrance hall, with only her own cape hanging up and her own wet tracks on the floor, already smelled like all hallways on rainy days, as if the merest touch of moisture brought out the old odors of rubbers and oilskins and the woollen steam of clothes and the smell of wetted dust.

It was all, she thought drearily, like the beginning of a movie — a sterile, lackluster scene with a lonely girl at a lonely table in the middle of it. From the high godlike angle of the camera she watched and pitied herself. But as the camera continued its steady quiet stare she grew afraid. She herself was part of the paralysis that gripped the hall and her home and the whole town. No effort of will could break the catalepsy that held her rigid there under the yellow lights in the empty room.

She was very close to terrified when the first feet scuffed on the porch and the door opened to show her the welcome heads and faces and the light-silvered streaks of rain.

There were several different kinds of people who went to the village dances, and several different reasons for going. Village people went because they liked the music and crowds and the sense of frolic. Many summer people — professors and economists and prep school masters and Hartford lawyers and writers and who not — went because they thought the dances quaint survivals of a simpler and more wholesome past. They came in droves, with an antiquarian interest in learning the figures of 'Duck to the Oyster' or the Portland Fancy. Though they habitually tangled up the sets beyond anyone's untangling, and irritated the village people halfway to homicide, they were very good-natured about the whole business. That was the principal quality of the older summer people, that invincible good nature in the face of failure or clumsiness. Their next most notable quality was their violence. When they learned anything they performed it with enormous expenditures of energy, and most of them carried bandannas to wipe off the sweat. Their wives wore dirndls and were as active as their husbands.

There was also the younger summer crowd, the boys crop-haired and brown, dressed in jeans and sneakers. They were wilder than their elders, and louder. Their girls wore tennis dresses and were tanned and solid-legged and with large lung space. This crowd had acquired somewhere the knowledge of how to do the Rhinelander, the Butterfly Polka, and the Varsoviana, and a good deal of their time was spent in trying to induce the orchestra to play appropriate music. When they succeeded, the rest of the village cleared off the floor. It wasn't safe to stay.

Altogether, young and old, the summer people constituted a muscular school of the dance. Their shirts stuck to their backs long before any villager began to get warm. When they swung their partners they cleared a space fifteen feet in diameter. When they promenaded they pranced; in a *dos à dos* or a grand right and left they minced and bounced. Their smiles stuck to their sweaty faces and their hair fell in their eyes and they were very happy and well-exercised. Also, they were invariably annoyed when the orchestra played anything but a square or contra dance. When waltzes or one-steps were being played, the summer people left the floor and hung around the fringes looking either aggrieved or amused.

But the village people, who thought square dances old-fashioned and were a little embarrassed to find them suddenly quaint, preferred 'Three O'Clock in the Morning' to the 'Wabash Cannonball,' and much preferred the freedom of the half-empty hall when a waltz was played to the chaos that ensued when the summer people charged joyfully into sets for a quadrille.

The youngest village crowd, especially the girls, liked foxtrots. When they got one — and they seldom did — they went at it with a cold ferocity that was almost terrifying. Most of the boys their age knew only square dances, or were too bashful to take a chance on anything new in front of all those eyes. So the girls danced together, just as they had done when they learned their steps in the school washroom during lunch hours. They went like tightly-wound dolls, very erect, staring straight ahead. Since most of the summer people withdrew from foxtrots as from waltzes and one-steps, the girls had a clear field to go whirling, knee-dipping, walking front, walking back. All over the floor their heads bobbed down as the knee-dip came. It was rather odd to watch, because the heads went down and came up again so stiffly, like the heads of base-weighted dolls that cannot be tipped over.

From the doorway, after Mrs. Bentham relieved her of ticket-taking, Helen watched one of these foxtrots. She had taken people's money, stamped their wrists 'Paid' in purple ink, smiled into many faces, made change and ac-

knowledged congratulations on her new job. Most of the
people she knew, both summer people and villagers,
were there, and all the things that had shaped and bounded her life. The solid respectability of the village, the
Pratts and the Benthams and the Browns, breathed the
same warm dust as the disreputables, the Mounts and
the Bradfords and the hot-eyed French youths from down
around the Corners.

She had seen James Mount come pushing through the
crowd, his saxophone held above his head and his toothless mouth a black hole of laughter. She had smelled his
whiskey breath ten feet away, and seen in his wake old
Will Bradford and James's adopted daughter Vina,
round-shouldered and insolent-eyed. A little pang had
touched Helen then, and it touched her again now as she
watched the high-school girls dance together in mechanical dips and turns while the summer people withdrew to
look on.

If you were a sensitive person, she thought, you would
always have to withdraw. You couldn't participate in
anything so clownish and clumsy.

The music stopped for an instant, then switched with
only the briefest break into 'Gone but not Forgotten.' Will
Bradford was out of tune with his fiddle, and James
missed notes now and then on his saxophone, and slid
frantically to pick them up. Helen watched him aim the
sax between his feet, directly at the Coca Cola bottle that
stood there. The bottle did not, she knew, contain Coca
Cola. Old Will Bradford played as if in his sleep. His
eyes were closed, his fiddle braced against his breastbone. A cigarette hung limply from one corner of his
mouth, and a long white ash grew on it until it fell and
dusted down the fiddle's smooth waist.

They were bad enough, two disreputable old ne'er-do-
wells, a kind of cross the village bore; there were better

orchestras available, but the village hired Will and James because if it didn't pay out in wages it would have to pay out in charity come winter. But bad as the two old men were, Vina Mount was worse. The chords of her piano marched along under the uncertain melody of sax and fiddle as if hammered out by a machine, defiantly three to the bar, perfect as a metronome, unfaltering and unchanging and grim. Vina didn't know more than a dozen chords, but those sufficed her. And above the music and the dancers and her own metronomic hands Vina's face looked out over the crowd and was superior to it. She played as if riding a bicycle no-hands, and her lips curled in a small, insolent, contemptuous smile. It struck Helen that Vina was the homeliest girl she had ever seen. Yet if rumors meant anything she had boys by the dozen chasing her, and there were bad stories about after dances at the Corners.

Helen leaned against the wall with her nails picking at the roughnesses in the plaster, and watched her village, her friends and neighbors, some of her relatives, her whole life, go past her: the high-school girls dipping and walking and dipping with frozen bodies and frozen faces, older people waltzing clumsily, lumpish young men hanging around the doorway leering in. There sat the orchestra — James Mount with his obscene old face and his winks and cackles, old Will sleepy and out of tune, Vina with her superior air and her dirty reputation and her dirty mechanical hands. There it was, and all around the wall the summer people taking it in, smiling and watching and whispering things to one another.

Quite abruptly she couldn't stand any more. She ducked into the hall and found her cape under the wad of wraps. As she went out the door into the rain she met Andrew Mount with one of the Swain girls, and though he was a nice boy, quite unlike his uncle James, she brushed past him with hardly more than a murmur of greeting.

For a minute she stood letting her eyes adjust to the outside. Close around her the rain fell straight down as if she stood under an umbrella in a shower bath, but beyond the reach of the porch light there was only a vague suggestion of rain. Across the road the windows of the primary room were scratched with faint glinting lines, and a puddle in the road glimmered as someone walked across the lighted windows. Helen pulled the cape over her hair and went across to the school.

The door was half ajar, propped with a rubber doorstop, and there was a smell of cigarette smoke and an angle of light from the primary room. Helen looked in. Mattie Prosser and another girl — the one who had come up a week or so ago as secretary or something to Mrs. Weld — were sitting in the front row of desks smoking and talking. Mattie's hand made a lightning dart out of sight, then came up again. She laughed.

'Scare a person to death! I can't get used to the notion I'm a free woman.' Her hair was mussed, there was a cardboard box of odds and ends on the teacher's desk, and the wastebasket was full. The secretary was a big Swedish-looking girl, so healthy that Helen felt puny just looking at her.

'I saw your car and the lights,' Helen said. 'I thought maybe I could help.'

'All done,' Mattie said. She drew on her cigarette, looking at Helen sideways. 'When it means shaking the dust of Westwick we don't fool around.'

The secretary laughed. Her teeth were as perfect and strong as the rest of her, and she opened her mouth when she laughed so that Helen saw her pink tongue moving inside. 'You sure encourage the incoming teacher,' she said.

'She knows all about it,' said Mattie. 'This is her home town. That makes a big difference.'

'Does it?' Helen said.

'Oh, sure. If I'd been teaching in my home town I wouldn't have felt like I did here, like being in jail. I'd have known more people, there'd have been ways of getting away. Teaching in your home town's a lot different.'

'I suppose,' Helen said. 'You aren't going to teach at all any more.'

Mattie Prosser looked at her ring. So did Flo Barnes, the secretary. So did Helen. Mattie looked up at the ceiling and stretched her legs under the desk and blew smoke straight up. 'Not a single teach.'

Envy crept into Helen's voice in spite of everything she did to hold it under. 'Living in Laconia,' she said. 'What I wouldn't give to be living somewhere like that.'

'Oh, but this is your home,' Mattie said. 'It's always better in your home town, you'll see. You're lots more your own boss.'

Over Mattie's half-reclining body Helen's eyes met those of the secretary. The white teeth made a smile and a question. 'How come you're not at the dance?'

'I was. I took tickets till nine-thirty.'

'Don't you dance yourself?'

Helen looked at her. 'No. Who'd want to jerk around to one of those Moose Pond waltzes?'

'I thought these were square dances.'

'About half, they are. When they play a quadrille or anything the summer people mess it all up.'

'Sounds like a gay time.'

'That's why I left,' Helen said.

She looked curiously at Mattie Prosser, the sleeves of her sweater pushed up above her elbows, a smudge on one brown arm. 'I should think you'd feel funny, smoking in the schoolhouse.'

'Annie doesn't live here any more,' Mattie said, and stretched her eyebrows in amusement.

'Just the same, what if somebody came in — Martin Bentham, or Mr. Tait?'

'Who's Mr. Tait?'

'The new minister. He's nice, he really is. Haven't you met him?'

Mattie stood up and stretched, and the secretary watched her, her teeth showing. 'To think I'm never going to have that pleasure,' Mattie said. 'And all the other pleasures I'll be missing. No more playing for school cantatas. No more yanking James Mount's overgrown kids in to the principal. No more accidental BM's in the front row.' She did a little adagio down the aisle.

'But of course,' she said, and danced back to pat Helen's arm, 'it's different when it's your home town. If this was my home town I'd feel a lot different about it.'

'Yes,' Helen said. 'I guess so.'

'You even went to school in this room, didn't you?'

'I was in this room four years,' Helen said. 'Miss Barnes is sitting at my old desk.'

'Flo,' the secretary said.

'What?'

'Call me Flo.'

Her smile was direct, frank, very healthy. Her eyebrows were darker than her hair, straight dark lines making a T with the straight line of her nose. Her cheeks were naturally rosy, without rouge.

'I suppose I should lock this place up,' Mattie said. 'I've still got to drive to Lancaster tonight.'

The secretary slid out of the child-size desk and straightened her linen suit over her hips. She was large, but well-made, and her suit made her look slimmer than she was. She moved purposefully, every slightest motion giving the impression of vitality and health. 'Anyway *we'll* still be here,' she said.

'How long will you be around?' Helen asked.

'Labor Day, probably.'

'Stop in at the post office sometime,' Helen said. 'Most of the time I'm not working, just sitting there.'

'Like to swim?' Flo Barnes said. 'Or row?'

'I'm not very good at anything, but I like to.'

'I'll be around,' Flo said. 'We can drum up something to do.'

'Mattie,' Helen said, 'I hope you're awfully happy.'

'Can't help myself,' Mattie said, and hugged her. 'Don't you pay any attention to how I talk about your new job. You'll have fun at it.' She gathered up her box of odds and ends. 'How about you, Flo? Can I drop you anywhere?'

'Maybe I'll go have a look at the dance,' Flo said. 'You going back, Helen?'

'I guess not. I've got two or three things I ought to do here.'

They both looked at her before they turned to the door. 'Don't forget to lock up,' Mattie said. 'Mr. Pond'd get it if we left the place open.'

'I'll be sure.'

They went out, and she heard their steps in the hall, their voices. After a pause there came the burr of the starter. The row of tulip-pot silhouettes pasted against the windows leaped into enormous shadow on the ceiling as Mattie switched on her lights. Then the shadows marched smoothly into the corner, melted into a moving band, and were gone.

The room went back to the dusty yellow light that had illuminated it before. Its emptiness came forward and demanded recognition. Empty rows of seats stretched back to blackboards patched with the crayon pictures of generations of first graders, the stereotypes of pumpkins, black witches on broomsticks, Thanksgiving turkeys with their tails spread, little Dutch girls all cut from one sheet, with their shoulders and feet joined. Somewhere among those stale first-grade repetitions might be some Dutch girl or witch-on-a-broomstick that she herself had cut out when she was six or seven. The thought brought her a kind of anguish. How was it going to be to teach among all these identical fetishes and know that some of them were your own? How was it going to be to reproduce in new generations of first-graders the automatic responses and the customary reactions and the orthodoxies of habit and belief and acceptance, knowing all the time that what you were doing to them had been deliberately done to you?

In your own home town, she said, it's different. You feel at home there, you know people. It's fun to teach where you know everyone and can live at home. Just think, you'll be teaching in the same room where you started school. . . .

She swung around, wondering what had possessed her to tell Mattie and Flo that she had things to do here. In an effort to recall whatever impulse had moved her, she let her eye travel over the entire room, the blackboard full of cutouts; the side board neatly cleaned with a kerosened rag, ready for the next term; the carved desks and the worn floor and the teacher's platform and the half-seen opening of the cloakroom near the door. She saw herself too, as she had seen herself in the middle of the empty Grange Hall, herself a cutout as repetitious as any Dutch girl. From an immense remoteness she looked down on herself there, and the fear and loneliness that filled her were like the loneliness and fear she had felt the first time she had ever entered that room.

There was no ceiling to the room any more. She looked down as she might have looked down on a stage from up among the ropes and pulleys and batteries of lights.

She saw with the camera's eye, and now the camera began to play tricks with her. Her own figure in the white raincape was still there, but there were two other figures, a bulky older woman and a child perhaps six years old.

They moved quietly in from the hall door, hand in hand. The child clung closely to her mother, and at the last minute, when they were about to come into the open space before the teacher's desk, she broke suddenly and fled into the cloakroom, dragging her mother along. As she turned the corner out of sight the camera caught her face convulsed with crying.

For some time, perhaps a minute, the camera remained focused on the doorless opening to the cloakroom. Then it moved down like a slow hawk swooping, planed smoothly in. In the dusk under the rows of coats and lunch pails and bonnets with strings, among the muddied rubbers, the shadowy mother bent over the shadowy child. Now for the first time there was sound. The child was sobbing, 'I can't, Mumma, I can't!'

'Now you go right in,' her mother said. 'Mumma'll go with you, there's no reason to be scary. Miss Bramwell ain't goin' to bite you.' By a curious anachronism the woman was too old, was well past fifty, was fat and shapeless, though she was clearly the child's mother. When she turned her face and talked seriously to her daughter she showed the pink gums and chalky regularity of her store teeth.

The child turned her face into her mother's dress and sobbed.

The woman shook her gently. 'Why is it you're so scary, Helen? Why, you want to go to school. All the other younguns goin'. You know you want to go. Now why don't you just go in there brave as pie and sit down and no more fuss?'

She whistled on the s's, and shoved with her thumb
against the upper plate. The child clung to her legs, still
sobbing. Finally the mother stooped to take her by the
shoulders.

'Teacher won't hurt you. Teacher's there to learn you
to read and write and figure.'

The little girl continued to sob and cling. 'Folks'll
think you're a baby,' the mother said. 'Folks'll think you
ain't a big girl.'

The child would not move her face from the muffling
dress.

'If you don't go to school,' the mother said, 'you'll never
be smart. Folks'll say, "Look at that Helen Barlow, she
don't know two and two. She's the dumbest girl in the
village. Father's a selectman, lives in a big house, but she
don't know nothing."'

The child crowded against the woman's legs until the
mother had to put out a hand to the wall to keep from
toppling. The fat hand shook the child again, not gently
this time, and the mother-voice was hard. 'Good land,
ain't it enough to have one in the family this way? Are
you goin' in there now or do I have to carry you in?'

She rose, creaking her stiffened knees, and started to
lead the girl out into the primary room. The moment they
approached the opening the child hung back with frantic
strength. The mother grappled with her, lost her hold,
and had to follow back into the protective shadow of the
cloakroom. For some time she stood looking down at
her daughter. Twice she opened her mouth to say something, and twice she shut her lips again. Finally she
kneeled down.

'Helen,' she said solemnly. 'There's only one thing for
us to do.'

The child's face was a pale blur with big terrified
eyes. She did not answer.

'We're goin' to have to ask God's help,' Mrs. Barlow said. 'We're goin' to have to pray to God to see if he thinks a little girl should stay away from school and make her Mumma ashamed and make her family a laughing-stock in the village.' She put her hand on the child's head. 'Get down like you was sayin' your prayers.'

The child stared with swimming eyes, swallowed, and got down onto her knees. Her eyes clung to her mother's face, but when her mother's head bent, the girl's bent unwillingly also.

'Dear God,' Mrs. Barlow said, 'we come to Thee to ask what to do. We want to know if it's right a child should refuse to go to school with the other children. We want to know if there's any reason she should be afraid of her teacher and disobey her Mumma. Guide this little child, Lord, and make her know which way it's right for her to go. Teach her to be worthy in all things. Make her honor and obey her parents and be obedient in Thy sight. We ask you not to punish this little child, Lord, but to show her how to act right. We ask it in Christ's name, Amen.'

The child's head was down, and her breath caught in occasional wheezy sobs. The two were silent for a moment. Then the mother spoke in her normal, non-praying voice. 'See, Helen? God wants you to be a good girl.'

When she climbed painfully to her feet again and tugged, the child rose obediently. This time they walked straight into the primary room before the teacher and all the seated children with the watching eyes. The camera, backing away smoothly before them, focused steadily on the child's immense blank eyes and bitten lip, on her skin white as paper and her weak little pointed chin. She came forward in a somnambulist's walk and turned down the middle aisle between the watching children and slid into an empty desk and folded her hands in a tight little ball on the desk and looked at them steadily with her blank eyes.

The camera moved backward and upward, planing away; the little white face diminished and wavered like something seen through water, and shrank until it was like a white tulip, and still shrank until the face was gone entirely, and only the terror that had been in it was left.

Helen moved quickly to the hall door. Her fingers found the switch and dropped the primary room back into darkness. The front door resisted her: she had to bend and lift the rubber-ended doorstop with her hand before she could slam the door to upon the dark interior of the school.

She felt that she might almost be crying, though with the rain on her face she couldn't be sure. Deliberately she pulled the hood off her hair, and with her face tipped back to get the comfort of the rain she walked up the puddled road, through the square, up the street under the loom of the hill, on up the steep muddy drive, forcing herself to walk slowly, and saying to herself, 'What's the matter with me? Oh, what's the matter with me, anyway?' Her hands, almost lost down under the cape, felt wet, cold, and small, like the hands of a child.

When she slipped into the kitchen she could see through the dining-room door that her father was still reading. Beyond him, in the parlor, his sofa bed was made up, with the sheet turned back. The old man did not pay the least attention to the noise she made in the kitchen.

Helen felt again how cold her hands were (a drowned person's hands would feel like that) when she took off the raincape and patted her wet hair with the roller towel beside the sink. A wild, irresponsible impulse to sneak back of the stove, where she used to hide when she was a child, brushed her mind. Back there it would be warm and dark and snug, and from there she could hear the noises people made, and see their legs go back and forth, and smell the things they cooked, and hear the crash of the wood they dropped into the woodbox, without ever show-ing herself. Her cat used to come in there too, balancing his vertical tail and rubbing against the stove-leg, and she could capture him and hold her face against his fur.

Almost in flight, she went into the dining room. 'Hello, Pa.'

The white-bristled dewlap stretched, the quick, half-lidded eyes looked at her as bright as the eyes of a wood-chuck. In the deep chair, with his thick-ankled feet in wool socks and slippers stretched out over the footstool, he looked a little like a sunning woodchuck at the mouth of his burrow, his body relaxed but his eyes vigilant.

'Thought you was to the dance.'

'I got tired of it.'

George Barlow read a while. Then, 'See your Ma there?'

'She must have come after I left. I was over at the school a while.'

'She didn't come home with you?'

'No.'

Abruptly he was reading again. Helen had a feeling he had dived down his hole, and that if she watched she would see his questing nose, his whiskers, his bright but-ton eyes, pop warily up again when he thought he was safe. Sure enough, when she looked again there was his eye over the paper.

'Is there anything you want, Pa?'

The eye disappeared.

Helen crossed the room, half intending to go up to bed, but passing the stair door before her intention crystallized. On the wall at a level with her eyes was a picture of a child with braids down her back, a plaid tam on her head, and books under her arm. She studied the face a minute. It was the wistful, timid face of the child in the cloakroom. She jerked past it and went on, running her fingers along the plate board at the top of the wainscoting.

Again she stopped, this time before her framed diploma from the University of New Hampshire. There were the four free, the four good years of her life, reduced to scribbles on parchment, mounted under glass, and bound in black wood like a mourning band. The four good years, the four dead years. She would have liked to yank the diploma off the wall, but nobody in the whole village, least of all her mother, would have understood an act like that. Within the black frame was one evidence of the family's respectability, the right to hold up the head, the authorization to take pride, the compensation for her father's helplessness. It would not do to pull the family's respectability off the wall, any more than it would have done to refuse the village school when Mattie gave it up. On what grounds could she possibly have refused it? On the plea that she wanted to go to New York or Boston? Or that she preferred to stay on in the post office at a half-time job? It wouldn't do. God and her mother wanted her to be a good girl.

'Pa,' she said, turning.

Her father's eye did not lift above the paper.

'Pa, can you think what it would be like to walk again? To be free and active the way you used to be, and get out of your chair and work and hunt and fish again?'

The paper dropped slightly, and the gray old head, the grizzled chaps, the bright unwinking eye looked out, the features of a very old, very wise woodchuck in a very secure burrow.

'What in thunder put that in your head?' he said. It was not his usual grunting voice.

She was standing at his feet, the slippered feet that stuck up like the feet of an effigy on a tomb. They looked unwithered, thick-ankled, strong, as if they should be able to get up and walk away any time. She took the big toe of one between thumb and forefinger and waggled it. The toe twitched away angrily.

'I don't know,' Helen said. 'I just got wondering what it must be like for you, never to be able to move out of one place.' Before his glare she bent a little. 'I don't know, Pa, I just . . .'

Her voice trailed off, for in the instant when they looked eye into eye there was something in the old man's face, something he might have said, something they both knew. Then the sound of footsteps on the porch broke their look. Their heads swung toward the kitchen door, and when Helen looked back the half-terrified, half-angry expression was gone from her father's gray face. His head had ducked between his shoulders and he was sliding a perceptible inch or two deeper into his chair.

2

A Girl Named Liebowitz

WHEN HAROLD SWETT told Abe the girl was there Abe didn't believe him. They were leaning on the picket fence in front of Harold's place, just talking and watching the summer people gather outside the post office waiting for the afternoon mail.

'It's a fact,' Harold said. 'Her name's Liebowitz.'

'Listen,' Abe said. 'You are a great kidder. You like to string people. What should a girl named Liebowitz be doing in that inn?'

Harold pushed the beak of his greasy cotton cap upward off his brows. He grinned at Abe. 'That's what quite a few people are asking.'

Abe bristled. 'They wouldn't put her out. Not even those Browns.'

'Don't s'pose they will,' Harold said. 'Wouldn't've let her in in the first place if Connie hadn't sent her up. Their own daughter's friend from New York.' He began to laugh almost soundlessly. 'All those "restricted clientèle" ads. All that exclusiveness. That old front porch crowd is fit to bust.'

Abe jerked his elbows off the fence and stared up at the wide-porched inn, set snobbishly high above its fastidious lawns. 'You know something?' he said to Harold. 'You got any idea what it is? It's a hell of a thing.'

'I thought it was funny,' Harold said.

'Sure, it's very funny. She must be an innocent or why

20

would she come here? Why wouldn't she go to the Cat-
skills where it is possible to go?'

'Oh, she'll figure things out,' Harold said.

'Sure she'll figure them out. You don't know how it is
to figure things out. How would you?'

Harold shrugged and scratched at the mat of hair showing above his open shirt collar. 'Maybe it ain't funny for
her,' he said, 'but it's a hell of a fine joke on Herb Brown.'

Abe took off his hat and puckered up his face. 'I don't
get you,' he said. 'Is it a joke people should be snobs?
Maybe you think a pogrom is a joke. I wish you had been
brought up in Russia with me. I could tell you some funny
jokes.'

'Keep your shirt on, Abe,' Harold said. He pushed
Abe's chest lightly and went into the shed. Abe remained
by the fence, looking up the terraced hill at the Westwick
Inn. Maybe it was a funny joke the girl should be there,
but he didn't like to think of it.

When the dinner bell bonged at six, shadowy outlines
rose from porch chairs and went inside. Three or four
people crossed from Bentham's store. Abe, hanging
around the creamery on the northwest corner of the square,
watched the empty porches and decided that he was a
fool. What was there to see? A girl named Liebowitz from
New York, taking a vacation in a New Hampshire village
where Jewish people had never come for vacations. The
Browns had let her in, okay, because she was a friend of
their daughter's. But now what would she do? There were
no dance-halls in this quiet place. There was the lake, but
what fun was it to swim alone? There was walking in the
hills, there were rowboats and horses for hire, but again,
what fun were they alone? If she went to the tennis courts
or golf course she would be snubbed faster even than at
the inn. So in a day or two she would see that she had

made a bad mistake and would go home. Meantime, what
did he expect to see by hanging around the creamery
while sensible people ate their suppers?

The thought of food sent him into Bentham's, where
he caught Martin Bentham just closing up, and bought
two rolls and a slice of cheese. Out against the creamery
wall again he ate them quickly and drank from the tap
that jutted from the cement foundation. After ten minutes or so he had a second drink, and a little later a third.

He was just rising from the third drink when the screen
slammed and he turned and knew instantly that this was
the girl. She had a square face, reddish or brownish hair,
high coloring. She wore a green blouse, and she was
grown up but still young looking, maybe twenty-five. She
hesitated a moment as if deciding which way to walk, and
then came down into the square and started up the county
road between school and Grange Hall. She did not seem
to pay much attention to things she passed, even the immense schoolhouse woodpile. That, Abe had noticed,
always stopped city people the first time. The Liebowitz
girl went straight by without turning her head. Abe knew
because by then he was following her.

He followed her past the Charbon farm, down the
swale where the brook came down, up the road a mile between the hills and the lake. When he saw that she was
turning up Peter Dow's road he hesitated. If he turned
in there after her he would certainly be following this
girl. Up to this point he could have been merely taking
an after-dinner stroll. She had already disappeared in the
woodsy little trail when he came up and leaned on the
turnstile. He got angry with himself, leaning there. Since
when is it against the rules to walk in Dow's road? he
asked himself. Is Peter Dow the kind of a person to object if people walk in his road? He went through the stile.

The road curved back along the shoulder of the hill,

climbing into heavy timber. There was at least an hour until real sunset, but the sun was gone here, and the trail was a somber, gray-columned tunnel with hemlock branches interlocking overhead. The girl's sharp heel tracks were punched in the damp ground.

Up where the sun was still shining, on the brow of the hill, he found her sitting under a tree at the edge of the meadow. She was off the road a few yards, so that when he popped up along the bank he startled both himself and her. Staring at her glassily, he got an impression of very curly light-red hair and hazel eyes that did not look friendly. They were, in fact, so hostile that when Abe managed to break the stare and say something he said the first thing that came into his head, something foolish.

'Are you in some trouble?'

'No.'

Abe grunted, hung there a moment, and walked on. Up above her a little way, behind a fringe of cedar and spruce, he sat down on a stone and cursed himself. Follow the girl two miles and then ask a silly question and walk on past. Through the low cedars he watched the glimmer of her green blouse and wondered what she had thought when he popped up over the bank and opened his mouth on those foolish words. What would she think if he went back? He threw a handful of pebbles into the trees and muttered. He could not go back now. He could sit here like a fungus on a log, and when she decided to go home he could follow at a respectful distance, like the cat's tail.

Below him the hill flowed in unbroken treetops to the tape of the county road, and beyond the road it pitched steeply into the lake. Abe could see the mouth of the brook and a delta of beach. Back toward town, Charbon's meadow was hobnailed with haycocks. Straight ahead Weld's Island rose roundly wooded from the glassy water.

It was a fine view, the best around. The girl was lucky to have stumbled on it alone. It irritated him that she should have found it without help, and with a painful curiosity he wondered how it looked to eyes fresh from New York.

The ribbons of cloud over the ridge were flushing pink. Abe stood up and dusted his hands on the seat of his pants. Before he could weaken he started down the trail again, taking pains to kick around with his feet and make a lot of noise.

By the time he was under the bank again and looking up at her they had been watching each other for a minute or two. With his stick planted in the road and his feet braced, Abe put his shoulders back and faced her. Because he felt awkward, he shouted. 'Do you know the way back? In fifteen minutes it is getting dark. Can you walk back in the dark, tell me yes or no?'

The girl stood up. Her eyes were not hostile now. Even under the shadow of the tree they were curiously light-filled. 'I don't know,' she said. 'Unless it gets dark awful fast here . . .'

'I can walk back with you,' Abe said. 'That is the way I am going.' Her eyes shone and swam so that he had to look over her shoulder, and he shouted again. 'Unless you would rather walk alone.'

The girl watched him, half smiling, saying nothing. Abe put his hand against his breastbone and bent a little. 'My name is Kaplan,' he said. 'I heard you were in town and when I saw you leave the inn I followed you. If that makes you mad, I will leave and you can go home alone.'

'I don't understand,' Miss Liebowitz said. Her face, wide-jawed and quite pretty, was screwed into a puzzled frown, but her eyes were still full of light.

'If it makes you scared,' Abe said. 'You don't know me . . . I have followed you out walking. How do you know why I followed you?'

Her lips twitched. 'Because my name's Liebowitz,' she said.

'How did you guess it!' When she laughed he frowned. 'How did you know I would follow somebody named Liebowitz?' Then he opened his mouth and nodded several times, laughing. 'Ah, ah,' he said. 'When I tell you my name is Kaplan, that did it, eh?'

'I knew it the minute you opened your mouth, the first time you came by,' she said.

At his puzzled stare she laughed aloud. 'Your accent! My goodness, was I surprised! Here I think I'm up in New Hampshire where everybody says 'twan't and 'twasn't, and I run right into somebody with an accent like East Eighteenth Street.'

'I have never been on East Eighteenth Street,' Abe said.

'Maybe not, but you talk just like it. For that matter,' she said, 'I was never so glad to hear a Jewish accent in my life.'

Abe slapped his hands together. 'Now we have both been surprised, eh? This afternoon I heard there was this person named Liebowitz staying at the inn. How do I know who she is? She may be some millionaire, she may be a hunchback, she may be anything. But never since I came here has anybody with a name like Liebowitz stayed in the village. The summer people keep it that way, like a suburb of New Haven or Montclair. So I thought you might be lonesome and I followed you.'

They were walking slowly down the trail. When she didn't answer he looked up. 'All right,' he said violently. 'You don't believe it. It makes a bad story. All right.'

'I believe it,' the girl said. 'Why did you think I might be lonesome?'

Abe shrugged. 'I have lived here five years, I have been lonesome most of the time.'

'Why do you live here then?'

He looked at her in disgust. 'Go back to Boston, maybe? Go down and sit cross-legged and sew all day for some tailor shop that cheats its customers and robs its help? Live in a hole in the wall and work in a disease factory? Ha! That makes fine sense. Don't make me laugh!'

'Well, you don't have to bite me,' Miss Liebowitz said mildly. 'You live here for your health, is that it?'

'I live here because I wouldn't live anywhere else,' Abe said. 'That has nothing to do with being lonesome.'

They walked silently for a while. The view dropped behind the trees, the road passed through scattered cedars and entered the hemlocks. It was so dusky that the girl stumbled, and Abe offered her a stiff arm. From the hill springs came down; the dark was musical with the sound of water. Once something moved and snapped twigs off in the brush, and Miss Liebowitz's hand convulsively grabbed Abe's elbow. Abe considered telling her that the noise was undoubtedly made by one of John LaPere's calves, but it was pleasanter to let her believe there might be dangers. All down through the shadowy tunnel of the dugway he kept his arm stiff for her to cling to.

'You were a friend of Connie Brown,' he said finally.

'Yes, we both worked in Garbstein's, on the Bowery. Wholesale wedding gowns.'

'So that is why you are up here,' he said. 'There had to be some reason. Here is no summer resort. Here it is mainly university people, deans and college presidents and professors and some writers, very quiet, as I told you, like a suburb of New Haven or Montclair. They are very fussy about keeping the place unspoiled. Not even a movie is here.'

'Who'd go to a movie on his vacation anyway?' Miss Liebowitz said. Abe winced and bristled at the edged voice. All right, he said to himself. So you are from New

York. Oh, yes. But Miss Liebowitz was still talking. 'Connie used to get so homesick she'd almost die. She used to tell me how the hayfields looked across the lake with the late sun on them, and how there'd be whole fields absolutely yellow with kale. She made it sound just like heaven.'

'And it isn't so heavenly,' Abe said. 'You don't find it quite like paradise, is that so?'

They emerged from the hemlocks into lighter dusk. The road bent down through a bog toward the county road. 'I think,' Miss Liebowitz said with solemnity, 'that from up there on the hill it's the most beautiful thing I ever saw in my life.'

'Ha!' Abe said. He had been waiting for it, hoping she would say it. For a while he had thought that maybe her New York superiority would make her look on all this as just the sticks, Hickville.

Through the bog faint fireflies coasted around them, and a damp, sweetish odor rose like mist from the ground. Abe dragged his hand and caught a handful of fern and held it under Miss Liebowitz's nose. 'Sweet fern,' he said.

Out on the county road he relaxed his arm, thinking she might want to let go, but she kept hold of it. 'Connie Brown,' he said, 'got out of the village because she thought it was stuffy. Some do, quite a lot I guess. So she went down to be somebody's maid, and then she took a job. Now you tell me she is homesick. Well, it is funny, but it is what I would expect. She was a nice girl. But how do you like her family, eh?'

'It sounds as if you didn't.'

'You are right,' Abe said. 'You are absolutely right. Snobs are bad enough, but little people who kiss the feet of snobs, those are something else. They make you feel unwelcome at that inn, isn't it so?'

The girl's eyes turned to brush his face; he felt them

like a flash in the near dark. He heard her snort through
her nose, a soft angry sound. 'They put me at a separate
table,' she said.

Abe stopped short in the road. 'Akh!' he said. 'It's a
shame you went there.' His legs moved again, and he
went shaking his head and muttering. With his stick he
switched the weeds beside the road. 'Pah!' he said. 'Such
people!'

'That's one reason I was surprised at your accent,' she
said. 'I thought you must live here, because you weren't
at the inn, but if people in town feel that way I didn't
see why you *would* live here.'

'Don't go by me,' Abe said. He bent to peer into her
face. 'You're not orthodox, eh?' He waved his arm to
forestall a reply. 'No one could be orthodox and live at
that inn. So you are like me, maybe, a bad Jew. Not be-
lieving in this kosher business, I live where I please. Second, I have a usefulness here. I am a tailor, a mechanic.
All summer, for the summer people, I make clothes. In
the old country I am a military tailor, I know my business.' Not hard, but solidly, he hit himself on the chest.
'So I am not a summer person, but I make my living from
summer people. I am not a native, but I live here all the
time. I live between the two of them like a mouse between two walls.'

He ran his hand through his hair and brandished his
stick. 'I do not call myself a Jew,' he said. 'All that religious business I throw out the window.' He took her
arm and lowered his voice. 'Let me tell you something I
remember from Russia. I am brought up by my grandfather in Kharkov. My parents are dead, I never knew
them. Every Sabbath we go to the synagogue, hours at
a time, nothing but hard seats and a cantor droning. I am
seven years old, maybe eight. I wiggle, or fall asleep, or
scrape my feet. My grandfather is an old man, very re-

ligious. He would not lift his voice to scold me in the synagogue, so when I wiggle or make a noise he just hits me across the face. I never went away from that synagogue without blood on my mouth. And that is religion. You should hit a seven-year-old child because he can't stay awake. That is the kind of people who love God.'

There was quite a long silence. Then Miss Liebowitz's sympathetic voice said, 'I think that's terrible. No wonder you're not religious. But it's funny you should be an orphan. I am, too. I was brought up in an asylum. I guess you could say my religious education has just been neglected.'

'That's fine,' Abe said. 'It would be good if everybody had it neglected. You know what that religious stuff made out of me? A revolutionist.' He turned and laughed softly. 'No less, a revolutionist. When I was thirteen I ran away to Odessa, a long way, and apprenticed myself to a tailor. All day I would sew, and all night I would try to learn something, and finally I started going to meetings. By the time I was sixteen I was a revolutionist, oh, I tell you! Work all day, go to meetings all night, pass resolutions and print pamphlets and study Marx and all that foolishness. I thought it was excitement to be always running away from police.'

She was watching him. 'Are you still a revolutionist?'

'Akh!' Abe said. 'All that is a waste of time.'

They topped the rise behind the school. The lights of the village lay to their left in a horn-shaped constellation along the shore. They could hear a girl's laugh across the water. 'So what are you going to do about the Browns?' Abe said. 'You wouldn't let the snobs freeze you out.'

Miss Liebowitz moved her head. In the dark she seemed close and warm, and Abe swallowed. 'I don't know,' she said. 'It's no fun having a vacation where you get pushed around. I might go to a place down in the Berkshires where some of the girls go.'

'You shouldn't do that,' Abe said earnestly. 'Let them run you out? You wouldn't be such a spineless thing. People here are mostly okay. You should stay and have a good time.'

'People here are okay,' Miss Liebowitz said, 'but you've been lonesome ever since you came.'

Abe shrugged. 'Is anybody ever not lonesome? I don't know.' He felt suddenly sad and tired and as if it weren't worth talking any more. 'Sure, I admit it,' he said. 'Sure, I'm lonesome, why not?'

Off across the water a girl laughed again, and he felt Miss Liebowitz shiver. 'So I'm lonesome,' he said angrily. 'What is that to anyone else?'

They came down the hill, walking carefully in the dark. At the foot of the slope Abe stopped. 'No matter what you do tomorrow,' he said, 'you don't want to go back to the inn yet. You haven't seen the lake.'

'I saw it from up on the hill.'

'Oh, up on the hill!' Abe said. 'That isn't seeing anything.' When he started to urge her down a path to the left, she held back, and for a minute he saw it as it might look to her: a strange man trying to get a girl off into the woods. He dropped her elbow. 'Of course, maybe you're scared,' he said. 'There is nothing to be scared of. See, this is a path down to the lake.'

Stepping in front of her, he scratched a match on his shoe. The yellow flame bloomed weakly, brought up the weathered rails and the sagging cross of the turnstile, the dark of trees. With the sulphur smell in his nostrils Abe waited.

'What would I be scared of?' Miss Liebowitz said, and again the scorn in her voice set Abe's teeth on edge. Once in a while that New York superiority was more than a man should take quietly. 'And my name is Ruth,' she said. Without his guiding hand she groped her way off the road and put her hands on the turnstile. 'Ummmm!' she said, and lifted her face. 'Isn't that a *heavenly* smell!'

'Cedars and firs,' Abe said. He was walking so anxiously close that he bumped into her twice. 'You'll see,' he said. 'This village isn't as bad as it looks from that inn. There are fine people here, lots of them, good friends of mine, summer people and natives and all kinds. For instance, I can borrow a rowboat. Would you like to take a row on the lake? I can borrow a rowboat as easy as you would borrow a pencil.'

They came out of the woods, the dark cool smell of water was in their faces, and as their feet left the packed ground and found hollow planks there was a steely, fleeting, visible-and-gone-again movement of light from the surface of the lake. Under the planks the water stirred like something sleepy and alive. A jangle of laughter and falsetto yips came across from the lost shadow of the far shore.

Abe put his hands on Ruth Liebowitz's shoulders and pressed down, as if to settle her feet firmly onto the dock. 'Wait here. Just wait a minute, please,' he said stammering, and was gone.

She waited a good while above the uneasy stirring of the water, hearing the rodentlike gnawings and lappings under the dock and trying to see into the dark. The cool breath of the lake touched her again, and she shivered, wishing she had stopped at the inn for a coat. For a moment she contemplated leaving, just going on back to her room, but that would have been mean. He was such a funny, pompous, angry, nice man, and so kind of pathetic.

She turned to look the way he had gone. A light

bobbed toward her, the wide-thrust yellow light of a swinging lantern. Kaplan came up, breathing hard, saying, 'Ah, ah, I didn't like to keep you waiting, I hope it wasn't long.' Shadows tipped and swung around him as he stooped and hunted for something at the edge of the dock. She heard him grunt, saw him pulling on a rope. A pulley rose dripping to the surface as the line fed through it, and the sharp nose of a white rowboat slid into the lantern light, the oily water parting with deep glints of lemon and ruby, lifting the boat a little as Abe held its bow against the planks.

Kaplan stepped in after her, set the lantern in the bottom, and settled himself to rowing. The lantern threw a diffused glow upward on his pleased and satisfied smile. As he swung the oars he kept nodding at her, and his large even teeth glinted. 'You see?' he said. 'What did I tell you?'

'Tell me about what?'

'About the lake. About rowing at night.'

'You didn't tell me anything about it.'

Rowing, he bent so that his puzzled eyebrows netted light as a spiderweb nets dew. 'I didn't tell you? Then how did I persuade you to come out here?'

'You didn't. You just went and got the lantern and brought me.'

He stopped rowing. 'This is funny. Do you want to go back?'

'Why, because you didn't persuade me first?'

'I don't know what is the matter with my head,' he said, and beat it softly with his fist.

She laughed aloud. A little thrill went through her at the thought that maybe someone, maybe a couple in love, somewhere around the lake, would hear her laugh across the water and it would say something to them of love and pleasure and the sadness of being young at night, the way the other girl's laugh had spoken to her. 'I wouldn't go back for anything,' she said.

Kaplan looked relieved and rowed again. 'It's really funny, no kidding. You live alone, you never know when you've said something and when you've just thought it. Plenty of things you want to say bad enough, you just have them on your mind and never quite know whether you've said them or not. Did you ever do that?'

Ruth never had, but she thought it was interesting because it showed how really all by himself he was. She told him about Garbstein's, how it was the other way around there. A lot of things you shouldn't say you just spilled out, talking with the girls, and first thing you knew they had you all by heart. Still, she guessed it was better than having no one to talk with at all.

'Well,' Kaplan said, 'I apologize. I am sorry. I thought I told you how I liked to row at night and how the stars slide down the little hills of water the oars make, and then whirl just under the surface. I had a whole speech. I never said any of that?'

'No. Go ahead, though. It sounds as if maybe you wrote poetry about it.'

'Poetry?' Abe said, and stopped rowing to make a repudiating gesture with one hand. 'Not poetry, not me. Poetry is all right, there is a girl in the village writes some, but not me.'

As he bent and lifted the lantern the light spread out wide, but showed no shore. The dragging oars cut the water as if it were gelatinous. 'I can show you how I like it best,' Kaplan said. 'The light spoils it.'

Ruth said nothing. She was leaning over the gunwale, looking down into the green-amber gelatinous water with the light drowning in it far down. A miraculous trailing frond of water weed flowed across the light and was gone again.

'Have I your permission?' Kaplan's angry voice said.

She jerked her head up. He was still holding the lantern high, ready to lift the shade and blow out the light.

'Oh!' she said. 'Oh, sure, certainly.'

Now that they were out in open water a faint light seemed to come from somewhere, out of the sky or from the lake itself, and Ruth made out the dark shore on the right, the cloudy sky with only an occasional star showing. In the almost-luminous water she saw once or twice the thing Kaplan had mentioned — the stars that slid down the glassy hill of water before the oar blades and floated just under the whirlpooled surface.

She sighed, listening to the regular *creak* and *chock* of the rowing. 'You know,' she said, 'I never had a boatride at night, never in my whole life. Not in a little boat like this.'

'It is something I like,' Kaplan said. 'When I am lonesome, I borrow this boat. Having friends here, I don't have to own one. All I have to be is a good borrower, leave it tied up and not dirtied.'

'It seems funny, you being up here,' Ruth said. 'Somehow it doesn't seem right that Jewish people should *live* in the country. Generally if they get out at all it's just for a vacation, like me, but here you live here the year around.'

'I am a bad Jew,' Kaplan said.

'And you know the names of things, like a country person. You know sweet fern and what kind of trees things are. You must have lived in the country in Russia, didn't you?'

'I told you,' Kaplan said. 'Kharkov. And that is not country. That was a ghetto. When I was a child I was in jail.'

'You mean when you were a revolutionist?'

'No, no, that isn't what I mean.' Talking with his hands,

he splashed her skirt with water. 'As a child I lived as if in jail. Stone, iron, synagogues, my grandfather, beatings and black bread. That is a black place, that Russia. Maybe it is better now, I don't know.'

'I guess orphans have it about the same anywhere,' Ruth said. 'Poor orphans, at least.'

The rowing sounds went on in the cool silence. Near the boat a fish splashed heavily, and in the stillness that followed, there was a noise of frogs somewhere under the black shore. A little dog was yipping off on the hill.

'You hear that?' Kaplan said. 'That is a fox.'

'Really?' Ruth said. 'It sounded just like a little dog.'

Kaplan's misty figure half rose on the thwart, and his coat fell softly into her lap. 'Put this on,' he said. 'You'll be cold.'

They went in silence again, and Ruth sat remembering how Connie had been homesick for this lake and the farms and the village and country things. She wondered if it were possible ever to be homesick for an orphans' home or a settlement house or the face of old Mrs. Malevinsky, for the baking brick walls and the breathless windows on the airwells and the shoeless people on the steps, for the loud boys and the tipped ashcans and the black and dirty snow. It seemed to her that Connie had grown up infinitely richer, and for a moment, holding Kaplan's coat around her shoulders, she felt almost the pang of homesickness she wanted. But it was Connie's homesickness she felt, not her own, and she knew that if she had grown up Connie Brown she would never have left this place even for New York.

In the dark she even felt her eyes sting with tears, and she didn't know what for, unless it was for all homesickness and all loneliness and the memory of her own stony childhood or the black-bread-and-beatings childhood of Abe Kaplan. Perhaps the tears that wet her eyes were for the low dark line of shore and the almost-invisible water, for the bark of a fox on the hill and the chorus of frogs under the bank, for beauty that she felt and yet did not know. It seemed to her pathetic, almost a personal wrong, that she should have grown up unable to tell the bark of a fox from the bark of a dog, and not know sweet fern when she smelled it.

It was late when they came back, groping toward shore with nothing to guide them except two arc lights back on the village street, several hundred yards from the lake. Ruth couldn't see the dock, the beach, anything. Land was a dike of shadow that might be rods away or might be a boat-length. Abe lighted the lantern and stood up to hold it high. All it did for Ruth was dazzle her and hide the shore in an obscurity of light rather than an obscurity of darkness, but Kaplan grunted and sat down, and after three or four strokes the bow choked suddenly in sand.

Ruth stood on the beach while he pulled the boat to the dock and tied it up. The gestures of his enormous shadow were polite and jerky as he moved around the lantern. Then the lantern rose and came toward her and they started up toward the village lights. Clods in the road, insects that came flying, the posts of a roadside fence, came out of the dark to stare palely.

When they struck the square Kaplan took a good hold on Ruth's elbow and walked her up the street under the hill. They were, she saw, almost directly under the high spire of the church. From down below it looked amazingly high, carrying the hill upward in a thin pointer against a blackboard speckled with stars. Abe walked her up the road a few yards and held the lantern high. She saw first a woodpile with an axe stuck in the block, its new handle white as china. Beyond the woodpile was a gray tent with a patched roof and wooden sides. A stovepipe came up through a tin patch on the roof, and the front flaps were tied down across a framed doorway. Behind the tent the hill went up in a dark, almost vertical wall.

The lantern swung down, lighted briefly on tall grass and a half-strangled squash vine with yellow flowers on it. 'This is where I live,' Kaplan said. The note of brusqueness or anger, which hadn't been in his voice for more than an hour, was back. He stood close and shouted at her, 'This is where I have lived for five years!'

'In a *tent?*'

'Well,' he said, 'if I want to live in a tent whose business is it?'

'Nobody's, only . . . '

'So anybody who thinks it is funny can mind his own business,' Kaplan said. 'I could build a house if I wanted to. I like this.'

Impatiently he steered Ruth down to the square, where the one arc light spread a misty yellow light around. A single globe burned above the doorway of the inn.

'I could build a house,' Kaplan said. 'As a matter of fact, I have thought of it. But when you get a house you get water pipes to freeze. It seems like a lot of trouble.' The lantern swung in a wide gesture. 'It would be easy enough, don't fool yourself. Friends I have got here would help, it would go up like nothing.'

He was walking sideways and staring at her. With the light on his face from below and his big eyebrows full of it he looked like a comic mask. 'Well, I should think . . . ' she said.

'All right, I will tell you,' Abe said. 'I had reasons for living in a tent. When I came up here I was sick. Boston did that to me — tuberculosis. All the first winter I slept in that tent with all my clothes and an overcoat on and quilts over my head. And when I had done it once I could do it again. I could have built a house any time, but the last two winters I went to Florida instead and kept a little cleaning and pressing shop. By now, instead of Saint Petersburg I am thinking of a house.'

Stamping past the post office he snorted as if his nostrils were obstructed. 'So that is why you see me living in a tent,' he said.

On the lawn before the dark inn they faced each other like awkward high-school children after a date. Finally Abe reached out and shook her hand — not pressed it or squeezed it, but shook it as if he were greeeting a farmer friend. 'Well,' he said, 'I have enjoyed meeting you. I hope you are not mad because I followed you.'

'Of course not,' she said. 'It's been lots of fun.'

'Also I hope you will stay right here until you have had your vacation. This is not a summer resort, but there are some things we could do.'

He was looking at her so earnestly, his teeth showing in a formal smile, his body inclined from the waist, that she didn't know quite how to answer. He wasn't her notion of a Romeo, but still he was terribly nice, really . . . He was still shaking her hand.

'I don't know,' she said, 'It's hard to decide.'

'I insist. You should stay.'

'Well,' she said, mocking him, 'if you *insist!*'

He dropped her hand and stood back and when she went in the door of the porch he was still standing there with his hand raised in farewell, up to his knees in the round shadow of the lantern base.

The next morning, Saturday, it was raining when Abe appeared after breakfast. As he was talking with Ruth at one end of the porch, away from the inn guests, Mrs. Brown came down the stairs. She was a drab little farm wife, too busy for her strength, and everything worried her. She wondered now what Miss Liebowitz and Abe had in mind. Maybe they would like a picnic lunch made up.

Abe looked at her, and as he looked his elbow jerked outward and his lips began to stammer. But he didn't say anything nasty. He just nodded down at the dripping maples and the gray slant of rain over the square and said, 'Does it look like picnics?'

He was still looking at the landlady in triumph, daring her to reply, when he had another thought. He frowned at Mrs. Brown, who stood there as if not quite sure how to excuse herself. 'We changed our minds,' he said. 'You should put up a lunch for Miss Liebowitz, yes.' He added, holding Mrs. Brown's eye, 'A good one, eh?'

Mrs. Brown went away. 'Where do I come in on this?' Ruth said. 'Do I have anything to say about where I eat?'

'Not today.' He smacked his hands together, beaming at her. 'Today you will see how the other half lives.'

There were eyes on them from down the porch. Abe cleared his throat noisily, and smiled at Ruth in a secret, confidential way. When Mrs. Brown finally came back with a basket he took it from her and hooked it over his arm. 'I put in an extra half of chicken, Abe,' she said. 'I thought maybe you . . .'

'Thank you very much,' Abe said. 'Well, you won't see us again today. That will be good, eh?'

Ruth yanked him outside before he could say anything else. She did not like to watch the helpless, worried face of Mrs. Brown, and her thin pointed lips feeling for words to say, reaching out like a snail's foot to see what was rough, what sharp, what safe; or hear the thin tired voice feeling its way through an empty sentence to die on an unfinished phrase. Ruth felt sorry for Mrs. Brown. Snobbery should be administered by people who believed in it.

'Where are we going?' she said.

'Up to my place.'

Together, Abe holding his umbrella over them, running sideways with the basket of lunch on his other arm, his feet slipping and swerving in the puddles, they ran down into the square and up the shining wet road.

The floor of Abe's tent was raised, and it was snugger inside than Ruth had expected. The roof did not leak at all, though it had been raining for over an hour. The bed, back against the rear wall, made a sofa with an auto robe over it, and there were two chairs, a dropleaf table, and a small square stove, and along the other side an ironing board and a rack made of galvanized pipe, on which hung dresses and suits with cleaner's slips pinned to them. The stove was still warm from Abe's breakfast fire, and even with the flaps down there was a pleasant gray light. The roof moved now and then under a blast of wind and rain, but altogether it was warmer, lighter, and pleasanter than she would ever have anticipated.

Abe stirred around, putting wood on the fire, moving chairs. As he reached out and tied back one of the door flaps he nodded to her. 'In case people went by,' he said. 'It would look better, you understand. People come here all the time with cleaning and mending.'

Even though she did not like the draft on her ankles, Ruth nodded. He was so fussy about little things like this that he amused her. 'Punctilio in a tent,' she said.

'Eh?'

'Nothing. I should think you'd get awful cold in the winter.'

Abe shrugged himself into a canvas chair. 'A few times I have seen it forty below. That is cold, I tell you. I bank up the sidewalls with cedar branches, and I keep the stove redhot and on really cold days I run an oil heater too, but forty below, that is too cold. You can't sit around, no matter how much you have on. Somewhere the cold will find a crack and get at you. I spill water on the floor, it freezes *sssssssppt!* like that. The store is a better place to sit those days.'

His eyebrows cocked up at her, his large brown eyes met hers almost as if pleading. 'Of course, with a house, that is a different thing. Wind does not blow through solid walls, and a big kitchen stove keeps things warm and heats water, and in the living room can be a heating stove that burns big chunks. It's easy then, it's like pie.'

'Well, I don't know,' she said. 'I should think you'd miss books, and music, and things like that. I would. In New York I only live three blocks from a branch of the New York Public, and I read all the time. I couldn't live without books. I should think you'd just perish.'

'Books?' Abe said. 'I've got books.' He reached under the bed, saying, 'Sorry, excuse me, please,' as he moved her feet aside, and pulled out a long narrow box. Inside were books. He pulled them out one at a time, blew dust from them, whacked them on his bent knee. 'Sumner, *Folkways,*' he said, and passed it over. 'John Reed, *A Daughter of the Revolution.*' He got out another. 'Lynd, *Middletown. The Writings of Nicolai Lenin.*'

Ruth held them in her lap, bending to see titles in the box. She never could help looking over people's books to see what they read. 'Have you got any novels?' she said. 'Galsworthy, or Aldous Huxley, or Sinclair Lewis, or Thomas Wolfe or anybody?'

'Novels?' Abe said, and brandished a book at her. 'Why should I waste time on novels? When I read I want to work my brains, get some exercise. I read serious liter-ature. Novels, no. I haven't got novels.'

Ruth's brows drew down, and she looked at him hard. 'What do you mean, waste time on novels? You don't mean to say you don't think novels are worth reading — good novels?'

'Well,' Abe said, 'what are brains for? To be used, eh? And what works your brain reading a story about somebody? Why not read something that tells you something?' He stuck a book in her face. 'Here, here is *The Rise of American Civilization*, here is a book that tells you something. What do you know about this country from reading novels?'

'I wouldn't attempt to tell you, because you wouldn't understand,' Ruth said tartly. 'But anybody with any sense can learn more from novels than he can from all the textbooks in your box. Novels give you an understanding of people, they open your eyes to all kinds of things. Who do you think Sinclair Lewis is, some writer of children's books, maybe?'

'I suppose he is some novelist,' Abe said, and shrugged.

'You suppose,' Ruth said. 'You don't know. You sit up here in your canvas house and read your textbooks and stuff your head with sawdust when you could be reading something good like *Arrowsmith* or the *Forsyte Saga*.'

'Say, listen!' Abe said. 'Sawdust, is it? Let me tell you. Into this tent, every summer now for five years, come all sorts of people, fine people, college professors and economists and writers of history and all kinds. How many college presidents do you know, ha? I know three. I make their clothes. How many historians do you know? None? Almost every day comes in here Stephen Dow, the best historian in America except maybe Beard. Every day I talk to him, I argue with him, I sharpen my brains discussing things with him and with deans from Harvard and Princeton and Yale. I sit here and stuff myself with sawdust, eh? Let me tell you, Miss Liebowitz . . .'

'Tell it to the Marines,' Ruth Liebowitz said through her teeth. She stood up and grabbed Abe's umbrella. 'I guess I don't have to stay here and be yelled at — and in a tent at that.'

She started out, Abe right with her. 'A tent is as good a place for brains to grow as anywhere else, even maybe Rockefeller Center,' he shouted. 'This tent is always full of brains. Is it religion you want to discuss? All right, I will discuss it. Is it economics? All right. Is it revolution? I am an old revolutionary, I know all about that business. Is it history? Okay, I have read history. But if it is novels, I resign. Novels I do not consider brains. Storytelling is for children's bedtimes and silly women.'

'Oh, it is!' Ruth said, because she was so mad she couldn't think of anything else to say. She ducked out through the flap and stood for a moment on the single step with the rain in her face while she fought the umbrella open. Abe came up behind her and spread his hands, grinning. 'Say now, listen . . .'

But Ruth pulled the black umbrella close down over her head and marched out the path through the grass, hopped the muddy stream flowing down the roadside ditch, and went on down the road to the inn.

About eleven o'clock the rain blew to a stop, the clouds fogged off northwestward leaving pools of blue sky, the maples along the street dripped quietly. Abe sat in the tent and read in the book he had happened to have in his hand when Ruth Liebowitz left. It was Beard, and Beard was a great historian. But his eyes kept lifting from the page, looking outside into the clearing weather. Twice he waved at people going by; once a cottager brought a child's coat for mending. The blue pools in the sky grew, the roiled clouds thinned.

Abe looked over his shoulder at the picnic basket. He was getting hungry, and there was a whole chicken in there, bread and butter, maybe pickles, potato salad, pie or cake. It would serve the girl right if he ate everything. But he kept thinking that any time she went into that dining room she would meet the snobbery naked and unmistakable, and if he didn't get the basket to her she would have to eat in the dining room. At the same time, suppose he went up to the inn carrying this basket. What kind of nonsense would that look like, the two of them starting on a picnic in the pouring rain, and a half hour later the girl coming home alone, and an hour after that Abe Kaplan with the untouched picnic basket? There were enough ways of making a fool of yourself without trying that one.

He threw the Beard angrily into the box and kicked the box under the bed. Angrily he clapped his hat on his head and went down the rainwashed street and up the U-drive to the inn. At the door, kicking his feet back and forth on the steel mat, he looked through the screen and saw Mrs. Brown in the kitchen and beckoned her.

'Hello,' he said, when she came. 'Would you maybe go to Miss Liebowitz's room and ask her to come down? It is important I should see her. As a special favor to me, please.'

He saw bewilderment spreading in Mrs. Brown's face, and it enraged him. 'Miss Liebowitz came home because she was not feeling well. But tell her please it is important I should see her here a minute.'

He stepped back and out on the lawn. 'I will be by the croquet place,' he said. He got a mallet and started a croquet ball around the terrace. The ball kicked up a rising trail of drops, and left a dark streak on the wet lawn. Abe played carefully all the way around, hit the home stake and started off again, and he was almost around the second time when the screen clicked.

Ruth Liebowitz came out on the step, her lively eyes very careful and cool and polite like the eyes of a clerk who must wait on everyone but who does not like the person she is waiting on now. Abe beckoned. Miss Liebowitz did not move. Using his mallet like a cane, he went and planted himself before her. 'I appreciate it that you would come down,' he said. 'Would you walk this way, please, so we can talk?'

'We can talk here.'

'Not confidentially,' Abe said, and looked at the bridge table set up down the porch.

Miss Liebowitz languidly stepped down and followed him over to the croquet wickets. Her eyes were still cold.

'Now look,' Abe said. 'It is like this. You shouldn't get mad at a little argument. Every day I have arguments ten times worse. Does anybody get mad? Not once. We laugh and part friends.'

'Maybe so,' said Miss Liebowitz indifferently, 'but I did not come up here on my vacation to be insulted.'

'Oh, insulted!' Abe had lifted his spread hand to count off some logic for her, but something in her eye stopped him. He let the hand drop. 'If you're insulted, I am sorry,' he said. 'Novels or history, what does it matter? If it is novels you want, you should come not to me but to the village library, which is open Wednesday and Saturday afternoons. If it is history or religion or arguments you want, I am your man.'

'All right,' she said. 'Is that all you came to tell me?'

Abe stiffened his back. 'There is one other thing. Up at my place is that basket. I didn't bring it here because that would look funny. But I thought now the rain has stopped you might rather eat that than eat at the inn. So if you will tell me some place you want it, I will take it there.'

Ruth Liebowitz looked down over the square. Her nostrils pinched in momentarily. 'I guess we'll just forget the lunch. I wouldn't want to bother you.'

'It's no bother.'

'It's a lot of trouble to go to for a woman who reads *novels*.'

Abe blinked, but let it pass, and the moment it passed he knew that everything was all right again. Ruth Liebowitz smiled, her eyes filled with light, her good broad fresh face crinkled and curved, and they stood on the croquet ground laughing at each other.

'Well,' Abe said, 'that is some relief, I tell you. I thought you would hold those novels against me all my life.'

'I will, if you ever say anything like that again. You were positively insulting. Besides, you were absolutely wrong.'

'Yes,' Abe said. 'I suppose. I remember something about sawdust, too. But I tell you, this is no place to squabble. We can take that basket and eat down by the lake. And after lunch I will do penance, I will take you to the library and let you see some novels.'

The library occupied the front half of the firehouse — a bare room with shelves around three sides, and a table and a chair for old Mrs. Budd. Ruth was squatting against the wall reading titles on the lower shelf when she heard the door open and heard Abe's voice in loud enthusiastic greeting. She turned to see him shaking hands with two very tall men and a pretty woman in a red corduroy suit.

'Well, well, well!' he said. 'Hello, hello! Just the people I was looking for. How are you today, eh? I want you to meet somebody, a friend of mine.'

Ruth stood up and fixed her face for introductions, and Abe rushed to grab her arm and lead her up to the older man. 'Mr. Stephen Dow,' he said, 'this is Miss Ruth Liebowitz, a friend of mine from New York.'

The old man had a graven, rosy face and pure white hair, and his hands were brown from the sun. His smile was kindly and warm, his voice a resonant bass. Ruth shook his hand diffidently, feeling young and shy and a little ashamed of Abe's boisterousness, and wondering where she had seen the old man before. His face and voice were both familiar. . . .

'And Mr. and Mrs. Peter Dow,' Abe said. 'Last night when you went walking you walked up their road.'

'Oh, yes,' Ruth said. 'The view is lovely from up there.' She shook hands with Mrs. Dow, and with almost a pang noted her vivid smile, the bright, intelligent, well-cared-for, well-loved charm she wore as casually as the red corduroy. Peter Dow was very tall and rawboned, with a long homely face and a big laugh. But where had she seen the old man?

'Oh, I know!' she said. 'I knew I'd seen you before. I heard you lecture once at the New School.'

Abe was standing back, unable to conceal his pride at having brought these friends of his together. 'New School, is it? Have you lectured at the New School, Mr. Stephen Dow?'

'I'm afraid I have, Abe,' Mr. Dow said. 'Is it something I should be ashamed of?' He winked at Ruth Liebowitz.

'Maybe, maybe not,' Abe said. 'Tell me this. Did you lecture on history, or did you lecture on novels?'

'I might have lectured on either. When did you hear me?'

'Last winter,' Ruth said. 'About February, I think.'

'Then it was history. Am I in bad?'

'Oh, Abe!' Ruth said.

'No,' Abe chortled. 'You are in good. Miss Liebowitz is a novel reader, she thinks history is sawdust.'

'Isn't it?' Peter Dow asked, as if surprised. He in turn winked at Ruth Liebowitz. His wife laughed. 'Ask Dad what he comes in here for twice a week,' Peter said. 'Go on, ask him. Embarrass him.'

'All right,' Abe said, grinning. 'What are you after to read? I suppose it is novels.'

Stephen Dow bent over close to Abe's ear. 'I hate to admit it, but the village is so full of professors who donate their summer books to the library that this little room we're in right now is probably the best library of detective novels in America. I come in twice a week and take away three at a time.'

Ruth pointed her finger at Abe and screamed with laughter. For a minute she had a horrid cold feeling that she was being loud, but Peter Dow and all the rest were laughing too. 'We had an argument,' Ruth said. 'You know how he loves to argue! Well, you know what he told me? He said novels were for children's bedtimes and silly women. And here he respects you more than anybody in the village, and you read six mysteries a week!'

'And you,' said Stephen Dow gravely, 'a confirmed novel reader, attend lectures on American history at the New School for Social Research.'

'Oh, yes,' she said, not quite sure how to take him. 'I used to take courses there all the time. I think it's wonderful.'

Abe was trying to make himself heard. From the librarian's table old Emma Budd stared bleakly across the room. 'All right, all right,' Abe said. 'So you jumped on me two onto one. All right. I give up. But the question is does reading use your brains, and there I won't give up. You read novels in your spare time, I play croquet or go for a walk. But in our serious times when it means brains should be used, we all study history, even you, my friend Miss Liebowitz from New York.'

He skipped about them, his face stretched with a delighted grin. Ruth looked at the Dows and saw that they all liked him; they were amused by him and they liked him. For the first time since she had met him she began to think that perhaps he *did* have friends up here, perhaps he did have some kind of good life. It made her feel good just to see how much he liked and admired the Dows, and they kidded Abe and gathered up the old man's detective stories and walked to the door with their hands on his shoulders.

'I tell you,' he said when they were gone, 'those are fine people. The very best in the world. That is what it means to be civilized. To be as good as the best, but not hold yourself above anybody.'

'Old Mr. Dow is a very distinguished-looking man,' Ruth said.

'Looking?' Abe said. 'He is more than looking. He *is* distinguished. Also he is one of my good friends. We argue every day when he comes down for his mail. There are others too, professors and writers. In the New School you can hear them lecture, but here I can argue with them every day.'

'That must be fun for them,' Ruth said.

He grunted. 'You bet it is fun for them. I give them as good as I get, I tell you. Such arguments we have.' With a strange little smile he fell silent, watching her sidelong. 'There are worse places in the United States to live,' he said at last. 'This might look like Hickville, but all summer it is full of brains, and even in winter there are plenty of fine people.'

'Well,' she said, 'you'll convince me when you show me a Philharmonic or a Carnegie Hall. You produce some good music and I'll move right into the inn and stay the year around. They'd be delighted to have me, I'm sure.'

'Music?' Abe said. 'Music, hey? You like music? Say, listen! What are you doing tomorrow night?'

'I don't know. Maybe you think you can talk me into going out with you again.'

'Say, where would you be in this village if I hadn't shown up?'

'I wouldn't be in this village. I'd be down in the Berk-shires.'

'Maybe you're right,' Abe said. 'Should I take it as a compliment that you stayed, answer me.'

'I may not stay much longer.'

'But you have to stay until tomorrow night, anyway,' he said. 'Tomorrow we will go to the Westwick Philhar-monic. You wait. I will show you this place has every-thing New York has except maybe Chinatown and the Rockettes.'

The sun was still over an hour high when he picked her up Sunday evening. They were delayed ten minutes while he introduced her to four farmers in front of the creamery — farmers who grinned sourly and looked at the ground and said monosyllabic words in accents so marked she could hardly understand them.

'They don't fall all over themselves being cordial,' she said when they were walking again.

'That's just the way they are.'

'Well,' she said, 'what are they that way *for?*'

'Why are you the way you are?' Abe said. 'People are different. Farmers don't mix with summer people much.'

'Why not?'

'Maybe they are snobs. Maybe the summer people are snobs. Maybe nobody likes to let anybody else into his gang. I don't know. Here it is just like anywhere else. The natives are one crowd, they keep to themselves pret-ty much. The summer people are all pretty much one kind, and they make this place in the summer like New Haven. There are summer people who want to get in with the natives and can't make it, and natives who want to be like summer people and aren't accepted. There is even one woman, you will see her place tonight, who has spent fifty thousand dollars around here trying to get herself accepted among the university people. But they won't have any of her. She is just a rich widow, why should they let her in? It is like totemism, or Calvinism. You have to be elected, or born lucky.'

They were at the dock by now. A man she recognized as Martin Bentham was putting his two daughters and his tall thin wife into a rowboat. Abe pulled in the white boat they had used before, got her settled in the stern, and dug out the oars.

'Where is this music?' she said. 'Across the lake somewhere? What's all the mystery?'

'Here,' Abe said, and tossed her an auto robe. 'You can sit on this now. Maybe later you'll need it.'

Once they got out in the open lake Ruth could see rowboats, canoes, two or three sailboats, all coming like toy boats pulled on strings toward the big island that cut the lake almost in two. She could imagine some Gulliver on the island with all the strings in his hands. Abe laid to his oars. The sun was behind the hill, but the broad field of mackerel sky was purest silver and blue.

Two boys in a double kayak, their paddles dipping in swift unison, shot past them and pulled away. A sailboat far out tacked and cut into the procession as smoothly as a gull. Ruth relaxed and let her fingers trail over the edge. From up ahead around the point of the island something — radio or orchestra — opened the *Egmont* Overture.

'Well, my goodness!' she said, and sat up straight. 'You really weren't fooling.'

'Why should I be fooling?' She could see how even her momentary excitement tickled him. 'Every Sunday, unless it rains, we have such a concert. Summer people put up money for records, it is a big music library now, and Mrs. Weld, this widow I told you about, she plays the concerts from her dock. You can hear it clear across the lake, it is some kind of big expensive machine with a fancy speaker.'

'I thought the summer crowd wouldn't accept her?' Ruth said.

'She is another kind of fish, another tribe,' Abe said. 'She should go somewhere else in the summer, that's all. She thinks the way to show off big is to get a big speedboat with an American flag on it. What she doesn't get through her head is that all these professors think there shouldn't even be fishing motors on the lake. They sit out in their think-houses and they want it quiet. It's the same with everything Mrs. Weld does. She tries like anything but she does everything wrong. All the professors think she's vulgar.'

He pulled into position a hundred yards off the wide dock, lifted the rock-anchor from the bottom, and paid out clothesline until the gray rope slackened and bent in the green water. People were coming through the cedars on shore, and boats were anchoring all around them. Abe fussily helped her get down in the bottom and folded the robe over her. The *Egmont* Overture had been over three or four minutes when a man's voice said over a public-address system, 'The first number on tonight's program will be Tchaikowsky's Sixth Symphony, the *Pathétique,* played by Leopold Stokowski and the Philadelphia Symphony Orchestra.'

'That other, that was the theme song,' Abe said. 'They always start with that. People never pay any attention.'

Ruth was snuggling into the angle of thwart and gunwale, huddling the robe around her and getting set. 'Tchaikowsky!' she said. 'This is wonderful! Imagine! Oh, I just *love* the *Pathétique!'*

'All right,' Abe said. 'How is it? Is it all right? Is Westwick as good as New York, or isn't it? Where can you sit in a rowboat and listen to concerts in New York?'

'Shhhhhhh!' she said fiercely. She closed her eyes to listen better.

Now as the light faded the mackerel sky went deep rose along its fluted edges, and then dulled to gray. A whisper of after-sunset breeze stirred wavelets against the sides of boats and rocked the quiet canoes and flapped the edge of a furled sheet on a sailboat. The stirrings and low talk in the boats fell away to a murmur, to silence; the music grew stronger across the water. The sense of being among people was lost; boats dissolved gradually in the dusk, and except when someone on the dock changed records there was no light except a remote glimmer from the cottage back among the cedars. Over the liquid world the music crept like some soft whimpering beast, self-pitying and affectionate.

When it was finished there was movement, the clunk of an oar against a boat, voices, a widely-spaced spatter of applause. A boy swung his canoe closer inshore, keeping the paddle blade deep in the water and paddling with a swift figure-eight motion. Ruth Liebowitz sighed.

'That was wonderful,' she said. 'Oh, I think this is simply a *grand* idea.'

'Every Sunday, all summer long,' Abe said.

The announcer, his voice too big for the intimate dark, announced the Fifth and Sixth Brandenburg Concertos by Johann Sebastian Bach. Ruth looked up at Abe on the center thwart, his battered hat pulled around his ears and his coat collar up. The sky was blue and dark behind him.

'You're cold up there. Why don't you come down and use part of the blanket?'

'I'm not cold.'

'Don't be silly. My one hand I had out is like ice. Come on, there's plenty of room. I don't want to sit here snug while you freeze.'

'I'm not freezing. I'm perfectly . . .'

'Shhhhh!' she said. 'Come down here.

He came, crawling along the teetery boat, and slid cautiously down, and she folded the robe over him and wriggled her shoulder solidly snug against his. 'Now, isn't that better?' she whispered.

Across the water the Bach was beginning, cool and precise on the surface, but with a pulse in it like the regular warm pulse of the blood.

3

Fox in the Hayfield

FOR THREE DAYS they had been clearing Peter Dow's hill-side, topping cedars and thinning out small trees and widening the steep footpath. Their hours were warm with sun and the smell of summer woods. Sometimes they came upon patches of wild strawberries in sunny openings, and crouched to pick a handful. The ground was glossy with trillium, and the flower shafts of greater Solomon's seal stood up from the throats of the plants. The cedars were edged with a lace of new growth.

At midday they had lunch on Peter Dow's porch. This was the third time Andy had eaten with the Dows, and he liked it. He could sit and look down over layers of blue air, over the light-sown summer hilltops, and see far off the bare granite peaks of the White Mountains. Stepping closer, getting darker and more distinct with each crest, the minor ridges of hills came in folds of blue toward him until the foot of the last range touched the shore of the lake. A boat rowing in the south channel around Weld Island was like a legged waterbug from this height.

Mrs. Dow brought coffee and left them, and for a while they sat sipping, just looking out at the view. Just as Andy was beginning to feel halfway at ease, and to feel that his embarrassment at eating with summer people would eventually disappear if he let it alone, Peter Dow startled him with his booming voice. 'Well, Andy, would

you be as big a fool as I was, and build a house so high
on a hill you had to pack in food on your back every time
rain washed the road?'

'It's nice to look at,' Andy said cautiously. 'Wind'd
blow like sixty up here in winter, though.'

'That's the penalty you pay for seeing a long way,' Mr.
Dow said. He examined his hands, stained with pitch
and as calloused as a farmer's. Andy watched him, thinking that he neither looked nor talked like the headmaster
of Dryden Academy. He talked just like anybody, and he
could work like a horse. But he had a habit of speaking
sometimes as if he meant more than he said. He fixed
Andy with a quizzical eye. 'The village of Westwick is
a sample of what happens when people make a virtue
of staying out of the wind,' he said.

'E-yeah,' Andy said doubtfully. Mr. Dow boomed out
a laugh and slapped the boy's leg and rose.

'You're too agreeable when I run down your village.
Why don't you ask me how come I've spent almost every
summer for forty years in it?' Lifting his head, he sniffed
the air and looked amazed. 'How would you like to pitch
hay for Thurson this afternoon instead of clearing any
more?'

'All right with me.'

'I owe him a few days' work. Let's take him two hands
instead of one.'

'There's only one thing,' Andy said.

'What?'

'Mr. Richie might think if I'm out haying I ought to
be haying for him. He's short of help down there as 'tis.'

'The hell with Mr. Richie,' Peter Dow said. 'If he's
willing to hire you out like a livery horse it's none of his
business where I work you.'

At the crossing of the brook behind his house, Mr. Dow
took out his knife and cut a willow switch and walked

along peeling it carefully. Up along the meadow he slashed the heads off daisies with it. 'Tell me something,' he said.

'E-yeah?'

'Does Richie take the wages you make when you work out?'

'He puts half the money away for me.'

'And keeps the other half?'

'I guess.'

'That's interesting,' Mr. Dow said. 'How old are you?'

'Sixteen.'

'Graduated from high school pretty young, didn't you?'

'They let me skip a couple of grades.'

Mr. Dow began whacking at daisies again. On the other side of the meadow they looked over the snake fence into the thigh-deep timothy with the wind loose over it. The whole field lay on a slope facing east and north. The north end of the village, the flash of water from the old mill dam, the looping road to the Corners, the long trough of the valley of the Ammosaukee, and beyond all those the rampart of Sunday Mountain, lay out like something painted. The lower half of the field had been mown. Mrs. Ed Thurson, in a flowered dress and a big hat, was riding the rake, and her husband, bare to the waist and with his head done up in a red bandanna, was cocking up. Above them the haywagon leaned on the hill behind a span of black and white oxen. Every color was sharp and clean. Even the slopes of Sunday, fifteen miles away, glinted bright emerald where the sun picked out meadows among the timber.

'Where else would you see a sight like that?' Peter Dow said. 'It might as well be the year 1800.'

As they threw their legs over the snake fence the schoolmaster's big hand reached out and tried to push Andy from the top rail. For a moment they sparred, grinning

and watchful, until Andy leaped sideways and got clear.
While they walked down the fence along the edge of the
timothy he was thinking — feeling, rather, as he felt the
sun and the drift of wind and the perfect haying weather
— that of all the people he knew Peter Dow was the one
he respected most and liked most. A city man, he could
do practically anything a farmer could do, and he could
do so much more that a farmer couldn't even imagine.
And he had a way of making even a half-mile walk an
occasion of special friendliness.

Thurson's piratical figure came up the hill brandishing
a hay fork. He lobbed it like a spear, and Andy caught
it before it dug into the ground. Thurson did not ask
what Andy wanted to do, nor did Andy ask him. He simply fell to cocking up, swirling the hay into place and
locking it there with a jab of fork and foot. But there was
a special joking tone in Ed Thurson's voice as he spoke to
Peter Dow.

'Don't s'pose you know how to pitch on.'

'Don't know much,' Dow said. 'But I reckon if you can
do it I can learn.'

Thurson forked a whole haycock up onto the wagon
and vaulted up after it. He spit on his hands and rubbed
them on his pants. 'All right, Mr. Dow,' he said. 'Let the
sonofabitchin' hay fly.'

About three, Mrs. Thurson finished raking and turned
her horse toward the barn. The first load went in right
behind her. By the time the second load was on the
wagon Andy had finished cocking up. After that he and
Mr. Dow kept Thurson humping. Ed would touch his
fork to where he wanted hay, and up it would come, a
strong, thatched forkful. Corner to corner to middle to
corner, they laid it where Ed wanted it, and faster than
he could take it sometimes. They tried to make him holler
for time, but he waded around neck deep in the upbuild-

ing hay and managed somehow to make his loads, and
when he set the teeth of the hayfork into the load and
ran the great gobbets high into the mow where Andy and
Mr. Dow stood ready to mow up, he got even by dumping
hay on their heads a quarter ton at a time.

As the fifth load turned on the precarious hill and
started toward the barn, Peter Dow tossed his fork up on
top. 'You can mow this one up alone,' he said. 'See you
tomorrow.'

He sat down on a ledge of outcropping stone that went
like a wall across the field, and Andy sprawled in the stubble. They were both sweating after the furious pitching
on. 'At forty-two,' Mr. Dow said, 'you don't rally as you
did at twenty. But I think maybe we made Ed Thurson
hurry just a little, at that.'

Andy said nothing. Pretty soon he should be getting
back for chores, but he was willing to kill a few minutes
just resting here with Mr. Dow. He looked down to the
foot of the meadow, dammed by snake fence and cedar
swamp, and up to where another higher outcrop of stone
made a wall across the top. When he became aware of
Mr. Dow again he found the schoolmaster watching him,
leaning back on his elbows and fishing for a cigarette.

'I've been making myself a snoop,' Dow said. 'Asking
questions about you.'

'Me?'

'I find that you're the brightest boy who ever graduated from the local high school.'

Andy grunted, embarrassed, and could not hold Mr.
Dow's eye. 'You have the further reputation of being
about as good help as there is in the village,' Dow said.
'I know you're a good hay hand and a good hand in the
woods. Mose Thatcher says he'd rather have you on his
ice-cutting crew than any grown man in the village. Moreover, they say, you're a slow-boil sort of boy, you keep
your mouth shut and don't talk away your time.'

For a painful instant Andy met the blue eyes set in wrinkles of brown skin. His own face was warm with creeping blood. 'People expect things of you,' Mr. Dow said. 'So I've been wondering if you ever thought about going to college.'

Very carefully Andy rolled over on his belly and propped himself on his elbows. Had he ever thought about it? What else filled the time between bedtime and sleep? He studied the stubble under his nose. 'How could I?' he said.

'No money?'

'Well, that. Mr. Richie too. He takes care of me, you might say.'

'You might say,' Mr. Dow said, and knocked one bony hand lightly against the ground. 'Do you earn your keep?'

'I guess.'

'You could earn it at college too, if you had to.'

'Maybe,' Andy said. 'But . . . '

'Richie has never adopted you, has he?'

'No, not exactly. He . . . brought me up after my mother died.' He was hunting words carefully, because he did not know how much Mr. Dow knew. Everybody in the village knew well enough, but summer people lived in another world, and maybe Mr. Dow didn't.

'How long have you lived with Richie?'

'Since I was ten.'

'How long have you been working out?'

'The last couple of years.'

'But you've done the chores right along.'

'Oh, yes, right from the start I did chores.' He looked again, briefly, at Mr. Dow's long face. 'I couldn't get into a college, could I? Aren't there college boards, and Latin, and stuff like that?'

'Coming from this high school, you'd have to tutor or study for the boards,' Mr. Dow said. His mouth was humorous. 'Where are you planning to go?'

Andy felt the heat beating back into his face. It was a joke, then. 'I guess you know where I'll be going,' he said.

Abstractedly burying his cigarette butt, Peter Dow looked over the meadow. His face wrinkled into a grimace, the same sort of grimace Andy had seen him put on when he talked in town meeting. 'You just sit still,' the schoolmaster said. 'Don't move fast, or startle me. I feel a proposition coming on.'

He spoke slowly, as if he were talking to himself, or making a speech to an audience he couldn't see. 'There is the obligation that goes with having brains, for one thing,' he said. 'An intelligent man in a community like this touches maybe a hundred people. Intelligence of the same grade in a larger world can touch millions. This business of mousetraps and the world beating a path to your door has something to it, or used to have, but in our time you can't afford to wait twenty years for the world to come pounding through the brush. The world needs mousetraps too desperately.'

It came to Andy quietly, while he watched Mr. Dow talk and listened to the seriousness in the big quiet voice: This is what it might have meant to have a father. But immediately upon that thought came the images of some of the farmers he knew, the fathers of his friends. They gave their boys something, but not this.

' . . . loved this place,' Mr. Dow was saying. 'I do. But my reasons are special, I wasn't born into this and I don't have to stay. This is a static society, Andy, a dying village in a dying state. In spite of everything wonderful in it, stability, laboriousness, traditions as binding as laws, the whole state's in a backwater. It's a little tribal backwater, a survival, and it doesn't lead anywhere. History touched it once, in the Revolution, and hasn't touched it since. Whether we like it or not, the world went another way.'

'E-yeah,' Andy said, and dug in the matted grassroots with a sliver of sharp stone.

'If you left here,' Mr. Dow said, 'you wouldn't be any happier. Maybe you wouldn't be as happy, because the world you'd go into wouldn't be as certain of its values as this one is. But I'm not talking about money or fame or happiness or anything personal to you. I'm not speaking of rewards, but of what you do to earn the rewards, the obligation you owe the world for endowing you with brains. You just can't develop far enough in a society this narrow and this static. Does that make any sense to you?'

'I guess so, yes.'

'I doubt it,' Peter Dow said. 'It wouldn't have to me at sixteen. At sixteen I thought of nothing but girls and football. I flatter you by assuming that you're a better man for your age than I was.'

'Ahh!' Andy said, and let a smile slip sideways over to Peter Dow. Peter Dow slapped dust from his overalls and laughed.

'You'd make a good farmer,' he said. 'You might even get a farm around here and make it pay. A few do. But I'm advising you to get out of here and go to college.'

Andy dug at the matted roots, keeping his face down. His mind kept wanting to bound away like a lively horse, but he kept snubbing it in. 'I'd like to, no question,' he said cautiously. 'But you said I'd have to study somewhere to pass the boards. How . . .'

'That's the proposition,' Peter Dow said. 'I've got as many chores at home as Allan Richie has. We've also got a spare room. And one of the pleasant things about being headmaster of a school is that you can generally arrange a scholarship for somebody good.'

'Scholarship?' Andy said. 'At Dryden?' His head was up now, and his mind was on its hind legs.

'After a year you'd be in shape to take the exams,' Mr.

Dow said. 'If you come out as I hope you will, we can
try to wangle something for you at college — Harvard or
Yale or Princeton or Williams or wherever you decide to
go.'

'Harvard, Yale, Princeton?' Andy said. 'Thunderation,
you don't expect me to get into one of those!'

'Why not?' said Mr. Dow. 'I did.'

Andy sank back on his elbows, chewing a hay stem and
letting his mind loose to run as it wanted to. To go down
country, live with the Dows, go to a school like Dryden
(it was all monumental granite out of the quarries at
Milford, the way his mind saw it, with a mile-long arch of
elms). To go to classes with boys who had had that sort
of chance all their lives, to go into the library and take
out any book he wanted, and know that anything he
wanted was likely to be there. . . .

It did not occur to him to doubt that he could do it.
Mr. Dow thought he could; he himself knew he could.
But then it turned strange on him, a daydream he would
have to put aside, a vision with a sour ending, and it
seemed to him incredible that he should be lying there in
the stubble taking it seriously, letting himself get taken
in.

'I'd be scared green, probably,' he said.

'Of course,' Peter Dow said.

Andy had expected something else, encouragement perhaps. He rolled again onto his belly and stared across
the stubble to the bright cutbank of unmown grass halfway up the slope, and beyond the cutbank to the undula-
tions of timothy shadowed by the lightest possible of
winds. He watched a tiny stir begin far up, under the
topmost outcrop of ledge. It twisted down a dip in the
field, faded as the breeze lost itself or went dead, reap-
peared farther down. It came neither straight nor fast,
but it came almost as if it had purpose, winding a narrow
shadowy stir down the field.

Andy watched it half-aware, wondering how Mr. Richie would react to a notion like this, estimating how much there might be put away from his working for the past two years.

'What if Mr. Richie wouldn't let me go?' he said.

'Why shouldn't he?'

'Well, I owe him something, I guess. He's kept me for six years.'

'And had your services,' Peter Dow said. 'I can't answer that one, Andy. That's between you and Richie. I'd say the account was more than even, but I don't know.'

The wandering shimmer of wind had come down almost to the mown edge, and was moving erratically as if unwilling to spill over and be lost. Andy's eyes followed it while he thought. He opened his mouth to speak, and then abruptly the wall of grass parted, thirty feet from where he lay, and the face of a fox looked out.

Everything about it was pointed: the sharp nose, sharp ears, sharp eyes in which a pointed light like candleflame glittered. No other part of the fox was visible except that questing alert face, abrupt as a question mark, shocking as an idea that comes suddenly and by stealth.

Andy moved slowly, laying a hand on Mr. Dow's foot. 'Look!' he whispered.

But when Mr. Dow turned his head the wall of grass was empty. The tips waved gently, as if brushed by wind, for only a moment. The movement of the retreating fox blended with the wind shadows and was gone.

'What was it?'

'Fox.' Andy took his hand off Mr. Dow's foot and stood up. The sharp face was still a presence in his mind; he still felt cold from the suddenness and stealth of its appearance. It was perfectly clear to him what he should make of this visitation, and when he turned his head and saw Mr. Dow watching him he felt guilty, as if he had been trapped in something.

'Just poked his head out and disappeared again,' he said, knowing as he said it that Mr. Dow was not fooled. Something had come into their conversation, an intrusion had been made, a warning given.

'I'd have to talk it over with Mr. Richie,' he said desperately. 'He's . . . I don't know. He might not think it was the thing to do. I could let you know.' His eyes searched Mr. Dow's long seamed face and he felt like crawling under something. 'I thank you for thinking of it,' he said. 'It was nice of you. I could let you know.'

'No hurry,' Mr. Dow said. 'We're not going back until the middle of September.'

'E-yeah,' the boy said. 'Well, thanks, Mr. Dow.' He looked uncertainly down the meadow. 'I guess I might's well go home this side, it's shorter.'

He nodded and strode off down the meadow, just ready to break into a run to jolt the kinks out of himself, when he heard Peter Dow yelling. 'Don't take that proposition too solemnly, eh? Some of it might even be fun!'

Andy walked steadily, neither hurrying nor lagging. There was a bar of fatigue across the small of his back, and his mind was sore with the things that fretted it. Going downhill, he dropped steadily into twilight; only the hilltops over toward Sunday were still sunlit.

When he hit the road that ran up around the hill to George Pembrook's farm, he moved into deeper twilight under the maples. He was late for chores, and Mr. Richie would be mad, but still he did not hurry. Walking, he watched the sun lift off the hilltops, and by the time he came to the junction with the swamp road the color was all gone, the green hills and the farms had gone slate-colored and cold, the valleys between the ridges were beginning to fill with gray mist.

It was such a cold, pallid, dead light that Andy moved his shoulders inside his shirt. His mother had always hated that time of evening when the light went and the gray came up out of the ground and the warmth left the earth. He remembered her saying that the world went as gray sometimes in the dusk as if it had been brushed by the wing of the angel of death.

So by the side door his thoughts finally came out in the open. The shame that had come out of hiding when the fox thrust its questing muzzle out of the timothy was acknowledged now. And when his mother's mood came across to him from other gray twilight days years ago she was close to him in fact as well as in thought. On the left, through the hedgerow of spruce and chokecherry and cedar bordering the road, he saw the white rails of the cemetery fence and the steep slope of cemetery hill.

Without any conscious intention, he stopped at the gate. The cemetery climbed steeply, a broken ladder of granite and marble handholds, almost to the top of the low ridge. Along the ridge was a fringe of black spruce, and over the tips of the spruce, embedded in the metallic sky, a steely chip of moon looked straight down between the gravestones into Andy's face.

With his foot on the lowest rail he stood watching, and the curious feeling grew in him that the dead were watching too, that from the steep burial ground they observed him like spectators from an amphitheater. Men who had fought in the Revolution lay there, and women who had died under the knives of the Iroquois. Men who had helped blaze Hazen's Road to Canada and farmers who had heated musket barrels at Lundy's Lane were side by side with Grand Army men and hired hands who had died last year in an accident with a potato digger. Father, grandfather, great-grandfather, great-great-grandfather, they lay there freed from time, and looked down from

their spruce-and-moon-tipped hill on what had always
been there:

A village no bigger, no wealthier, no different in appearance from what it had been in the years after the
Revolution when the first houses went up along Broken-
Musket Brook. Men whose names were Bradford and
Wills and Page and Calvert and Hunt and Mount and
Goodale and Kent, the same names the earliest gravestones carried. A village, still half-colonial, clustered
around its square; and around it, on the hills, farms that
were still half wilderness after a hundred and sixty years.

Nothing changed in Westwick. The teachers read off
the same names from the roll, the farms went on from
father to son to grandson, the girls married local boys so
that everybody was everybody else's cousin. Nothing
changed, unless it grew a little tireder and older and less
patient with intruders and intrusive ideas; unless all those
calm eyes from the burial ground weighed more heavily
on the village as the generations passed; unless under the
pressure of the static years little by little of what had
been won from the wilderness was given up.

Back in the hills, too far off the roads for profitable
farming, too far off for farm women to keep their sanity,
too far for the school team or the snowplow to reach in
bad weather, abandoned houses and barns the color of
tarnished silver rotted slowly in the quiet, and every summer the goldenglow sprang up tall and yellow around
their untrodden doors, and little by little the spruce
marched in from the woods and engulfed the meadows,
took them back. Every year the banks gave up on some
of those farms, tired of the struggle to find a tenant; and
every year the hedgehogs found new sheds to nest and
gnaw in undisturbed. Every spring the hazel brush was
closer to screening off the blind openings of what had
once been roads.

Everybody in Westwick worked hard, worked himself to the bone, barring a few like his uncle, James Mount. And most found themselves poorer in the end than in the beginning, their whole lifetime of callousness and rheumatism gone in the effort simply to hold their father's ground, or not quite hold it.

The dead watched from their stony hillside, his mother among them, and his father whom he had never known. They waited unhurriedly to see what he would do. They spoke neither advice nor warning, unless everything he knew of their lives was a warning, unless the sharp face of Mr. Richie which poked into his thoughts as suddenly and alertly as the foxhead emerging from the grass was a warning. Mr. Richie, old Foxy Grandpa, was certainly warning enough. And how had he happened to get tied up with Mr. Richie? How had his mother happened to die as she had died, in disgrace and alone? It was all there, every shameful detail of it, waiting just behind a little door in his mind.

He was looking at the Foxy Grandpa book that Mr. Richie had given him when he heard the lock click. Instantly he shoved the book under him and crowded back against the wall, his feet just sticking over the edge of the cot, his arms hugged tight around his body. In his terror his body felt small and insufficient, hardly enough to hang onto.

They came in just the way they had come in every day since they brought him here, Mr. Richie first, then the insurance detective from Concord; Mr. Richie's sharp little face poked forward, smiling, his eyebrows moving up and down, and the detective behind him tall and solemn, red-nosed, with his handkerchief in his hand. The detective had hay fever, and his eyes always looked red-rimmed like a hound's. The boy watched them come in and shut the door; he felt the rough plaster wall through his shirt, and the bulge of the overall straps up his spine.

Mr. Richie sat down and thumped his knees. 'Well, Bub,' he said cheerfully. The detective also sat down, blowing his nose. It was all the same as it had been before. In a minute they would start asking him, and prodding him, and sticking their faces out at him, trying to make him say something that hadn't happened.

'Treating you all right?' Mr. Richie said. His little fox-face was grinning, and he twinkled under white eyebrows.

The boy nodded.

'You like being in jail, uh?' the detective said.

Andy shook his head.

'Now looky here, Bub,' Mr. Richie said, 'We ain't tryin' to be mean to you. You just tell us the truth about how that fire started and you'll be out of here in a minute.'

'I already told you!' the boy squeaked.

'You told us something,' the detective said. 'How about telling us the truth?'

Without taking his sharp blue twinkling eyes off the boy, Mr. Richie dug into his pocket, got a cigar, bit off the end and spit it out, found a match, lighted it under his chair, puffed, and said through the smoke, 'Still an accident, was it?'

Andy nodded.

'You just went down with a candle to the barn and the swallows flapped around the light and scared you and you dropped the candle and run and that set the barn afire.'

The boy nodded, swallowing.

'You lived on a farm all your life,' the detective said heavily, 'and you don't know no better'n to go into a haymow with a candle. You don't know swallows'll fly at a light. You don't know enough to make sure a light's out before you go.'

The boy said nothing.

'Why'd they send you down there with a candle?' the detective said harshly, and stuck his face forward.

'There wasn't any oil for the lantern.'

''Tisn't as if Branch Willard was any kin of yours,' Mr. Richie said mildly. 'He ain't but your stepfather. You don't have to protect him. He never treated you very good anyway, did he?'

Andy did not answer.

'*Did he?*' the detective said.

The boy jumped, but said nothing.

'Why hadn't Branch put any hay into that barn yet?' the detective said.

'He had.'

''Bout five load,' the detective said. 'You think we're silly, boy? Everybody's got a barnful of hay in, and here's Willard with a twenty-acre meadow he hasn't touched.'

'I guess he was busy,' Andy said, and drew his knees up under his chin, crowding himself against the wall. 'He was selling the calves.'

'And you know why,' the detective said. He blew his nose, wrenching the end harshly. 'He wanted 'em out of that barn when he burned it down. He wanted his insurance but he didn't want to lose his stock.'

The boy hiccoughed. A nerve in his cheek twitched, and he put his hand over his face. He looked at Mr. Richie for help, but Mr. Richie was rolling his cigar in his lips and looking out the window.

'He's a slick one,' the detective said. 'I never seen any slicker trick. Sending a kid down to the mow with a candle and then saying the swallows scared him. He sent you, didn't he?'

The boy kept still.

'*Didn't* he?'

'Yes, but . . .'

'What for?'

'Some pitchforks.'

'What'd he want of them after dark?'

'I don't know.'

'Savin' his pitchforks too,' the detective said. He leaned back and reached for his handkerchief.

Mr. Richie blew half a dozen rings and said, ''Tisn't as open and shut as all that, Rufe. How in thunder would he know the swallows'd fly down and scare the boy? How'd he know the boy'd drop his candle and run?'

'There's a fifty-fifty chance of a fire any time you send a kid into a mow with a candle,' the detective said.

Andy was grateful to Mr. Richie. Mr. Richie lived in the village, and even if he did sell insurance and even if he had been helping the detective all along, he was somebody familiar at least. And he wasn't as rough as the detective, and he smiled all the time.

'Just the same,' Mr. Richie said, standing up and pointing the cigar at him, 'we know Branch Willard burned down that barn a-purpose. You might as well tell us.'

'I told you already,' Andy said. 'Honest, Mr. Richie . . .'

'We might's well go,' Mr. Richie said, and put the cigar back in his mouth.

The detective rose grumbling. 'Three days,' he said. 'Three days in this damn place where every meadow looks as if it'd been planted to goldenrod. You'll never get anything out of this kid.'

'Never did expect to,' said Mr. Richie cheerfully.

'Then what are we keeping him for?'

'Got a right to hold him,' Mr. Richie said. 'Long as he says it was him set the barn afire we got a right to hold him.'

'What good will that do?'

Mr. Richie held the door open and twinkled past the detective at the boy. 'Trouble with you,' he said, 'you ain't got the imagination to bait a hook.' The door snapped shut behind them, and Mr. Richie's voice went down the hall. 'If you was Martha Mount, and you'd married a good-for-nothing like Branch, and he had an insurance fire, and they come and put your boy in jail for it, what would you . . . ?'

The voice dwindled and went away, and Andy relaxed a little against the wall. He pulled the Foxy Grandpa book from under him and looked at it stupidly. What if Branch had wanted to burn the barn down? But he couldn't have. Everything had happened just as Andy had told them. Big with terror as that night was, he went over it, trying to remember something new.

He went out with the candle after Branch shook the oil can and found it empty, and went creeping through the blackness that blanketed sky and ground. Holding his hand around the candle flame to shield it from the wind that wandered down the hill toward the swamp, he went in the cow stable and through the milk room and up the ladder to the high drive. Then just as he stuck the candle on a beam the things came, beating at the light, at his head, flapping around him with batlike squeaking noises, and he screamed and ran through the black mow, banging into the double doors, ripping a fingernail getting the bars up. Then he ran across the back lot toward the kitchen window, and slammed into a leaning wireless fencepost in the dark, knocking his wind out, and the next he remembered was Mumma picking him up off the back stoop and carrying him inside. He was still crying, not yet over his scare, when Branch came running in the back door and said the barn was afire. His candle must have dropped off the beam into the hay.

So it had been an accident, plain as that. How was he

to know the terrible fluttering things were only swallows? The memory of the awful black loom of the mow, and of the unseen squeaking things that swooped down, contracted his whole body like a chill. He flapped the pages of the Foxy Grandpa book.

He wondered if the detective would put him in jail for a long time. He thought that probably Mr. Richie wouldn't let him. Mr. Richie was too jolly to let a boy be put in jail for an accident. Mr. Richie was always making jokes. Andy remembered the way the men in the store had laughed one day when Mr. Richie was telling about a joke he played on a city man. The city man had bought a cow and had brought it to Mr. Richie to make sure he hadn't got stung. Mr. Richie had looked the cow over, opened her mouth and looked in, and said, 'My gosh, man, this cow ain't got any teeth in her upper jaw. She'll starve to death in a week.' The city man was so ashamed to have been beaten in a deal that he sold the cow to Mr. Richie for forty dollars, to make beef out of, and when he found out how Mr. Richie had fooled him he sold his cottage and moved away and never came back.

Mr. Richie wouldn't let him get put in jail for very long. Maybe Mumma would come and get him out. That was what Mr. Richie seemed to expect. Only why didn't Mr. Richie go up to the farm and see Mumma if that was what he wanted? He swallowed as he remembered how the two men had come up to the farm three days ago and asked a few questions and taken him away, and how Mumma had hung onto him and cried. He shut his eyes tight to squeeze the two big tears that oozed into his eyes.

Lying down on the cot, he craned under to look at the rusty springs, put his hand tentatively around the iron leg. Then he sat up and listened. Someone was coming again.

The door opened, and it was Mumma. 'Andy!' she said.

'Oh, poor Andy boy!' She grabbed him in her arms and hugged him, and he smelled the store smell of her shirt-waist. 'Have they scared you?' she said. 'Have they been mean to you?'

'They keep trying to make me say Branch burned down the barn on purpose.'

Her arms tightened. She kissed the top of his head, then held him away to look at him. There were tear streaks in the flour she had used to powder her face. 'Did they feed you?' she said. 'Did you have enough to eat? You look thin.'

'Oh, yuh,' he said vaguely. He looked at the faces of Mr. Richie and the detective in the doorway. Mr. Richie winked at him.

'Do you mind staying here a little while longer?' Mumma said. 'I want to talk to Mr. Richie.'

'Can't I go?'

'I'd rather you stayed here,' she said.

'Mumma! Don't you tell them anything just to get me out! They tried to make me say it wasn't an accident, but it was.'

'Don't you worry,' Mumma said. Her eyes blinked and she turned away. 'I'll be back in a little while, Andy.' She turned back, took him by the shoulders and shook him gently. 'You won't mind, just for a few minutes, will you?'

They were some time coming back, and when they came he saw that his mother had been crying again. The boy stood up, and his mother came across the room very fast and hugged him tightly. Her voice sounded choked. 'You'll hate your Mumma,' she said. 'That's what I can't stand, you'll hate your Mumma.'

He clung to her, trying to look into her face, but she kept her head turned. Mr. Richie had lighted another cigar.

'They're going to put your Mumma in jail,' she said.

Andy's eyes went from his mother's twisted, averted face to Mr. Richie's. 'You don't have to pretend any more, Bub,' Mr. Richie said. 'Your Mumma's told us all about it.'

'But it was the things!' Andy said. 'The swallows, they came down and knocked the candle over . . .'

'And it went out,' the detective said. 'Branch went out afterwards and stuck a match in the hay, like he'd been plannin' all the time and then plannin' to lay it on you for bein' careless.'

Andy's hands clenched in his mother's coat. 'Mumma, he didn't, did he?'

She nodded.

'But why are they going to put you in jail?' he wailed. 'You never did it, it was Branch.'

'I helped him,' she said. 'You'll never forgive me, Andy, but I was even going to help him lay it onto you, because I thought if it was an accident and we didn't blame you for it you wouldn't feel bad. If there'd been any other way we could see . . . We were awful hard up, Andy.'

The boy wet his lips. 'Why don't they put Branch in jail?'

'He's left. I don't know where. They'll put him in too if they can catch him.'

He stood very still, letting the detective's long face and hound-eyes, Mr. Richie's lips with the cigar between them, his mother's pale flour-streaked face twisted with crying, go around him in a confused blur. It was all a part, a continuation of the terror he had felt when he went out into the pitch blackness with his candle. It had sent him blind and screaming across the high drive under the black loft when the things came down, it had left him throat-dry and frozen when he looked out and saw the flames licking from both doors of the barn and knew that he had done it. It had been with him for three days in the jail while the detective's face and Mr. Richie's face thrust out at him, sharp-lipped, saying sharp words.

'I'm ashamed, Andy,' his mother said. 'I'm so ashamed I could die.'

He swallowed, only half hearing her, and a thought came beating down like the terrifying wings from the dark mow. 'What'll I do?' he said. 'Where'll I go, Mumma?'

Mr. Richie smiled and winked. 'Your Mumma and I talked it over,' he said. 'You're comin' to live with me. I ain't so mean I can see a boy thrown out in the world like that. You'll go to school in the village. Think you can make yourself useful enough to earn your keep?' He smiled widely and winked again, his fox-face full of good humor and friendliness.

Andy tugged at his mother's coat, still watching Mr. Richie. 'Mumma?'

'Mr. Richie's very kind to offer it,' she said. 'He'll take care of you till I come back, and you'll be a good boy, won't you?'

Andy looked at Mr. Richie's lips. Mr. Richie's hand came up and took the cigar out of them, and the lips smiled. The boy stared at him, hardly seeing him at all, seeing only the smiling lips. He smelled the store smell of his mother's clothes.

'Yes,' he said. He laid his face against the store smell, and his fingers dragged at the coat. With his eyes shut tight he screamed into the muffling cloth, 'But I'll hate him! I'll hate him as long as I live!'

And there she lay among the quiet dead, her bequest to her son not even a dying farm with a sagging barn and meadows grown to paintbrush and redtop, but only a shame that all the village knew, a heritage as heavy and inescapable as a mortgage. When your mother dies in prison you start your life not merely empty-handed but with your hands tied.

Suppose he stayed and did his best to live down that shame, what then? Eventually, maybe, he could get together the down payment on a farm, and from there he could fight back to where his father had been fifteen years ago — chiseling at the face of a hard country and picking at the durable surface of a debt, marrying a second cousin and leaving his children the shelter of his roof and the burden of his obligations, and eventually joining the others of his name under the granite and marble hill.

Andy sighed. His eyes, staring up the broken tiers of stone to the ridge and the moon-tipped spruce, caught a movement along the black horizon, and a deer went up over the ridge, clearly outlined, delicate-footed and jerky, and dropped out of sight on the other side.

It would be so wonderful if he could do that, climb up out of this and escape, just go over the ridge and never have to look back. . . .

He looked around quickly, afraid that someone might be watching him. It was almost wholly dark in the road. The sky was laced with branches. Between the trunks of the roadside trees he could look down toward Calvert's and see the valley filling with slatey mist. At a dogtrot he started down the last quarter-mile to the village.

4

White Mouse

IN HER MIND, deep in the defensive skull, Helen Barlow had a hiding place. When she was in it, it was like being in the lagoon of an atoll behind protective reefs, or in a hidden valley among mountains.

Often she induced herself into this place, saying open sesames before the entrance. Any passage of sibilant, lulling poetry would do, but the one she liked most, the one that brought tears to her eyes with its sweetness, was from Tennyson's 'Lotus Eaters.'

'There is sweet music here,' she would say in her mind, and the spell would begin.

> There is sweet music here that softer falls
> Than petals from blown roses on the grass,
> Or night-dews on still waters between walls
> Of shadowy granite, in a gleaming pass;
> Music that gentlier on the spirit lies,
> Than tired eyelids upon tired eyes. . .

Like a sleep that she could summon at will, like a drugged dream, the private world would open and let her in. Sometimes she went to bed early for the sake of lying warm in bed and inducing her day-dreams. But sometimes she slipped into the hiding-place without conscious intention, when she was bored or tired or waiting, and then there was always the danger of awaking to find that she had been watched. She hated the thought of that as she would have hated the thought of being spied on in the bathroom.

This time she awoke with her heart fluttering and found her mother already standing, the congregation already moving up the aisle. Quickly Helen stood up and sidled into the stream of people, holding back there to let her mother go ahead. In the jam at the door, where Mr. Tait was shaking hands with people, she got shoved against her mother's broad back, and with something like loathing she felt the rubbery roll of flesh across the fat woman's shoulder blades above the constriction of the corset.

She shook hands with Mr. Tait and got his warm paternal smile and stepped down to the lawn. A voice said, 'Have a nice sleep?' and she turned to see Flo Barnes. In the ten days since Helen had seen her, the secretary had got startlingly tanned. Among the golden-tan of the cottagers and the sun-hating whiteness of the village women she looked like a barbaric foreigner. In her dark face her eyes were like blue ice, her teeth dazzling.

'Oh!' Helen said. 'Hello. You scared me.' She laughed an abrupt little cautious laugh. 'What do you mean, sleep?'

'I was watching you. You were a million miles away.'

'I didn't mean to be. I don't even think I was.'

'You were, all right,' Flo said. 'You were lucky.'

With a smile in the corners of her mouth she looked around at the crowd, and Helen, seeing for a moment with the outsider's eyes, noticed the black straw bonnets with violets or daisies on them, looking, she thought, straight out of the 1910 Sears Roebuck catalogue. She saw the stiff heavy suits of the men, the differences of ease and grace, even in this ultimate Christian citadel of village life, between the city people and the villagers.

'Quite a little town,' Flo said. 'Utterly unspoiled. I can see how Mattie felt.'

Helen let her eyes meet those of the secretary. More bitterness than she intended must have been in the look, for one of the level brows above the ice-blue eyes went up. The red mouth twitched.

'But it's your home town,' Flo said. 'That makes a lot of difference.'

Helen swung around and started across the lawn. Flo followed. At the roadway she began to laugh.

'Did I say something funny?' Helen said. She was angry at being spied on, angry that this woman in two minutes should know more about what she felt than anyone else in the village. There was something so irritatingly adept in the way that confession, if it was a confession, had been extracted. The wire loop had been lowered, the fish had swum in, and up it came with the wire around its gills.

Miss Barnes was still laughing. She seemed greatly amused. 'A bird in a gilded cage,' she said. 'Why don't you get out of this jerk town if that's the way you feel? What's holding you, the golden opportunities?'

'Oh, you don't know!'

They were already at the drive that continued up the crest of the hill to Helen's house, and she stopped uncertainly, searching the other woman's brown face. For no reason she could name, she felt all gone to pieces inside. 'This is where I live,' she said lamely, and after a moment added, 'Would you come in a while?'

'You don't want to go in. Why don't you come and paddle around with me? I came over in a kayak.'

'Oh, I couldn't.'

'Why not?'

'Dinner's in about an hour.'

'Skip dinner. I've got some candy bars in the boat.'

'Oh no, I . . .'

'Go get your bathing suit and come along.'

'I really couldn't stay out but a little while . . . '

'That isn't important,' Flo said. 'Run in and get your suit. Let's go somewhere where we can talk.'

On the north side of the lake, where Weld Island squeezed in within a quarter mile of shore, there was a stretch of almost a mile of steep shore without a single cottage. A New York millionaire had bought it as a wedding present for his daughter years before, and the daughter had never come back to claim it. From waterline to county road the hill was clothed in belts of heavy timber, maple and beech and hemlock stepping down to a strip of tall cedars along the shore. Many of the cedars had been undermined by waves and ice and had fallen outward, some of them clear in, some only far enough to lean precariously against the air. Those which had fallen outward, some of them clear in, some only far from floating free, made underwater gardens, and perch swam through their branches and around the stubs of old waterlogged cedars from many years ago that now lay on the rocky bottom, brown and wavery through ten feet of clear water. Above these submarine gardens the lean-ing cedars made another sort of garden in the air, and a boat or canoe drifting between the branches was like the perch that glided underneath. It was fairly easy, if you leaned over the side of a quiet boat and let your eyes go out of focus, to confuse the subaqueous gardens with the aerial gardens above, and the reflection of the hanging cedars and the wavering shapes of the sunken ones swam together into a single image.

Helen and Flo Barnes, resting after the hard paddle against the open-lake wind around the point, came through the cedar gardens as quietly as the perch. The kayak, low in the water, rode its own reflection, and a face that leaned over to look into the water, or a hand trailed over the side, met a face or hand coming up. For a long time Helen hung over the gunwale looking deep into her own eyes, and seeing beyond the reflection of her face the hallucinatory sunken snags and the drowned cedar fronds and the bright quick perch.

Flo moved her paddle against the boat, and a frog hit the water from shore. Helen saw his green shape kick itself down angling until he sprawled on the bottom. His human-looking hind legs and long webbed feet trailed out behind. She could see the bump of his eyes move as if he were looking up at her. When she dropped her hand in the water the frog swam away in a spurt of sand, and she lost him among the shifting light-shadows on the bottom.

'How about a swim?' Flo said.

Helen turned, her eyes still misty and her mind dazed with the remoteness that came over her sometimes. As her eyes and mind cleared, she saw Flo Barnes, strong and confident and armored against weakness or regret or indecision, and the realization of the woman's tidal strength and confidence and resourcefulness brought her a pang of envy so black and ugly that she turned her face aside.

'All right,' she said. 'Shall we go over to the Welds'?'

'What's the matter with here?'

'Where would we dress?'

'We might dress in the woods here, but the rocks are better.'

'But they're in plain sight!'

'Not all of them, they're not,' Flo said. 'Before anybody is up in the morning I swim out to the rocks and back. There's a good place.'

'But . . .'

'What are you scared of?' Flo said. Swinging the kayak on a stiff left paddle she shot it out of the cedars toward the turtleback granite rocks a hundred yards offshore.

Helen helped pull the kayak up out of the water, and stood up in her bare feet. On the rock she felt as exposed as a mouse in a white empty room. With her toes gripping the granite she looked at the secretary, who went on unbuttoning the front of her white dress while nodding down between the two biggest rocks.

'Right down there. You stand in the water and the rocks hide you from shore. Throw your clothes up here.'

Obediently Helen scrambled down until the cold water tightened around her ankles. The angle of the rock shielded her on three sides, but left her exposed to the open lake. There were three boats in sight, far out. She laughed a little, nervously. 'This needs a front door.'

Flo leaned over the rock. Her dress was unbuttoned to the waist; below the taut brassiere her stomach was as brown as her face. 'Lord's sake,' she said, 'those boats are a half mile away!'

Helen stood hesitating. She would almost as soon have undressed before an open window in the village square. The sense of unbearably bright light on her made her fingers clumsy, but she stepped out of her pants and into her bathing suit, pulled the suit up around her waist, and then quickly pulled the dress over her head. With a last wriggle she unhooked the brassiere and pulled the straps of the suit over her shoulders and was safe.

Flo Barnes slid down over the rock in her underwear, and unhurried, with no attempt to hide either from Helen or the open eye of the lake, she stripped and tossed her underwear up with her dress. She filled her lungs with air, stood on tiptoe in the water and stretched, with her arms over her head. All unconcerned she exposed herself, front, back, and sides, and Helen's fascinated eyes saw that she was not tanned as a bather gets tanned, from the breast up and the thighs down. She was evenly brown all over.

Standing like a ship's figurehead, strong and shapely and the color of stained wood, Flo slanted an oblique look at Helen. 'You'll remember me next time!'

Helen flushed painfully. 'I'm sorry. I didn't . . . You're so brown.'

She slid up until her back was against the sloping rock, and Flo took one white ankle in her big brown hand, squeezed it, moved down over the slim arch. 'Pretty little feet,' she said. 'You're like a white mouse.'

'Get your suit on and let's swim.'

'Suit? Are you nervous?'

Flo dove in and switched in the water and came up facing Helen, flinging her short mop of water-dark hair sideways out of her eyes. Treading water, her body was foreshortened, and looked wide and blocky. 'Come on, mouse,' she said.

Careful to keep her hair dry, Helen slipped in and swam twice around the rocks. Flo played around her, swimming breast stroke, crawl, dog paddle, putting her face in the water and blowing like a playful horse in a trough, chugging around Helen with a burst of speed, beaver diving, rolling over and over. Later they stretched out in the water with their hands on the shelf where they had dressed and their feet kicking gently. The tightness in Helen's chest had gone, and her blood was racing. She felt alive and happy and not nervous any more about Flo's nakedness and the possible eyes on shore or in the boats. She looked at the secretary, and Flo rolled in the water slowly, an inexpressibly voluptuous movement like some blonde Juno yielding herself to wantonness, and stretched her arm against Helen's, brown against white. 'We make a nice contrast.'

'I feel like a slug,' Helen said. 'How did you get so brown in a few days?'

'I lie out on the roof after lunch. The old lady and all

the family retainers are believers in the afternoon nap. Come over sometime. I'll get you brown.'

Helen met the ice-blue eyes, almost too blue to be looked into, for only a moment. She felt tingly and excited, and kicked her feet in the water so that her palms pushed against the granite. 'I freckle,' she said. 'I burn and blister and then I freckle.'

Flo's hand moved and touched Helen's shoulder. 'You've got a nice skin. You come over, I'll guarantee to get you brown.'

'I guess I'm not the type,' Helen said, and laughed a little. The secretary snorted into the water and rolled over on her back with the back of her head on the ledge and the water lapping at her ears. Her nipples, contracted in the water, were puckery red buds. She smiled slowly, watching Helen.

'Just a little white mouse,' she said into the air, absently. 'Scared of people, scared of excitement, scared of herself, scared of anything new. Why don't you get out of this place and learn not to be scared of things?'

'Yes?' Helen said. 'How?'

'Just go. You know you hate this stuffy little burg. You're just scared to cut loose.'

'Who'd look after my family?'

'Can't your family look after themselves?'

'My father's paralyzed.'

'Oh,' Flo said. 'What, stroke?'

'I guess.'

'You guess? Don't you know?'

'He'd never let us call a doctor,' Helen said. 'He just came home one day saying he felt terrible, and next morning he couldn't move his legs. He's never been up since.'

'How long have you been Winnie the Breadwinner?'

'Oh, I'm no breadwinner,' Helen said. 'I guess we're

pretty well off, actually. It's just . . . I was in my last year of college. I had to come home. I never would have finished, only they let me do the last semester by correspondence, I was so close. That was four years ago.'

Talking about it agitated her so that she had to crawl out on the sun-warmed rock. The sleek mermaid shape of Flo Barnes slid out after her, and Helen looked in alarm at the distant boats, then over toward shore where walkers might be passing, or boys fishing. Flo watched her with amused eyes.

'What would you do?' she said abruptly. 'If you could do exactly what you wanted to, what would you do?'

'I wouldn't even dare think about it.'

'Come on, you think about it all the time. What?'

'I honestly don't know. It's so impossible.'

'Forget how impossible it is. You've got some notion.'

'Well,' Helen said, and looked almost coquettishly at the other woman, the straight T of brows and nose, the strong throat, the sprawling naked body. Without real embarrassment or any other cause she felt herself going dull red. 'I don't know,' she said. 'I'd get away.'

'Where to?'

'I don't know. New York. Boston, maybe.'

'And do what? Get a job?'

'I suppose I'd have to. But all I can do is teach, or do some kind of clerical work. Neither one appeals to me, though.' She shook her shoulders. 'I don't know, honestly. It's all so silly.'

The secretary's hand came out and took hold of Helen's instep, shook her foot slowly. She was smiling a strange warm smile. 'So what is it?'

Letting her knee wobble as Flo wagged her foot, Helen put her face down on the other knee and smiled and shook her head. 'I bet if I told you you'd think I was the craziest person in New Hampshire.'

'I guess not,' Flo said. 'I think you're all right, see?'

'I *am* crazy, though,' Helen said. 'I know it, but I can't help it.' She took a deep breath, glancing sideways into the secretary's face. 'I want to write poetry,' she said. She ducked her head as she said it, hugging her knees. A flaw of wind crossed the rock and goosepimples popped out on her arms and legs. 'I guess that's crazy enough to hold you!' she said, and with her hot cheek pressed against her knees she looked up again sideways at the woman who was so thoroughly everything Helen Barlow was not — who was poetry in herself, and didn't have to hunt in secret places for words to put her longings into.

'Sure,' Flo said, her mouth smiling faintly, her eyes on Helen's face. 'Of course, I should have seen it. You naturally would, it's in everything you do. Everything about you is frail and white and dainty. It wouldn't be natural if you *didn't* write poetry.'

'I have for a long time,' Helen said gratefully.

'Publish any?'

Helen held up three fingers.

'Where? Could I see them?'

The conversation was getting painful and exciting and difficult, so that Helen bent her face away and studied the crystals like miniscule snowflakes in the granite at her feet. 'They were just in the Woodsville *Gazette*,' she said. 'I just got a notion once and sent them in and they printed them all. They weren't in any magazine.'

'Why don't you send in some more?'

'I'd rather — you know, the *Gazette* isn't such a good place to publish poetry. If I could get some in magazines, you know, where you could feel they were *really* published . . .'

'When can I see some of your poems?' Flo said.

'Oh, would you like to?' Helen said. 'Any time, if you'd really like to. I've got a notebook full of things.'

'That's a promise,' Flo said.

They were silent for a while in the baking heat of the rock. Out on the lake a fisherman shouted something to another boat, and the other boat answered. Clouds like sheep grazed along the crest of the western hill.

'Of course I'll never write anything worth reading,' Helen said. 'I'm no good. I just do it because I want to, for fun.'

'It sounds as if you had a lot of time to yourself,' Flo said, and the blue eyes sharpened, the strong neck bent a little with her intent stare.

Helen jerked her eyes away. 'Who would there be to spend time with?' she said bitterly. 'Last winter there was Mattie, at least. But now there won't be anybody. The other teachers are no good, they're as bad as the rest of the village.' She picked at the granite crystals with her nails and raised her eyes to Flo's face. 'Would you believe it,' she said, 'there's only one person in the village, outside the teachers, who's been to college, and he's an old turkey farmer out on the Corners road.'

She bit her words off before her voice got away from her entirely. After a little silence she heard Flo's soft warm voice. 'Poor kid!' it said, and the brown hand came out again to tighten around Helen's ankle.

As if that touch and those two words of sympathy were what she had been waiting for, Helen felt the words coming, welling up as water comes lifting in a pump, until they spilled over and poured in a stream. She felt the long-awaited luxury of tears coming up with the words, spilling over with them while she told Flo Barnes about the miserable shut-in winters, the narrow village piety eating on itself, needing victims to justify itself upon as acid needs metal before it can etch. She told about the house she lived in, the silent squeamish father and the mother whose life went always in the ways other people

directed, not in any way she thought up for herself. How
every move in the house was conditioned by what folks
would say, what the village would think. There was no
freedom, she cried; you couldn't live in the village unless
you lived by the village pattern, and their eyes were on
you all the time. . . .

While she poured this accumulated grievance into
Flo's listening sympathy, she felt the sun-warmed skin of
the secretary, and the arm that went around her shoulders.
Some time later, when she came out of her babble of
confession and complaint and tears and self-pity, she
moved with obscure shame out of the hugging arm. Flo
let her go.

'You've had it tough,' she said. 'I'm glad you got it off
your chest. It's holding in things like that that makes you
scared of everything. You get all wound up in yourself
and you're afraid to come out in the open.'

'I don't know why I told you all that,' Helen said, and
laughed and wiped a knuckle below her eyes. She looked
at the brown face of Flo Barnes with gratitude and affection and shyness.

Flo sat up straighter, yawned, scratched herself con-
tentedly on the thigh. 'You know something?' she said.
'You need treatment, honestly you do. You need to be
tossed right out into the world and made to swim. You've
been hiding too long in a mouse-hole.' Tapping her teeth
with her nails, she pretended to study Helen as a doctor
might before prescribing something. The skin around her
eyes crinkled.

'I'll bet you,' she said, 'that you don't dare take off
that suit and swim around the rock in the altogether, and
then climb up here on the rock and let the wind blow on
you a minute. I'll bet you don't dare.'

Her hand reached out impulsively to the shoulder strap,
but Helen resisted. Her face was hot again. 'Please!' she
said.

Flo let go, shrugged, stepped down onto the flooded shelf. 'Suit yourself. It's the only way you'll ever get out of this shrinking-mouse stage, though.'

She dove in and swam aimlessly around, watching the rock. Helen sat with her hand still on the shoulder strap. It was hard for her to breathe. The sunny air bore down on her with an inexorable weight, and it struck her with a peculiar impact of shame that it was Sunday. Out on the lake the three fishing boats had moved perceptibly closer to the tip of the island. She started to open her mouth to tell Flo Barnes that she wasn't afraid to, it was just that she . . . Just that she what? That she was afraid. She closed her mouth, watching Flo kick her brown legs froglike out where the rocks shelved off into deep green water. Flo's face was closed and expressionless. She filled her mouth with water and spouted it out. Every move she made, every flash of the brown body in the sun, spoke of health and freedom and bright physical enjoyment. Helen looked at her own white legs, at her white upper arms just beginning to grow unattractively pink with sunburn. The mouse had crept out of its hole for just a moment, but now when it heard a noise, saw sunshine and creatures playing, it shook with fright and started to creep back in.

In one wiggling, desperate motion she stripped the flowered rayon down and over her hips. In the ankle-deep water she forced herself to stand up straight and naked, fully exposed to the lake and the distant boats and the uncompromising sun and the eyes of Flo Barnes. With her arms stiff at her sides she stood there for what seemed minutes, and her voice was as stiff as her arms. 'Is this the way?'

From the water Flo was laughing. 'Now you're shouting!' she said. 'Now you're shouting, mouse. Oh, beautiful, beautiful!'

Helen dove, careless of her hair, and when she came up Flo was beside her. The secretary grabbed her, they sank bubbling, and as they sank Flo planted a wet kiss on Helen's lips. Their bodies touched, cool in the water.

Then they were on the surface again, laughing, and as if they had rehearsed it, as if they had planned a deliberate recklessness, they were off swimming, Flo pulling ahead and rolling over, waiting while Helen caught up, then sprinting again. They swam straight for the steep shore and the cedar gardens, and when they reached the first drowned tree they hung to the branches that grew up out of the water. Half in the sun, half in the cold grip of the water, they hung there with their heads close together, laughing and getting their breath.

5

The Alien Corn

THE FIRST SENSE of the enormity of what she had done, the first dismayed realization of how thoroughly she had given herself up into the hands of strangers, struck Ruth as the bus turned around the edge of the golf course and came down the easy slope toward the square. It passed the gray tent and the ragged woodpile, and it was while those images slid past her eyes and Abe was already standing up fussily, ready to get off before the bus stopped, that her belly froze with absolute panic. That ragged piece of cloth on a two-by-four frame, that was now home. Her life would now be circumscribed by patched canvas walls and a front yard grown knee high to witch grass; her world would be bounded by the unknown hills around this barely-known village. And beside her in the terrifying isolation of the new life would be the man now helping her down the aisle of the bus — a grizzled, middle-aged man, a gentle, impetuous, kind man, but a stranger.

They were the only passengers getting off. Ruth's knees almost buckled as her feet touched the ground, and Abe grabbed her elbow. Two village women in front of the post office stopped talking while they watched. Across the street Martin Bentham, carrying reels of barbed wire in the side door of his store, nodded his head gravely. Abe waved to him, started to haul Ruth across. But she held back, pulling loose from his hand.

'Please, Abe. Let's go right on home.'

'I just wanted to tell Martin Bentham . . . '

'Take me home, please!'

If he insisted any more, or asked for any explanations, she would fly apart like a smashed alarm clock. She saw his face pucker with anxiety, and then he picked up the suitcase and they went up the street past the two women, who eyed them as they passed. Abe lifted his hat ceremoniously, said, 'Hello, hello!' and steered Ruth past them. When they were past the last billow of the inn's lawn he hissed in alarm, 'What is it? Are you sick? I should have known it, that bus is bad on the curves. We should have come by train.'

'No,' she said. 'I'm not sick. I'll be all right.'

They stepped across the roadside ditch and she stood in the path, which was like a bald streak through a lank head of hair, while Abe fumbled the tent flaps open. In the few seconds she stood there, her eyes and ears registered and tested the village. Turning her back on the rank weedy hillside, she saw the boy who lived with Allan Richie spreading gravel on the driveway across the street, and she heard the stone-and-iron sound, the metallic dry swish, as he swung the loaded scoop sideways scattering gravel in a short, controlled arc. A tractor was coming across Pratt's meadow with a load of hay lumbering behind it, and over on the Corners road the noise of the mill was a busy irrelevance. She heard these sounds, and yet over them and under them, packing them in as if in cotton batting, there was a soft country quiet that dismayed her. The thought of what it might be like if the busy little noises stopped was terrifying. It was not her world: it was another planet, inhabited by strangers whose language she neither understood nor spoke. When Abe finally got the ties undone and pulled the flaps wide, she ducked in past him as if escaping something.

Inside the tent it was stifling. Layers of superheated

air pressed up toward the even fiercer heat that beat down on the canvas roof. The light was the kind of reddish, internal light she remembered from the beach, when she had lain for a long time with the sun beating on her closed eyelids.

Abe pushed a chair forward, and she sat down. She tried not to look at him, but he was hovering over her. 'This is not so good,' he was saying. 'Eh, will you tell me what is the matter, please?'

'It's hot,' Ruth said. Immediately he was at the back of the tent, leaning over the bed and tugging at the canvas. It came up above the board wall, letting a flat current of delicious cool air through the tent. Abe propped up the canvas with a stick and went around raising other openings at the sides. Then he tied back the front flaps so that Ruth could see out into the sun-whitened gravel street.

'Maybe if you should lie down,' he said. 'It is probably some stomach thing, something that upsets you.'

'I'll be all right. Just let me be a while.'

'Well, but I don't like this!' he said. 'I want to fix you up, whatever is the matter.'

'There's nothing the matter!' she said, almost in tears. 'Just let me alone, will you? Let me get myself together.'

She went over and lay face down on the bed, pressing her face into the auto robe. The robe was scratchy on her face, and warm as the coat of an animal, so that her face steamed slowly as her breath moistened the wool. But on the back of her neck she could feel the cooling draft from the raised tentwall, and after a few minutes she found that she was listening to hear what Abe was doing.

She heard the scrape of metal coat hangers on the pipe rack, the soft sound of a chair being moved, the crackle of paper thrust into the stove, and the careful clunk of the lid being replaced. She lifted her mouth off the wet wool and propped her face with her wrist. 'I'm sorry, Abe,' she said into the bed. 'I guess I just got scared all of a sudden.'

'Sure,' he said. 'Well, so long as you don't stay scared.'

'I'll be all right. It was just so strange, it hit me all at once.'

'Sure, sure.' His voice comforted her, though he did not come near. 'You lie there a while, you'll feel better.'

The small comforting sounds of his activities went on, and she lay with her face on her wrist, letting the breeze cool her blood gradually. A calf blatted somewhere, and a car came down the road in front. After it passed she could hear again the swish of gravel from the scoop shovel across the street, and at intervals the tearing snore of the saw from the mill. The country quiet was still there, but she began to be ashamed of the way it had frightened her. She supposed that being brought up among millions of people, in a place where noise never really stopped any time during the twenty-four hours, she would naturally be disturbed by quiet. In a little village like this there were so few people around that every move was noticeable; there was so little sound that every word would be heard.

Hearing the stealthy *sssssssp sssssssp* of the broom, she sat up. Abe, sweeping the tent floor, looked toward her guiltily.

'Oh, Abe,' she said, 'you don't have to do that!'

'Well,' he said, his eyes uncomfortably on her face, 'I thought, you aren't feeling good, and if somebody should come around . . .'

'Who's likely to come around?'

He shrugged. 'Anybody. Everybody. People bring work to be done, and now people will know we are married, and they may start making calls. It wouldn't do if some of these village housekeepers found dust on your floor, tent or no tent.'

'Well, you put that broom down,' Ruth said. She stood up and took it from him, and standing close to him, seeing his troubled eyes and his incorrigible hair, she leaned and kissed him. 'I'm all right now. I was just like a lost child for a minute.'

'I hope you're not sorry about what we have done,' Abe said. 'That is the only thing.'

She kissed him again till his gloom lightened and he smiled. 'How could I be sorry?' she said. 'I'm as glad as I can be.'

'This tent business, it's not good,' Abe said. 'I should bring a wife home to a tent. But listen. I'll talk to Curtin tonight, and we will have that house in the shake of a cow's tail.'

For some reason the tears that might have come at any time chose to come now. He huddled her in his arms, moving sideways so that no one from the street could look in and see, and his voice grumbled in her hair. He took the broom out of her fingers and threw it aside. 'Now that's enough,' he said softly. 'What is this business of crying? You are a bride, and brides should not cry any more than they should sweep floors.'

'Oh, Abe,' she said, 'I don't know why I'm acting this way! Why don't you just give me a dressing down? Really tell me off, I need it.'

'Listen,' he said. 'Anybody that could stand up and marry me is not anybody to be scared. What are you scared of? There is nobody here to hurt you. When you get used to these people you will find out they are people like anybody else, and they will like you and you will like them. Didn't I tell you I like this place? And in three weeks it won't be a tent any more.'

She laughed against his shoulder. 'Isn't it funny? Isn't

it a howl, Abe? Here I sell wedding gowns for six years, and have my model all picked out, with buttons all the way down the back and long sleeves with buttons to the wrist — all white satin, you'd have liked me in that. I could get it wholesale, too. So I get married in a gabardine suit and take a one-day wedding trip to Crawford Notch and come home to keep house in a tent!'

Abe did not say anything for some time. When she pulled back to look at him he drew down the corners of his mouth and said, 'That wedding trip, you understand about that. It is a question of a wedding trip or a house, and I thought maybe a house . . . It *had* to be a house.'

'And I'm going to love it,' she said. 'Where's that broom?'

In the midst of sweeping she looked across the tent at him and asked, 'Do you think somebody might really come, just to wish us well, sort of?'

'Why not? But if you'd rather not, I could let the flaps down. That would mean we were not at home.'

'Oh, no,' she said quickly. 'I think it might be nice. I don't much care who, it would just be sort of pleasant to have somebody drop in.'

That was at two-thirty. At three-fifteen Mrs. Martin Bentham, tall and thin and with a nose that looked as if it had been sharpened in a pencil sharpener, came up the hill with two pairs of trousers to be cleaned. She was suitably surprised when Abe told her the news — well, not really surprised, because she had expected something of the kind. She thought it was real nice they were married, and she sat for ten or fifteen minutes. When she had gone Ruth commented that she seemed very nice and friendly.

'Sure, why not?' Abe said. 'They are nice people, both of them. Maybe a little close to that religious crowd, but good honest high-grade people.' He twinkled his big eyebrows at her. 'But I should tell you,' he said. 'They don't usually bring their cleaning to me. Why do you suppose they should start now, eh?'

Ten minutes after Mrs. Bentham had left, a summer camper came in for a fitting. 'Where've you been?' he asked. 'I've been around twice in the last couple of days.'

Abe cleared his throat solidly. 'Hah! Where have I been? I have been off getting married. That surprises you, eh? Come in, come in, I want you to meet my wife!'

He presented Ruth with a flourish, and in a few minutes they got to be a very friendly threesome. All during the fitting the man talked over his shoulder to her, telling her jokingly that she should look out for Abe, how a few years ago he had been the biggest tom-catter in the county, running all over to church suppers and game suppers in his old Ford. The worst was the men's supper over in Sudbury Common. 'Those men's suppers used to be something,' the man said, and winked at Ruth. 'Abe had Parley Pugh with him coming back, and just at the head of the lake they hit a mailbox and turned over in the ditch. Parley got tossed out in the long grass, and he'd had so many at the supper he forgot all about Abe. He just took off and walked into town and went to bed. It wasn't till he woke next morning that he thought about Abe at all, and then he hopped in his truck and came tearing out with a posse. When they rolled the car over, there was old Abe, madder than sin. He'd been lying there on the ground, not hurt at all but pinned down so he couldn't wiggle, all night. He was about the frozenest, maddest, hung-overest man you ever did see.'

'Yes, yes, yes!' Abe was saying. He had stood back to see how the lapels set, but had forgotten what he was looking for. His grin was wide and delighted, and with a big needle stuck in his shirtfront and a piece of marking soap in his hand he circled the summer man and laughed and said, 'Yes, yes, I admit all that, but that was a long time ago. Now I have got rid of that Ford and got a wife I am a different man.'

When he left, the city man shook hands with Ruth again and wished her happiness. She thought he was charming. He was a professor from Princeton, Abe told her.

The afternoon became a levee. Abe sat at the entrance of the tent, sewing on a half-made coat, but when people came by in the road, by car or truck or bicycle or wagon, he rushed out like a highwayman and flagged them down. 'I want you to meet my wife,' he would say. 'You didn't think I would ever have a wife, eh? You thought I was too old to catch a wife, or too homely in the face? Well, there she is. I met her two weeks ago and now I am married to her, now I am stuck.'

His laughter was a contagion, his jokes outrageous, his generosity wouldn't let him rest ten seconds without try-ing to force on a visitor a drink of water, a bottle of coke, a chocolate — here, there are plenty! — a more comfort-able chair. He collared a Yale dean and a professor of Greek from Pennsylvania. He ran down two little girls in playsuits and shooed them in long enough for Ruth to hug them and give them each a chocolate. He overtook old Daniel Pratt, a bent, hairy man whose thumbless right hand hung down his middle like the furry paw of an animal. 'He is a rich peasant,' Abe said when the old man had gone on. 'I have seen plenty like him in Russia. They are rich and cautious and suspicious, and their whole life is a hanging onto things.'

About five all three Dows came by, and for a few min-utes the tent was full of the bass voices of the men and the vivid smile of Mary Dow. Following them there was an insurance man from Wolfeboro and a French farmer who prophesied fifteen children. There was a sweet old man

with great knobby arthritic hands, a cabinet-maker. There
was the boy, Andy Mount, who lived with Mr. Richie, a
grave, quiet boy with a lock of brown hair falling across
his forehead and a serious, almost disturbing way of looking at people. There was Helen Barlow, who worked in
the post office now but was going to teach the primary
room of the consolidated school in the fall. She lived
just up on top of the hill, next to the church. She and Ruth
got talking books, but just when Ruth was feeling that
she had found someone she would like to see a lot of,
Helen had to run down to help sort the mail. She prom-
ised to stop in sometime.

The closing whistle of the mill at the Corners shrieked
faintly as Abe led Ruth across the road to Harold Swett's,
and from across the fence introduced her to three high-
school boys who looked at her in quick, sidelong glances
and kidded Abe and smiled out of the corners of their
mouths slyly.

'Good Lord!' Ruth said, stretched out at last on the
bed. She fanned herself and blew out her breath. 'Now
I know how the President feels when they line up on the
White House lawn.'

'Well,' Abe said. 'Is it strange any more? Have people
come in to say congratulations?'

'A lot of them came with a rope around their necks.
Did you have to shanghai people?'

'I don't understand this word shanghai,' he said. 'But
I guess people came around.' He sat down and leaned
over her. 'How about it? Are you still scared?'

She shook her head back and forth. 'Just imagine,' she
said after a silence. 'In New York we could get married
and move into my apartment and nobody would even
look twice, they'd never even notice us. Everybody's so
wound up in his own business down there.'

'So up here everybody is wound up in other people's
business,' Abe said. 'This is better, eh?'

She put up her arms and hugged him. 'This is much better.'

After supper they talked to James Curtin about building the house. As they came back up the lake street toward the square several young men sitting on the steps of Bentham's closed-up store watched them, and Ruth heard their soft laughter. The annoyance she felt was only for a moment. They were like all young men anywhere, like boys in Washington Square whistling at the girls. Following close upon her annoyance came a warm rush of acceptance. This was going to be her village. Already the little square under the hill, the angled porches of the inn and the white fronts of store and creamery and post office, were familiar and comfortable. She had seen before, through the evenings of two weeks, how the dusk came on, and smelled how the night-smells sharpened. Along the street there was the pulse of fireflies in the grass.

They pulled chairs to the flaps and sat quietly, watching the street darken and the last child go trailing home. Lights went on in the Richie house, the Swett house, the Pratt house. The street light down by the post office spluttered on. A bat went past their faces, not so much seen as felt. Above them the gray, half-luminous canvas roof darkened slowly and disappeared. Abe's hand holding Ruth's was warm, but the air moving past the tent flaps and brushing their faces was cool, and smelled of grass.

Ruth stirred. 'Maybe we ought to shut our door and light a light, like everybody else.'

'What for? All a light does is make silhouettes.'

'What?'

'Sure. A tent is not like a house. You can see through it with a light on.'

'You mean you never had any lights?'

'Oh, sure. When I was alone. Not' — his hand went out in a flat gesture — 'now.'

'Listen,' he said, and hitched his chair closer. 'Maybe you will be mad about this, I don't know. But I should tell you. Around here it is a custom when people get married that they should be given a chivaree, and when you live in a tent that chivaree might be bad.'

'What is it? What do they do?'

'Do!' Abe said. 'Do, is it? Listen! Out here on the swamp road is a farmer, Albert Hall. Last fall he got married. Now when he brings his wife home, and that night they go to bed, there is a big row and twenty people hammer on his door and yell and raise hell wanting free drinks. But Albert is a pinch-penny. He told them to quit bothering people, he wouldn't buy drinks for any gang of good-for-nothings. So they knock his door in and kidnap his wife in her nightgown and the last Albert is seen he is running for the woods in his long underwear with ten people chasing him.'

He leaned back dramatically, and for an instant the picture of Abe loping through the square in his underwear pursued by a gang of young men was so ludicrous that a giggle burst from Ruth's lips. Abe was relieved. 'Well, I'm glad you think it is funny.'

'I don't think it's funny one bit,' she said. 'Haven't they got any respect for people's privacy?'

'It is no good to argue with them.'

'They wouldn't dare do anything like that to us,' she said.

Abe got up and walked through the tent. In the faint light from the street she saw him wince at some thought. 'They would dare anything,' he said. 'This is like a lynch mob, you understand, but good-natured. There is only one way, and that is to treat them fine. After all, they are your friends, they don't mean any harm. They are just young hell-raisers making a joke with newlyweds. If I was a young man I'd be out with them, probably. Once I was a young hell-raiser myself, a revolutionary running from the police and staying up all night.'

Crowding past her, he opened his wallet and peered into it, took out a bill and held it in his fingers, watching her steadily.

'There is another thing about this business,' he said. 'In a tent anything can happen. Even if I put out ten dollars for beer there is somebody who might pull the tent down, just to make fun. I think it is smart we should go to bed in our clothes tonight. Then they can't take us unprepared.'

'Well, I must say!' Ruth said, ready to laugh. 'Do I have to wrinkle up all my clothes just because a bunch of country jakes want to have fun?'

'I'll press your dress again in the morning,' Abe said humbly. 'It's a crazy thing, sure, but I don't like to think of you being kidnapped in your nightgown.'

She remembered the youths on Bentham's steps in the twilight, the watchful heads and the soft laughter. 'All right,' she said. 'You know what goes on in a place like this, I don't. But it sure seems to me the whole town is in on this wedding.'

She was embarrassed about going to the privy, and made an excuse to stay outside a while as if enjoying the night air. She came in with her whole mind full of dull wonder that she should find herself using an outhouse like some country bumpkin. And sleeping in her clothes because the yokels might come around and raise an uproar. She almost laughed.

The tent bloomed weakly with light, its end-pole and low board walls black against the lighted canvas, and she saw Abe's shadow stoop on the slanting cloth. While she creamed her face he turned down the covers, pulled the oilcloth-covered stool close for a bed table, and laid on it a ten-dollar bill and a nickel-plated flashlight.

'Now it is a cinch,' he said softly, as if in fear of being overheard. 'When they come, I will be already dressed. I get up, go to the door, make them a little speech, hand them the ten dollars and tell them to have a drink on us. Then they will probably make a little noise and go away. All they want is to raise a little hell and beat on tin pans and scare people, and then they will go and drink our health.'

'What if they decide to do more than that?' Ruth said. She saw the cloth roof move in a draft, and the candle flickered. Anybody could push right through this tent. And she and Abe weren't really part of the village. Would that lead the crowd to be easier or harder to handle?

'They won't do anything else,' Abe said. 'Wait and see.'

'Oh, I'll be waiting!' she said. 'I'll be right here when they come!'

They laughed together softly, and then Abe blew out the candle. Ruth kicked off her shoes and lay beside him in her clothes, and he pulled the auto robe up over them so its tickly fringe was against her throat. Lying there in the dark with their bribe ready on the stool, their ears pricking for foreign sounds in the village quiet, they both giggled, and they lay giggling and whispering for some time. Later Ruth realized that she had been asleep, she didn't know for how long. Abe was snoring gently. She rose on one elbow, wondering what had awakened her. She could see plainly in the tent, and realized that the moon must have risen. In the dimness she lay listening for several minutes, holding her breath, but except for the thin bark of a fox off beyond Pratt's hayfield she heard nothing that she could identify. Finally she lay down again, and when she awoke the second time the sun was shining on the patched and tarred canvas of the roof, and Abe was lying beside her looking straight upward, flexing his mouth, dry with sleep. The ten-dollar bill still lay under the flashlight on the stool.

Abe left it there. 'It's a country custom,' he said, shrugging. 'Part of it is to catch you when you're not ready. If they didn't come last night, they will come tonight. It is no fun unless you surprise people.'

That night they went to bed in their clothes again, and again the night passed without an alarm. In the morning Abe looked at Ruth a little furtively and spread out the bill to look at it. 'By golly, I never knew anybody so slow to get ten-dollars' worth of drinks. But it is nice to get all that sleep.'

'I've got permanent marks of buttons all over me,' Ruth said. 'I wish they'd make up their minds.' Looking at Abe, she wrinkled her brows in perplexity. Didn't he feel that this whole business was crazy, all this sleeping in clothes, no mention of making love . . .

'If you can stand it another night,' Abe said, as if he were reading her mind. His eyes were contrite and his voice humble. 'I know it is a funny way for a honeymoon. But if it should happen Albert Hall's way, that would be worse.'

'It's all right,' she said. 'It isn't your fault.'

That day Curtin's truck unloaded three loads of lumber, shingles, nails, and building paper under the hill beside the messy woodpile. Under the hot sun the smell of new boards was an intoxication. James Curtin arrived with a cone of heavy hard string on a stick, and measured off distances and drove in stakes. 'I can hardly wait,' Ruth said, hanging on Abe's arm. 'Won't it be fun when we can walk in and see where different rooms are going to be?'

'You won't have to wait long,' Abe said, and screwed up his eyebrows. 'And it is just such a night as tonight those hoodlums will choose to come hell-raising. They will think they have got us fooled now.'

The bill and the flashlight were on the stool again that night as Abe blew out the candle and rolled over to kiss Ruth clumsily. She lay quietly, staring at the low roof and thinking, hardly hearing him.

'Well, let them come,' he said, and relaxed back into the pillow. 'A man should not begrudge his friends a little fun. A man only knows two things, all his life he knows only those: how he is himself and how he fits with other people. Once you move into this village you are behind glass, everybody can see you, but that is all right. Anyway, this is how I feel about it. A man such as me, to get such a wife as you, is so lucky these hoodlums could come every night for a month and it would still be worth it, if it cost me ten dollars a night.'

Ruth lay awake a long time, letting her mind run. Outside the tent, across the road, was Pratt's pasture, and through the pasture or up the street or down from the darkness of the hill the young men could be coming now to perform their initiation ceremony on the newly married. Behind the piles of lumber boys might be crouching, hanging onto their laughter, waiting for the signal.

It was a Friday night. There was a dance at the Grange Hall, and her ears caught the occasional swift beat of country dance music. Her little illuminated clock, perched on the two-by-four ledge of the wall, told her that it was eleven. If they were coming they should be coming pretty soon, maybe at the intermission.

She waited, listening to Abe's soft snoring, thinking with an odd tenderness that it was appropriate he should snore, but snore quietly. He should have the fault, but in an inoffensive form. The illuminated dial staring in the gloom said eleven-twenty.

She waited, and fell asleep, and awoke starting at some noise. It came again, a clatter across the street, and her heart jumped with fear, as if it were murderers she lay expecting instead of village youths. Then the clatter ended with the grate of a key, and she knew that the noise had been Harold Swett stumbling up his porch stairs after a toot in Stafford. The moon could not yet have risen, for it was still very dark in the tent. The clock said one-fifteen.

The leap of her heart at Harold Swett's noise had awakened her thoroughly. She lay thinking of the girls at Garbstein's, and what they would say if they could see her now, and of her friend Lucille in the New York Public, with whom she used to go to concerts at the Lewisohn Stadium. She wondered whether or not the movers would really pack everything up carefully and not lose things, and she thought of Mrs. Bentham's handshake and the sly mouths of the schoolboys across Harold Swett's fence. The quiet slipped in from the pasture and the shadowed lumber piles like a threat; she had a feeling that if the moon should come up now she could hear it rise. And all around her, mile after mile in every direction, were black woods, empty black fields, black farmhouses, loneliness and this deathlike quiet. It seemed to her that of all the lonely darkened places in all the miles of those quiet hills, the loneliest was this tent in the middle of the village where she lay awake and listened to her husband's gentle snoring, and only that soft loose rasp of breath kept her from screaming and burying her head in the covers. In the still dark she cried.

The noise of sawing awakened her. The sun was gold on the canvas. 'Well, missus,' Abe said from the front flap. 'Your house is getting built while you sleep.'

She looked at the stool. The ten-dollar bill was gone. 'Did they come?' she said. 'Did they come and I not even wake up?'

Abe grimaced. His eyes darted out the flap, shifted back. 'Well,' he said, 'I decided if they did not want ten dollars we would use it ourselves.' He tapped his pocket and turned away, ducking out through the triangular opening. The sawing went on steadily, and now some-one began to drive spikes with a steady, even hammer, the sound of hammer on spike getting higher and higher in pitch until the final wet *chunk* as the hammer head found wood. Then a new one, starting lower and climb-ing to the finishing *chunk*.

Ruth laid aside the auto robe and sat up. Her mind registered the wrinkled dress, and with a wry little face, standing up to twist the dress straight around her hips, she said to herself, 'Well, well! All dressed up and no place to go!'

With the noise of the hammers and saws building her house it had been made irrevocable.

6

A-Plenty to Live Down

ALLAN RICHIE's little hayfield bordered the golf course,
and as he moved slowly along over the raked windrows,
driving by voice and hopping to make into a load the hay
poured in on him by the loader, Andy caught glimpses of
men and women walking with golf bags on their shoulders, or pushing little two-wheeled buggies full of clubs,
or standing spraddle-legged waggling a club back and
forth. He had no contempt for the game, as many people
in the village had. He was simply curious, unable to imagine what it would be like to walk three or four miles
knocking a little ball ahead of you.

He reached the end of a windrow and turned, lurch-
ing, dragging the hay-loader around into line for the
backward tack. He forked the half-load even, tramped it
down. 'Gee-up!' he said.

The wagon rolled forward, the hay came in gobbets up
the moving belt of the loader. Slowly as the horses moved,
they brought up more hay than Andy could handle, and
he had to stop every few rods while he dug himself out.

'Gee-up!' he said again, and as they drifted a little off
line, 'Whoa-haw! Whoa-haw, there, Mae!' A waterfall of
hay smothered him, filling his mouth with dust and fine
twigs of grass, and he forked like mad getting out. At
the fence he drew up and smoothed out the load. He
was brushing haystems from his bare shoulders prepar-
atory to climbing down and unhitching the loader when

109

someone across the fence said, 'Looks like a good lively job.'

The boy scooped his forelock out of his eyes. An elderly man was sitting on one of the green benches while a younger companion set a ball on a little yellow peg. Beyond them a man and a woman dragged a doormat back and forth across the black sand green. The old man's face was pale and thin, and the hands that knocked a club up and down on the grass were ridged with cords, spotted with brown spots like big freckles. His eyes were blue and squinted. Andy knew him by sight. He was a man who had been financial advisor to a half-dozen South American governments.

'It isn't rightly a one-man job,' Andy said. 'Can be done, though.'

'Who drives the team?'

Andy was bent under, uncoupling the loader. 'I do.'

'And load the hay too?'

'Drive 'em by hollering at 'em,' Andy said. He stood up and shouted, 'Gee-up! Gee-up, there!' The team pulled the loaded wagon free. 'Whoa!' Andy said. He climbed up over the back of the rack and waded forward. Ordinarily he would have unwound the lines and driven back to the barn that way, but with the summer man watching he leaned on his fork and shouted at the near horse. 'Back up, Mae. Back up, now! Back!' The horse crowded her haunches into the single-tree and jockeyed backward. 'Haw-up!' Andy shouted. 'Haw, Mae! Haw, Milly girl. Haw, now! Gee-up, there!'

Neatly, aware of his own skill, he shouted the team away from the fence and started them down the field. He did not look back to see the effect of his driving on the golfers, but he did take out of his pocket the thing he had picked up from the mown grass when he stooped under the hayloader. It was a golf ball, nicked on one

side, but round and firm and heavy in his hand. He
hefted it, felt its surface dented with round craters, wondered how long it had taken someone to figure out just
what sort of ball was best for knocking around a lawn.
He had seen plenty of golf balls around the country club
service window, but he had never before had one in his
hand.

When he was halfway to the barn he looked back toward the old man and his companion, but they had both
hit their balls and were out of sight behind the knoll.
Andy flipped the ball into the air and caught it, then put
it back in his pocket, where it made a hard, unfamiliar
lump against his thigh.

By the time he had got the load mowed up it was
almost time for chores. He unhitched, watered the team,
grained them, threw down a mangerful of sweet fresh
hay.

The two cows were not yet in. Andy went to the ramp
of the high drive, saw them trailing single file up from
the lake shore, and opened the doors for them. In their
little interior pen the two Guernsey calves stuck square-
browed heads over the top rail and rolled their eyes white-
ly and lapped their tongues out. He let one have his finger for a minute, and laughed when the calf nursed it,
pressing it hard against the corrugated roof of its mouth.
'Boy, I bet you'd suck an axe-helve,' he said.

From the milkroom where he washed up, Andy saw Mr.
Richie out in the new gravel of the drive, looking across
at Abe Kaplan's half-painted little house against the hill.
He had not yet found his opportunity to bring up Mr.
Dow's proposition to the old man. As a matter of fact,
he had been afraid to. He was afraid to now. But
it was getting on toward the first of August. He
couldn't put it off forever, if he ever expected to go

down this fall. Pulling in his stomach and drawing his breath as if he were about to dive, he went out into the half court formed by house and stable with their connecting sheds. Mr. Richie was still there looking down into the square, his sharp chin thrust forward. It struck Andy that he had the kind of face that cried for a goatee, an Uncle Sam kind of face, the kind of face for a driver of hard bargains.

The square, he saw, was full of people, mainly summer people waiting for the mail. Henry Ball's car was parked among the others in front of the post office. The crowd filled the street in front of the post office and eddied clear across the street to the creamery and Bentham's store.

The old man shot him a sharp look as he came up, but his voice was mild. 'Mail's late.'

'E-yeah.'

'Get that meadow all in?'

'All I had mowed. There's about three loads to come in tomorrow.'

'Herbert Pratt wants to rent the loader.'

'I'll be through with it tomorrow afternoon.'

'Wants it tomorrow morning,' Allan said. 'You can pitch those last three on by hand, I guess.'

'I guess,' Andy said, and got his breath again. 'Mr. Richie . . .'

The old man took his eyes off the crowd in the square. 'Eh?'

'How much wages have I got saved up?'

Allan's head moved slightly forward, his chin moved slightly out. 'Don't know's I've counted 'em lately. Why?'

'I want to go to school this fall.'

Allan peered, suspicious of a joke, thrusting his narrow old white head further forward still. 'School? You finished school.'

'I finished high school. I want to go to college.'

He saw Allan's expression change, the outthrust lip and jaw relax slightly. The blue eyes under the slash of white eyebrows twinkled. 'Been talkin' to summer folks,' Allan said.

'Well . . .'

'I've got nothin' against summer folks,' Allan said. 'In their place. Some of 'em do well enough. But they're gettin' to stick their noses too much into how this village runs. Like that music thing.'

Now that he had made the opening move, Andy was willing to stall, though he had no intention of being side-tracked. 'What music thing?'

'That Sunday night music thing, over on Mrs. Weld's dock.'

'What about it?'

The chin went forward again, and for a moment Andy almost saw the little quivering goatee. 'Have you heard 'em?'

'A few times.'

'Like 'em? That kind of music tickle your taste? All that Wagner and Whatsisname?'

'All right, I guess,' Andy said. 'It sounds good over the water that way.'

'Not to some people, it don't,' Allan said. 'Whole village, practically. *And* Mrs. Weld. She can't get the kind of music she likes, not to save her, even if she does give the concerts off her dock. Schoolteachers run it their own way, set up a committee that votes her down. Votes the whole village down too.'

'They had the idea for the concerts in the first place,' Andy said.

Allan grunted. 'And packin' into the Westwick Association so they can vote down a movie picture house. Want to keep the town unspoiled. Vote down another service station. Same reason. Vote me down when I want to put up four little cottages down on my lake shore for over-night campers. Summer people don't want transients, outside the inn. Bring in the wrong kind of people.' He made a disgusted sound with his mouth. 'Might's well go down and get the mail, boy.'

Andy did not move. He kept his eyes steadily on Allan Richie's sharp face. There was a trembling going on somewhere under his ribs, and he scooped the forelock out of his eyes. The whole summer-people lecture had been an attempt to smoke-screen him, but he wasn't going to be smoke-screened. 'I mean it about going to college,' he said.

Now he was confronting not the twinkling Allan Richie but the hard-bargaining Allan Richie. The old face was hard as flint. 'You don't calculate that'll leave me out anything, I suppose.'

'I've worked all the time and done the chores. And since I've been hiring out you've had half my wages.'

'Enough to pay half your food and clothes.'

'All right,' Andy said steadily. 'Keep it all.'

Allan Richie turned away with a snort. Down in the square Alma Bentham came out of the post office lugging a bundle of papers, and a queue from the idling crowd followed her into the store. Allan swung around again.

'Damn it, boy, 'tisn't the money. But I would have expected you to act different. You know how I happened to take you in. You know how things was for you, and what happened to your Ma. You know about your whole family, for that matter. How much respect have folks got for your uncle James? Been on the town ever since I can remember, and a new kid every year. I didn't have to take you in. I could have said you were just another no-account member of the Mount family.'

'My mother wasn't no-account!'

'Never said she was,' Allan said. 'I was just talkin' the

way the village thinks. Folks'd say you had a-plenty to
live down, boy.'

'Maybe that's why I want to go to college.'

' 'Twouldn't be livin' it down to run away from it,' Allan
said.

They remained eye to eye, locked in a conflict as silent
and strenuous as if they had been straining every muscle
wrestling. Inside the house the telephone rang three
longs and a short, waited a moment, rang them again.
Allan turned around and went inside.

The holds had been disengaged so abruptly that Andy
took a minute to get his legs under him again. It was not
clear to him whether he had won or lost, or whether the
skirmish would be renewed again as soon as Allan finished
on the telephone. For a while he stood around waiting,
but when Allan did not appear he went down toward the
square with the vague intention of getting the mail. Milking could wait. As a matter of fact, maybe it could wait
indefinitely. The thought that perhaps the break had
been made, that perhaps this was all there was to getting
free, brought on the thought that perhaps Allan would
expect him to find some other place to sleep right away.
But that did not bother him long. Peter Dow might have
a place, or Mr. Mills might want somebody to do his
chores. It began to occur to him obliquely and tentatively that except in experience he was a man. He was as
big as a man, could do a man's work and assume a man's
responsibilities. Until now he had thought of school and
college as something he would have to do under Peter
Dow's wing. Now it was plain to him that if he had to he
could do it alone, without any help whatever.

Still, he looked carefully as he passed through the
crowd, hoping to see Peter Dow there. There was no
sign of him.

Inside the narrow alley before the glass-doored post-office boxes people were packed thickly. Children ducked in and out, and a dog started in but was dissuaded by a flick of skirts. Andy squeezed in, nodded to people he knew, turned the combination on Allan's box. As the door swung open he saw through into the inner office, saw Helen Barlow's sunburned arms sorting letters into the pigeonholes and the stooping back of Gaylord Brown as he sacked mail for the star route to Sudbury. Helen saw him looking in, and gave him an intent, concentrated smile. Evidently she had been swimming; her nose was as sunburned as her arms.

He took out the letters that were in the box and slammed the little glass door. Behind him he heard the stamp window slide up, which meant that all the mail had been distributed. People began getting into cars and stepping aboard bicycles. Two boys in shorts, with tennis rackets between their feet, sat on the edge of the sidewalk licking ice cream cones. The shadow of the creamery chimney lay almost across the square.

With the mail in his hip pocket Andy went across to Bentham's, nodding to Alma Bentham with a one-sided grin. He avoided looking at the summer girl she was talking with, and turned into the store without any real intention, unless it was that same half-wistful desire to see Peter Dow and be encouraged.

Two city women in jeans were buying groceries at the south counter. In the back room Martin Bentham was cutting a piece of glass for Albert Hall, and against the soda fountain three long-legged, brown-legged, T-shirt-and-shorts girls leaned to inhale from tall soda glasses. They leaned their chests against the fountain and braced their weight on backward-extended legs. Their three symmetrical hips jutted like the hips of resting horses.

Andy contemplated going out again, but he didn't like to give the impression of not knowing what he was after.

Neither did he like to have it appear that he had come in simply to stare at the three girls in shorts. But he was not unaware of them; he crowded over to the end of the fountain, as far from them as he could get, and waited until Margery Young looked his way.

'I'd like a tonic,' he said.

Now all three city girls were looking at him, their red mouths pursed on their straws. Andy flushed hotly, wishing he had never come in. 'Tonic' was a word that someone like old Daniel Pratt would have used. He should have asked for a coke or a root beer. Probably the girls thought he was some kind of quaint hick.

'Coke,' he said, and cleared his throat viciously. He pressed himself into the narrow space at the end of the fountain and drummed with his fingers on the marble slab and indifferently eyed the glass cupboard back of the fountain, filled with Climax and Prince Albert and Copenhagen snuff. Though he would not turn to look at the girls again, he felt that they were still watching him.

Margery brought the coke and he drank half of it at a gulp. In the reflecting glass of the tobacco case he saw the front door open and the familiar figure of his Uncle James come in. Hunching on the counter, Andy watched out of the corner of his eye. James went up to the grocery counter where Martin Bentham now was and laid a bill on the boards, keeping his fingers on it. His overalls were splattered with white paint, his hands were stained, there was paint in his hair. His toothless mouth was brown with tobacco.

'Looks like you'd been paintin',' Martin said.

James spread his stained hands, craned to look at his overalls. His mouth opened in a wide cackle of laughter. 'Brought away more'n I left behind,' he said. 'Gimme three-four loaves of bread and a peck of spuds.'

'Workin' steady these days?' Martin said.

'Steady's I can stand,' James said. 'Paint Abe Kaplan's place all day and blow my saxophone all night. If folks don't quit dancin' I'll be fallin' asleep and drowndin' in my paint bucket.'

Spotting Andy over at the fountain, he raised his hand and spread his mouth in greeting. His merry little eyes almost closed when he laughed. 'Hey there, Andrew,' he said. 'Where'd you find three such handsome girls? They all yours, or could a feller borrow one?'

Andy's neck burned. He tried to smile at the girls, but one glance at their faces, rounding in surprise and opening toward laughter, put him back in his coke glass.

'Needn't be bashful about it,' James said. He turned to Martin and cackled. 'Boy stands there surrounded with 'em like a dang Turk.'

'Lay off it,' Andy muttered. He tipped his glass and got a mouthful of ice, and rather than appear to be driven away by his uncle's kidding, he stayed leaning against the counter until James got his packages together and went out. But he was stiff with embarrassment, and to cover his shame at his disreputable uncle, he said to Margery, 'Haven't seen Mr. Dow, have you?'

'Which one?'

'Peter.'

'Not today.'

'Thanks.' He crowded out between the glove counter and the jutting hips of the girls. At the door he met Mrs. Emma Budd, who sailed in the screen door he held open without giving him a sign of recognition, though she had known him all his life. Mrs. Emma had seldom greeted anyone since George Budd traded her in on a giddy hussy of thirty-five from Lancaster. The hussy had died of pneumonia the first winter, but Mrs. Emma remained in the village, a scarred trunk in the burned-over forest of George's matrimony. People said she stayed alive only to plague George. She had even got herself put on the same telephone line, and no one could talk on George's line without hearing the quiet click of Emma's interest. She was lean, sapless, sour as vinegar, bitter as alum, vindictively pious and conscientiously unkind, and she had George's goat. For that matter, she had everybody's goat.

She came in past Andy leaning forward from the waist, her knotted hands swinging. Directly before her were the three cocked hips, the three pairs of long smooth brown legs. One of the girls straightened up and tucked her thin sweater inside the waistband of her shorts, patting her stomach with a sigh. Andy watched her; so did Emma Budd.

The old lady started back toward the meat counter on a course that took her within a few feet of the row of bare legs. She walked mincingly, as if there were electricity in the flooring, and her brown hands twitched. Her mouth worked on a kind of gasping smile, malevolent and triumphant and full of cunning.

As she passed the protruding hip of the last girl her hand darted out and one twiggy finger touched the startled bare skin.

'Run short of material?' Mrs. Budd said, and swept on to the meat counter without a backward glance.

Andy's eyes met the eyes of the girl who had been tagged. The girl's mouth was open. Andy snorted and let the screen door slam. As he hit the steps, exploding with mirth, he heard the three girls let go in high whinnying laughter inside the store.

He sat down on the steps, cleared of people now, and laughed to himself until he thought how he must look, and stopped. The girls came crowding out through the screen, looked quickly at him sitting there, and stormed off into the square, caving and staggering with laughter. They got on bicycles in front of the creamery and pedaled out the Sudbury road, standing up on the pedals and pumping hard, screaming to each other.

Andy watched them go, feeling a curious mixture of pleasure at the way they had been stabbed, and irritation at their hysterical self-conscious glee. He knew they would tell it a hundred times, and he knew how they would tell it. This old 'native' woman, prim as a doily and with a tongue like a rat-tailed file, comes in and sees us standing at the fountain having a soda. We're in shorts, all of us, and you know what she does? This will slay you. She comes right up to me, mumbling over her false teeth, and just as she passes me she puts out her finger and touches my leg and says . . .

The shrill laughter. The joy in the cottages and in the canoes and sailboats and on the porches and docks over the antics of the old native woman. The hilarity for weeks every time some fool kid reached out and pinched the bare leg of a girl and said, 'Run short of material, dearie?'

Mrs. Emma came out with a package and went around the corner to her tenement above the feed store. Andy sat on, thinking that little as he liked her, he liked the summer girls less. They made so obvious that ugly sense of difference, they opened their mouths and eyes and stared when his Uncle James came in and acted silly, they stood around like tourists in darkest Africa, rubbering at the queer natives.

The square was practically deserted. Two boys came down the county road on bicycles, pedaling furiously with their noses to their turned-down handlebars and the muscles bunching in their calves. With a brief swift rattle they were through the square and gone. Mrs. Bentham, coming out on her way home, looked at Andy curiously, and he knew she wondered why he wasn't at home doing the chores. The shadow of the creamery was gray over the whole square, and as he sat he heard the dinner bell sound up in the flame-windowed inn, and saw the figures rise from the porch chairs.

He had to make up his mind. If the break had been made, then he ought to be looking for a place to stay. If it hadn't, he ought to go back and resume that quiet wrestling with Mr. Richie. But he sat still with his head against the wall, watching the clouds blow over very fast, thin scuds of cloud, high up. Hunching up his feet so that he could hug his knees, he felt the hardness of the golf ball in his pocket and got it out, remembering how the professor of finance from Harvard, the money expert who was always being called to fly to Quito or Santiago or La Paz, had watched him with respect as he hollered the team away from the fence and down the meadow. There wasn't a man on the lake who could handle a team by voice, not even Peter Dow. Dozens of things he could do that a city man couldn't. It would be nice to get some camper on the other end of a crosscut, or put one to honing a scythe. If you were a good hand, there were a hundred things you could take pride in. You knew animals and tools and yourself. There might not be any money or future or fame in farming a place so stony it looked as if the devil had emptied his apron into it, but there was satisfaction. He thought of the farmers he knew, men like Donald Swain, most of them good men to work with, good with any tool from a saw to a shinhoe, who could doctor a horse or repair a tractor or set a straight line of fence or swing an axe from milking time to milking time, and do it the year around with no vacations and no two-month spells of rest with golf courses and sailboats. It might be a hard life, but it was a man's life. And it might look funny to city girls, but it was not something to laugh at. Maybe his uncle was, but there were things that were not.

He was bouncing the ball gently on the sidewalk, catching it and bouncing it and thinking about his uncle, and about what advice his mother might have given him if she were alive, and about what Nancy would say if he went over tonight and told her what he was puzzling over, when Helen Barlow came quickly out of the store.

She stopped at his sprawled feet, and he noticed that her neck was beginning to look a mite stringy. Not much — just enough to tell you she was getting along, twenty-four or five.

'Well, my goodness,' she said. 'Are you taking up golf now, Andrew?'

'Hadn't quite made up my mind,' Andy said. 'Think I should?'

He had the peculiar feeling that she was blinded by her own smiling, and couldn't see him. 'No reason why not,' she said.

'Any reason *to*?'

'Exercise.'

'E-yeah,' Andy said. 'Since Mr. Richie got the hayloader I don't seem to get my muscles shaken out, somehow.' He bounced the ball and it got away from him and rolled into the street. He did not stir after it, but half-lay on the steps, thinking that Helen had gone to college, almost the only person from the village who had. She ought to be able to tell him what it was like, what it was worth. But she was still smiling that dazzled smile, a smile she hid behind. A kind of funny girl, perfectly nice but a little odd, never ran much with other people. Maybe even a touch queer and separate like her father. And it wasn't that she wasn't pretty enough. He supposed she was as pretty a girl as there was in the village.

'I just found it up in the meadow,' he said.

She hesitated, as if not quite sure how to break off a conversation that had nothing in it for either of them. 'Haven't you got chores to do any more?'

'I was just considering them,' Andy said. 'Think I should take some action?'

'Shouldn't be surprised.'

'E-yeah,' he said, and stood up. 'Maybe you're right.'

She left behind her the impression of her bright, smiling, uncertain face. It was not a face you could see into. It was a mirror, not a window. Andy had a feeling as he watched her trim figure cross the square diagonally and go up the street toward the church that he knew exactly what was the matter with Helen Barlow. She was neither village folks nor summer folks; she had been successfully educated away from her own life but not into the other.

He stooped and picked up the golf ball, bounced it once, compressed his lips and stared up the street. Words Allan Richie had spoken to him returned to his mind. 'Folks'd say you had a-plenty to live down, boy, and you won't do it by runnin' away.'

Well, how did you live things down? How did you make up for a down-at-the-heel family and a disreputable hard-drinking old uncle like James? What could you do in your life to atone for the bad luck and shame that had followed your mother through most of hers?

The voice of Peter Dow was a strong one, and its arguments seductive. Given opportunities, he might be able to make something of himself, get to be a professor or a lawyer or a doctor. If you had any intelligence, you had an obligation to develop it to the limit, not let it rust like unused machinery in a leaky shed.

But he heard also the unanimous voice of the village. One of the Mounts getting too big for his breeches, thinking he can get to be a lawyer or a doctor. Village ain't good enough for Martha Mount's boy. Seems if something's wrong in the blood of that family. Never can settle down to anything.

The golf ball bounced crooked against the steps and

rolled into the street again. Andy swung his heavy shoe, intending to kick the thing clear across the square, but it dribbled weakly off the side of his foot and rolled to the corner of the building, where Norma Pratt's cocker spaniel appeared from nowhere and pounced on it.

'Go ahead,' Andy said, as the dog stood looking at him. 'Go ahead, you can have it. Eat the cover off the thing.'

He started walking fast up the street, straight up to Allan Richie's barn. He heard the sound of milking from the cow stable, and came in through the milk-room door to see the lantern hanging on a peg and Allan Richie squatting at Maggie's flank. The old narrow white head turned as he entered, but the even hiss of milk streams in the froth did not stop. Andy got another pail and hooked a stool by the leg.

'Reckoned maybe you weren't comin' back,' Allan said mildly.

Andy took the letters and the rolled paper out of his hip pocket and laid them on the ledge near the lantern. 'Went after the mail,' he said, and put his flat hand against Sally's hip to push her over. He reached the cloth from the rail between the stanchions and wiped off her bag and teats, and the cow turned her head as far as the stanchion would let her and watched him with wide, placid country eyes.

7

Interlude at Moonrise

THAT EVENING there was a church supper at which Helen was, as usual, supposed to supervise the high-school girls who waited on tables. But when she came home from the post office and found the kitchen empty, the stove ticking away its warmth, the smell of fresh-baked blueberry pies dissipating itself through the open window, she was overtaken by a strange feeling of helplessness, as if her muscles had forgotten how to obey her will, as if her mind were numbed and unable to function.

In the dining room her father sat, as he sat every evening of the year, looking through the Woodsville *Gazette*. He could have said hello when he heard the door open; he could have called out, 'That you, Helen?'; he could have made some gesture toward fatherliness. But he sat tucked away into his own peculiar isolation, and made no sign. How could he sit there so long — four years? How could he hold everything he needed in himself, and never spill a drop or give a drop away? How could he exist without belonging to something or someone besides himself?

She did not want to go to the church supper. The married women had their steamy, big-armed club in the kitchen; the high-school girls had a secret society in the pantry between kitchen and dining hall. Helen Barlow fell neatly between the two. In the whole village there was no one like her, a woman of twenty-five who yet belonged more with the girls than with the women. No one except poor Arlene Knight, with her cross eyes and her stuttering tongue.

Helen Barlow and Arlene Knight. Her lips twisted in a grimace, and in the same way that one can feel with salt-mouthed certainty the coming on of nausea, she felt the beginning of a headache. It would be stupid to go over now, ten or fifteen minutes late, and stand in the dining room with a glazed smile, looking out for coffee shortages or directing the girls to bring a new platter of chicken for the corner table. No matter what her mother would think, she wasn't going. Let Arlene run the waitresses. She loved to hustle people around and feel important.

Helen went into the dining room. 'Did Ma give you your supper?'

The bright eyes jerked up. 'Ain't heard me hollerin' for it, have you?'

'All right,' she said. 'I just wondered. I'm going upstairs.'

For the moment that he watched her she knew he was shuffling the possible reasons why she wasn't going to the supper. Then he ducked his head, and communication between them ceased. His face in profile looked like a pouty carving in weathered wood, done with such meticulous Japanese realism that even the grizzled whiskers were there, set in most cunningly and catching the light as if real.

She pulled down the shades so that no one could look in upon his privacy, which was all he had, and went up the dark narrow stairs.

Her room was almost dark. Its windows looked to the east and north, so that now only shadow came in past the neat tied-back curtains. The white walls were dusky, the corners lost. She guided herself to the bed by the glint of brass and lay down on the crazy-quilt coverlet. Among

the multitudinous small pieces of the quilt's pattern her
fingers found a piece of satin, and she hitched her body
until her face touched its flower-petal coolness.

A mood was on her, a peculiar, haunted, emptied mood,
as if she had been disemboweled. For a long time she
simply lay without thinking anything in particular, without wanting or feeling or hating anything in particular.
Her mind was a patchwork as crazy as the quilt she lay
on, a pastiche of Arlene's crossed eyes, envelopes type-
written and envelopes in longhand, Andrew Mount's serious face through the porthole of the box door, the look
of a fork in a big calloused hand, the church's great gran-
iteware coffee pot with a dishtowel wrapped around the
handle, and the strain of a girl's arm as she carried and
poured, deep trails through the snow at sugaring time,
and the ache in the shoulder from the weight of the full
sap buckets, the fierce primitive light from the fire under
the arch, and the weathered walls of the sugarhouse on
the old farm, years ago.

On the old farm, before her father rented it and moved
them into town, there had been a row of maples that
bloomed with flame in the fall and unraveled sticky fin-
ger-pointed leaves in mudtime. She could see them,
holding her eyes closed, and see the swing she had had,
made of an old tire on a rope. It seemed to her that she
had been very happy in that farmyard under that row of
old maples, and she remembered waiting for the mail-
man in the mornings, when she sat barely stirring in the
sagging tire and kept her toes against the ground and
saw how the dew was on the blackberry vines by the
fence, and felt the chill that would not go away until the
sun climbed higher. She saw too, with precise clarity, the
body of a woodchuck a fox had killed. She must have
come down the lane almost in time to interrupt the fight,
for when she got to the maples the chuck lay on its back,

its paws held in a ridiculous hands-up gesture. Its throat was bloody, and its yellow teeth showed. Its position was so helpless, it looked so utterly overpowered, that she looked in its face for signs of the anguish it must have felt when the needle teeth found its throat. But the chuck's face, with its rodent teeth protruding, had no expression whatever. It was just dead.

The memory of the chuck was too near her, and too unpleasant. She concentrated on the star-shaped patches of sky through the maples when she leaned back in the swing and looked upward. Lying quietly on her back, her hands over her head like the surrendered woodchuck's paws, she felt the words coming, and nursed them, listening to their flow. It was always the sound of a poem that came to her first. This one, she knew, wanted to be sad and gentle and nostalgic, like the sad rustling of leaves, so she let it come that way, shifting sounds around and trying them out in a whisper, until she had three lines. A fourth was necessary to complete the stanza, but nothing she tried seemed to suit. The fourth line had to say something definite, but she wasn't sure what she wanted it to say. To surprise the stanza into completing itself, she tried the first three lines almost aloud:

> The doves are mourning in the maples, love,
> The leaves are keening with a long lament,
> The willows weep beside the waters, love. . . .

The final line eluded her. She thought of getting up and getting the rhyming dictionary, but that would have meant putting on the light. She tried changing the third line, coming in by the side door:

> The winds are wailing in the willows, love. . . .

That was too violent, somehow. Her brain stuck, and

she jerked it free again. A line occurred to her, and she
tried it:

Weeping for that unkind note you sent.

It didn't satisfy her. It wasn't smooth enough and it
forced the poem to be about a broken love affair, and
she didn't want it to be about that. She tried another:

Once I too grieved, but now my grief is spent.

Her ear and her mind tentatively accepted it, went over
the whole stanza. It had the proper note of sadness rec-
onciled to its lot, of unhappiness bearing its burdens, and
it didn't bring in a troublesome lover and make the poem
sticky.

Her headache forgotten, she sat up with the intention
of writing the stanza down. In her mind she was already
showing it to Flo Barnes. She was already debating between sending it, when it was done, to the *Gazette,* which
would probably print it, or to some place like the *Atlantic.*
Even as she swung her legs down from the bed she was
imagining that letter, that formal but glowing paragraph:
'We are all greatly pleased by your poem, "September
Nocturne," and wish to buy it for the *Atlantic's* pages. It
occurs to us that you may have other poems which you
would be kind enough to let us see. . . .'

Then she noticed that the moon, almost full, was looking straight in her east window. The little white cell where
she most intimately lived was transformed by it. The top
of her desk under the window shone like some rich ori-
ental wood, with the moon's full image reflected in it.
Moonlight deepened the rag rug, lit expensive gleams
and glints on the walls, turned the foot of the brass bed-
stead into smooth gold.

As if a sound would disenchant her, Helen crossed to
the open window. Eastward the open, mown hilltop

spread bare as a lawn to the hedge of spruce at the far edge. She returned to the north window. Down over the hill she could see the silver roofs of the Richie and Swett places, and the street came silvery out of shadow and flowed into the quiet square. The square was white and deserted, and the inn's shadow lay half across it.

Back at the east window again, she looked at her arm, reaching to hold the curtain aside, and then down at her breast. Moonlight lay on her skin and on the white cotton of her dress like fine pallid dust.

She put her own stanza away and felt for the other, the remembered and romantic lines:

> Rose-bloom fell on her hands, together prest,
> And on her silver cross soft amethyst,
> And on her hair a glory, like a saint.

Tears came surprisingly to her eyes, and she was drawn again to the north window and the sunken, moon-drenched village. Moonlight on the transformed roofs and the enchanted square was too lovely and too sad. Moonlight was like poetry, like a magic that could lay glory on even Westwick Village, which she knew for a dowdy little prison colony. It could turn the front of Bentham's store into the pediment of a temple, and it could take her from her casement on waves of soft light, out over the silver roofs and angled shadows and the white streets, carry her light as down out of the village and through the world that spread moonlight-blasted and still to every horizon.

She sat there for a long time, stupefied with moonlight, riding the gable of the old house as Noah's wife might have ridden the prow of the Ark, dreaming of the flowered slopes of Ararat. Then the sound finally penetrated to her consciousness, and she realized that someone was knocking on the door downstairs.

Down the steep stair tunnel the dining room door was

half open. She heard the knocking again, and now her father was pounding in furious answer on the broad arm of his chair.

'Coming!' she said, and hurried down.

The knocking was coming from the front door, and her father was upset, glaring around over his shoulder at the disturbance. To open that door at all, his chair would have had to be moved. Helen ran to the kitchen door and stepped out onto the porch. 'Who is it?' she said. 'That door doesn't open.'

'Why don't you board it up, then?' Flo Barnes' voice said, and the secretary stepped out of the porch shadow and came along the edge of moonlight.

Helen's imagination caught at the strangeness of this meeting, both of them in white dresses, drenched in moonlight, both just at this edge where the moonlit world met the shadow. The moon glittered momentarily on Flo's white teeth, as if she had jewels in her mouth. She carried a book under her arm.

'I thought maybe I could talk you into going for a walk,' she said, and lifted a hand to sift the moonlight through her fingers.

'I wish I could,' Helen said, 'but my mother's over at the church supper, and I couldn't leave my father alone.'

'Couldn't he stay alone for an hour?'

'Not so loud,' Helen whispered. 'If I were just over at the church he'd put up with it, but if he knew I was really going away somewhere he'd be mad. He says what if he had another shock?'

'Yes,' Flo said. 'What if he did?' She seemed to be thinking, standing with her head dropped so that her whole face was in shadow, and the light cut obliquely across her short fair hair. The sounds of the church supper were momentarily loud, and then a car started and drowned them out. Helen was afraid she had of-

fended her friend. If things were as they ought to be, if
people had freedom to follow their impulses, they could
seize the opportunity of a great burst of moonlight like
this, and there would be no paralyzed old men, no grizzled Duties, sitting inside glaring at the unexpected
knocking on the front door.

'I might be able to go later,' she said timidly. 'Why
don't you come in and wait till Mom gets home?'

'I don't want to come in,' Flo said. 'My God, it rains
enough around here so it's a crime to waste even a minute
of a night like this.'

Helen dropped her head. 'I'm sorry. It's just Pa. But
it's nice from my room, too. I was sitting there watching
the moonlight when you knocked.'

'You were? Alone?'

'Of course,' Helen said curiously. 'I started to write a
poem, but when the moon came up I forgot all about it.'

'I've been reading your poems,' Flo said. 'They're fine.'

'Really? Did you really like any of them? If you didn't,
I wish you'd tell me, because I wouldn't want to go on
wasting . . .'

'I thought they were fine,' Flo said. 'Quite a lot of them
were like you.'

Such a wave of delighted embarrassment went through
Helen that she almost stammered and giggled. 'Silly and
sentimental and full of romantic nonsense? That's what
my professor at Durham used to say.'

'He was crazy,' Flo said shortly. Her shoulders moved
in a vigorous, thrusting gesture, as if she were going
through a door. 'Look, maybe I will come in, if we don't
have to sit around and make conversation with somebody
else. I want to talk with just you alone.'

As they went up the steps Helen said, 'It's funny, you
coming to the front door. Nobody except summer people
ever come to anybody's front door around here.'

'I should have known,' Flo said. 'This is a kitchen-door town.'

She seemed grumpy and abrupt, but not until she was standing at George Barlow's chair did Helen realize the full incongruity of Flo's presence here. Shooting a look at the secretary's tanned face and even teeth and short mane of blonde hair, she saw her with George Barlow's eyes as something strange and foreign and suspicious, a city importation. The old man was holding his paper down, looking fiercely over its top.

'Pa,' Helen said, 'this is Flo Barnes, a friend of mine. She works for Mrs. Weld, down at her camp.'

'How do you do?' Flo said. She put out her hand, and George Barlow's crooked fingers touched it reluctantly for a moment. There was a brief, awkward tableau with Flo smiling down on Helen's father, and her father looking pouty and disturbed, and Helen herself in the background unhappily conscious of how deep and wide was the abyss between them, how utterly incapable of being understood by either side, how immovable was his resentful suspicion and how caustic her city-bred contempt.

'We're going up to my room,' she said hurriedly. 'You call if you want anything.' His suspicious, intent frown followed them until the door closed.

Almost breathlessly, already forgetting her discomfort at the introduction of these two, she led Flo into the moonlit room. Bringing this outsider friend into it made it seem more than ever a virginal cell, immaculate and waiting. She was jumpy for fear Flo would not notice the room, the desk, the curtains, the pure whiteness of the walls, and because she could not wait for Flo to comment, she said something herself, her voice going fluty and artificial. 'Well, how do you like where I live?'

Flo was looking around with devouring intentness. She

moved to the bed, touched the crazy quilt, went around
the foot of the bed to the desk flanked by its two book-
cases. She put her own book on the desk and leaned to
look out over the dreaming, empty meadow. There were
voices from below: people beginning to go home from
the supper.

'It's like you,' Flo said, and her voice was so harsh that
Helen bent sideways, trying to see her face.

'That's what you said about the poems.'

'That's what I meant,' Flo said. She swung around with
her back to the window so that Helen could not see the
expression of her mouth or eyes, but her voice was bitter.
'There's a lot about you that's too good for this jerk town,
if you'd ever get the sense to realize it, and quit wasting
yourself on cheap people!'

Helen put her hands behind her, holding to the cold
brass foot of the bed. The attack was so sudden, the
switch from friendliness to contempt so abrupt, that her
heart seemed tangled in her chest, and she could force
out only a whisper.

'I . . . what do you mean?'

'Oh, don't be so innocent!' Flo said.

'I guess I just don't understand,' Helen said. She felt
pale and pinched-in, and in a moment she would cry.
With her back hard against the footrail she watched the
shadowy fury of Flo Barnes.

'I'm for Sunday afternoons, is that it?' Flo said. 'Week-
days you can hang around with your Brooklyn Jewess and
God knows who else. My God, is that the best you could
do?'

'Ruth Kaplan?' Helen said stupidly. Her mind was
running ahead and backward at the same time, trying to
anticipate Flo's attack and trying to remember when,
how, where, she might have said or done anything to
Ruth Kaplan that would warrant this. 'I've seen her in

the library a couple of times, and I had tea with her the other day up in her new house, but I can't . . . She likes books, she's read a lot. . . . '

'Oh,' Flo said. 'She's read a lot!'

'Yes, and she's nice!' Helen flared. 'Why shouldn't I talk to her all I want to? There are some people in this dirty place that think they're better than she is, just because she's Jewish, but if they'd just look they'd find she's more intelligent and more cultured than anybody in this village, even if she does have a Brooklyn accent, and I can't see . . . '

Flo's hand burned across Helen's cheek, and Helen backed away, her jaw locked with a paralysis that stopped her tongue and even prevented her crying. Her eyes filled, but she could make no sound, and as she backed away Flo followed her, and when her back was against the wall Flo slapped her again twice, swift hot blows that she could not defend herself against or understand. The secretary's face in the bluish twilight was convulsed with such fury that Helen turned away and hid her face in her arms against the wall. There was nothing in her whole mind but the sound of her own sobbing, a familiar, oddly comforting sound. Her body slipped against the smooth wall, and she let it go, slumping to the floor with her face still buried in her arms, the blows of her friend still burning in her skin.

She may have lain there for five minutes or for half an hour. When she came out of the dark place where everything else was obscured by the reassuring sound of her own grief, she realized that Flo was lifting at her armpits. She let herself be lifted and half carried to the bed, and she felt the springs sag as the other woman sat down beside her, but she lay quietly sobbing, pretending neither to know nor care what Flo Barnes did.

The secretary's hand lay lightly on her shoulder. It

patted her, then tightened convulsively, and when Flo
spoke Helen realized with a mean little thrill of triumph
that Flo was crying too. Her hands and her voice plucked
and beat and fumbled at Helen.

'Oh, dearest, dearest, I'm sorry I did that. I don't
know why I did. I wanted to hurt you and make you cry,
I was rotten jealous. I saw you talking with that woman
and laughing with her and I could have killed you both.
. . . Helen, don't cry any more. Forget everything I said
and did. I'll make it up to you . . . don't hate me for loving
you . . . for being jealous. . . .'

Her hands hauled at Helen's limp shoulders, pulled
her to a sitting position. The moon had climbed high
enough so that only a half pyramid of powdery light fell
at a steep angle onto the desk. The room was darker than
it had been, its white walls duskily staring.

'Look at me!' Flo said. 'Darling, look at me! Slap me if
you want, do anything to me, I'd love it. But don't hate
me. I couldn't stand it if you turned against me. I'd kill
myself . . .'

Helen sat quietly, looking down at the shadowy mosaic
of the crazy quilt. Flo's hands held her upper arms tightly, shaking them, and her talk babbled, intense and driven
and full of queer, unwomanly endearments. Abruptly the
secretary rose and went over to the desk. She came back
with the book in her hand, laid it in Helen's lap. Helen's
eyes were blurred with shadows and the long spell of
crying, and she couldn't see what it was. It felt heavy
and cool in her hands.

'I got it for you in Concord last week,' Flo whispered.
'I didn't mean to go crazy and lose my head. I wanted to
come and see you, that was all, and I brought you a present. I wanted you to love me, to think of me as your best
friend, I didn't want to drive you away.'

Helen said nothing. After a moment she rose and went

to the window, laid the book back on the desk. The escaping moon, like a convict taking one last look back before he disappeared over the wall, looked down on the gilt lettering of the title: *The Collected Poems of Elizabeth Barrett Browning.* Flo was behind her, leaning forward, eager, almost abject. Her hand came up to touch Helen's hair, and Helen bent her head away.

'Is it something you'll like?' Flo said. 'I don't know anything about poetry, but the woman said . . . I described you, she seemed to think this might be good.'

Still Helen said nothing. After a time Flo said, 'I know I've been a fool. I haven't any right to ask anything of you. But I wish . . .'

'Wish what?' Helen said. They were the first words she had spoken since Flo slapped her.

'I wish you'd let your hair down,' Flo's hurrying voice said. 'You've got luscious hair. I'd love to see it with the moon on it.'

Helen did not move or answer. She was looking across the meadow, where the shadowy hedge at the far side had drawn in and the light had taken on a quality almost like that of a pre-dawn twilight. It seemed as if at any moment the magic would flick off like stage floodlights, and trees and stubbly hayfields would spring back into reality again. She might have laughed at Flo's foolish solemn request except for the ache in her chest, a core of something undissolved by her weeping; for a moment her skin crawled, and she felt the presence of the secretary behind her as she had sometimes felt the presence of a formless, fearful Dark when she walked home late and alone.

But then the woman's voice came again, soft and pleading, full of contrition and love. 'Please?' it said. 'To show you don't hate me for what I did? Please?'

Helen's hands came up and felt for the pins. The firm bound weight of her hair loosened, spread, fell softly around her shoulders, and she shook it out with a little laugh, turning in the last steep beam of moonlight to face Flo Barnes.

As if he had seen her do it, her father began to shout and pound downstairs.

8

The Anti-Christ

AT SIX O'CLOCK on an August morning the light is gray and pearly. The leaves along the road to the Corners hang distinct and very still. The maples and gray beeches and split-barked yellow birches are motionless in every leaf, and not a needle quivers on the spruce that cross over the hill above the lake. There is no color in the sky, only cool gray light; the world is green and cool under it. If you listen you can hear the strokes of six o'clock from the old locomotive bell in the Catholic church at the Corners.

At this hour smokes are going up from the farms scattered over the hills, and a white river of mist is crawling down the valley of the Ammosaukee. A few minutes after six, the Toonerville whistles as it rounds into the big bend at the Corners, and ten minutes later it whistles again, trundling on across the Ammosaukee bridge and down the valley toward Stafford.

The cows stringing out into the meadows at every farm, their udders shrunken and empty, touch the grass with moist muzzles and snuff softly, dropping their heads to eat with the forward swing that lets their toothed lower jaws cut the grass. They pay no attention to the tooting of the Toonerville's short, comical whistle among the hills. Even if they are grazing in meadows that look down on the valley, and the mist lifts to show the little three-car train snorting across their vision like a cranky toy, they do not lift their heads.

By the time the train is gone, the long, sloping back of Sunday is furry with golden light and the western slope is almost black in the shadow. Some of the clarity is gone from the air, as if a fine mist of gold has been stirred up. The leaves still hang motionless.

Then a black Ford sedan climbs up out of the mist in the valley and comes fast along the county road. Cattle and deer grazing along Broken-Musket Brook lift their heads for it because of its speed and the air of purpose it wears. It swoops around the bends of the smooth blacktop, climbs under the still maples and beeches and birches west of the mill, speeds past the place where the piped spring gives its constant round inch of water to the roadside, crosses the bridge between mill and millpond, and then turns sharp right into the village.

This is Henry Ball, who drives the star route between the Corners and Sudbury Common. Every day, Sundays and holidays included, he comes like a messenger of morning. Until his car swings around the curve and comes up the street between the dock and the houses of John Mills and Parley Pugh, the village is barely yawning itself awake. A few smokes rising, a dog out early to course the street and inspect the inn's garbage cans, the far putt of a fisherman's motor on the lake, and that is all.

But when Henry stops in front of the post office the village stirs. Someone is sure to appear wanting to catch a ride up Sudbury way. The post office door opens and Gaylord Brown, the postmaster, comes out. Down the oblique church driveway Helen Barlow comes hurrying with a sweater across her shoulders, on her way to help with the sorting. Up on the hill the church is in full sun. Now a beam slips past the shadowed barrier of the inn and touches the creamery's white wall, and a little wind that will stir all the leaves comes up from somewhere and drifts down the awakening street.

Abe awoke when sun and breeze together touched the window curtains. For a while he lay getting his bearings, studying the raw-raftered pitch roof, the clean new wood with numbers and symbols left by the carpenters in black pencil or blue chalk. Through the cracks between the sheathing boards he saw the soft brown of shingles. He turned his head sideways; Ruth was still sleeping. She braided her hair at night into pigtails, and somehow the frizzy pigtails had curled down under her chin like the tiestrings of a bonnet. She looked about twelve years old.

He saw the sun at the window, the faint stirring of the new curtains, and the desire to get up was as strong in him as hunger. On such a morning only a fool or a sick man lay in bed. Cautiously he slid his feet out, felt for his slippers, eased his weight off the bed. Ruth still slept. He felt good, like a conspirator.

Carrying his clothes, he went down the half stairs through the tailor shop, which occupied the whole front half of the house, and into the dining room. It was only with an effort that he restrained himself from stumping his feet solidly into his shoes. For a moment he thought of getting breakfast, but then he reflected that with a wife he was not called upon to get breakfast, even when he got up early. Instead, he went to the front door and stood looking out.

He saw the sun take the village like a sliding flood. At about the time the yellow warmth reached the square at the bottom of the hill, Henry Ball's Ford was turning around and starting up toward Sudbury. Raoul LaPere, the handyman at the inn, came down across the square to the creamery. The chimneys of all the white strungout houses fumed in the still air. Abe twitched his nose. The smells of morning, smoke and coffee and the faint unnameable odors of breakfast, tantalized him. He went back inside and listened.

There was no sign or sound from upstairs. To kill time, he turned on the goose and pressed three pairs of trousers that had been brought in the day before. The smell of steamed wool filled the room — a good smell, familiar, mixed with a thousand associations. In the smell of wool and steam there was Russia, Boston, his old tent, a continuity that had lasted through twenty-five years. He was glad he had never changed jobs, and it pleased him to be curing this new house, only a week old, in the old smells, steam and scorch and beeswax and filler and cloth, good cloth.

The short counter by the west windows lured him, and he went over to finger the bolts of cloth there, feeling the tight, hard, unwrinkleable virtue of good worsted, the shaggy friendliness of Shetland. He bent his head to sniff the peaty, sheepy smell of his one remaining bolt of Harris tweed.

So he went sniffing around his new house, familiarizing himself with it, his nose isolating paint smell and new-lumber smell and cedar-shingle smell. In the middle of the room, itself bigger than his entire working and living quarters had been in the tent, he let his satisfaction swell. In such a house as this he could work all winter without freezing his hands. He could sit by his fire and read without a sheepskin on.

Absently, still sniffing for the present and the absent among the smells, he took the lid off his tobacco can and rolled a cigarette. Rolling his own was a concession he had made to the expensiveness of being a married man and a householder, and he was not good at it. He spilled crumbs of tobacco all over the congoleum rug, worked his thumbs awkwardly against the flimsy paper, and ended with a waddy and uneven thing that practically exploded when he lighted it. Warily he smoked the loose fuse of what was left, feeling good, feeling permanent and established. While he was smoking, Ruth's feet hit the floor upstairs, there was a loud, unbridled yawn, and she appeared at the top of the little stair, on the bedroom shelf seven feet above his head.

'For heaven's sakes,' she said. 'Up and working. Have you had breakfast?'

'No, how should I have breakfast? Am I a cook?'

'You managed all right till I came around.'

'Ah,' Abe said, 'but now I have a wife for those purposes. Now I am a mechanic again. My job is to make clothes.'

Ruth disappeared, talked unintelligibly all the time she was back on the sleeping shelf getting dressed, and came out still talking to slap down the stairs in her slippers.

'Could a man get a good morning kiss, maybe?' Abe said.

She stopped in the doorway to the living room, eyeing him and fending off his hands. 'I wish you'd find something to smoke besides that old shredded rope. And you ought to have better sense than to smoke before breakfast anyway. Smoking before breakfast gives you ulcers.'

'If breakfast was on time I wouldn't have to smoke,' he said. 'I could be stuffing my face.'

She escaped from him and whipped into the little kitchen. 'No fire?' she said. 'You yell for breakfast and you don't even build me a fire?'

'Oh, hell!' Abe said, and smacked his brow. 'I am such a man as will stand in his doorway and look at the smoke in every chimney in town and never think that his own is not smoking.'

Ruth laughed, but Abe kept talking seriously as he broke lath-ends and shingles into the firebox and built up the fire with bigger wood. 'No fooling, this is something I will remember. From now on I am not going to be the kind of a citizen whose chimney is cold when everybody else's smokes.'

About nine o'clock every summer morning young Mrs. Herbert Pratt let her cocker out for a run, and the fat shining little dog went like an auburn caterpillar up and down the road and around the square. Not everyone in Westwick looked with favor upon the cocker. He was a city-folks kind of dog; farmers and villagers kept beagles or hounds or farm shepherds. They watched this dog, owned by the town-bred wife of one of their own people, with some doubt and even with some asperity.

At first, when Herbert had brought it home, Martin Bentham and two or three other men had open-mindedly looked it over, had checked its deep mouth and big feet and had agreed that it looked like a retriever in spite of its small size. Still, there was nothing in the way the dog acted that made anyone believe it was good for anything. It was flighty, noisy, probably neurotic. Some people it fell all over in an anguish of affection; at the sight of others it fled home, into the house, and under a bed, where it lay making brave defiant noises until Norma Pratt coaxed it out.

Then one day at the dock, when Norma Pratt wasn't around to protect her pet, Parley Pugh picked it up and threw it ten feet into the lake to see what kind of stuff it was made of. Abe and Allan Richie and two or three city men stood and watched.

The cocker could swim, all right. It came up wet and plastered and set out for shore like a side-wheeler, its ears floating back like wings, its big feet chugging the water, its bulging eyes glaring at the safety of the dock. The dock was about ten inches above the water. Swimming strongly, the cocker came straight on. It made no attempt to climb or scramble up when it hit the planks. It simply hit them, nose on, at full speed. Its neck buckled, and it bounced, but its driving legs never faltered. It swam in and hit the dock again, beating like a fly against a screen. If Parley hadn't reached down and pulled it in by the scruff of the neck it would have stayed there slamming its nose against safety until it drowned.

After that the village had no respect for the dog, and when it caterpillared furry-footed up and down the hill on its morning run, no farmer or villager whistled at it or scratched its ears. The complete and disgraceful ineptitude of the spaniel was taken, moreover, as further evidence that city people lived in a strange and helpless world with different standards, and that even their pets, though perhaps all right in the city, were pretty comical when you brought them up country.

Actually there were three people, outside of summer people and Norma Pratt, to whom the cocker could look for a kind word. One was Helen Barlow, who loved any little soft animal; another was Ruth Kaplan, who had known a friend's cocker in New York; and the third was John Tait, who as the new pastor of an unfamiliar parish was engaged in being friendly with everyone, even the dogs.

The dog had run the length of the street through the ditch, had come bounding back up the other side with flapping ears, and had visited three telephone poles and a maple tree and the corner of Knight's culvert. Now he came across the street again to where Abe was fixing a length of plank as a bridge across the roadside ditch in front of his house. He stopped by Abe and wagged his whole hind end, the stub of his tail imperceptible among the silky red hair. Abe said, in the best village tradition, 'Get along, you imitation dog,' and the dog got. It bounded off, and at the bottom of the church driveway it met Mr. Tait coming down.

Mr. Tait put out his fingers and chirped with his lips. The dog slid to a halt and backed off. In a burst of feebleminded excitement it laid its chin to the ground and barked. Tait advanced, fingers outstretched. Finally he squatted down. The dog liked this. It went for Mr. Tait like an amorous lynx, tried to crawl into his squatting lap, fell through, and reared up to paw with muddy feet at Mr. Tait's shirt. Mr. Tait got up and walked on, brushing at his clothes, and the cocker sprang against the backs of his knees as if trying to hamstring him. By the time they got up to Abe the minister was making angry sweeping motions with his arms, trying to shoo the spaniel away.

'You imitation dog!' Abe said. 'Get along, out with you!' He waved his shovel. Across the street and down three houses, Mrs. Pratt came to the door and called. The cocker streaked for home, leaving Abe and Mr. Tait facing each other across the ditch.

Mr. Tait was a rather big man, wide-shouldered and wide-mouthed. He looked a little like William Jennings Bryan, who during the years of Abe's reading had slowly crystallized as the epitome of everything narrowly and pettishly denominational. Yet when the minister bent his head to see what damage the dog had done to his shirt-front, an unsuspected double chin mounded up above his collar, and his laugh was somehow a fat man's laugh. From across the ditch Abe watched him without enthusiasm, but without malice.

Mr. Tait took out a handkerchief and wet a corner with his tongue and worked on his shirt a minute. Then he laughed and came across Abe's plank with his hand out. Abe shook it. It was a big hand, with a hard, friendly grip.

'You're Kaplan, aren't you? I've been meaning to call, but you know how it is — new place, dozens of people to meet, especially when the summer folks are all here. I'm John Tait. I've just been called to this pastorate a few weeks ago.'

'Sure,' Abe said. 'I know. Pleased to meet you.'

The minister slouched, took off his hat, and ran his fingers through his curly hair. 'Well, it's a wonderful place,' he said. 'My wife and I keep congratulating ourselves that we couldn't have been called to a place with finer people in it. Every day we meet new ones, splendid people.'

'There are some fine people here, yes,' Abe said.

Mr. Tait put his hat on the back of his head and his two hands in his hip pockets, leaving the thumbs out. He looked straight at Abe, meeting his eyes easily as he talked. 'You're not native to these parts.'

'You mean was I born here?'

'Yes.'

Abe laughed. 'How should I be born here? No, I was born in Russia.'

The wide smile widened. 'Then we're both still company,' Mr. Tait said. 'I gather it takes a long time before a newcomer is accepted as part of a village like this.'

'Say,' Abe told him, 'that's the truth, without kidding. Even when you are born here sometimes you're not a native. You know that story about the man who bought a farm up by Huckleberry Pond? He lived there fifteen years, maybe. All his kids were born there. But everybody still called them city folks. So he got mad and one day he asked a neighbor what it took to be a member of the community, like you might say. He didn't care about himself, but what was the matter with his kids? You know what the neighbor said?'

'No.' The minister was listening politely and intently.

'He said, "Cat kin have kittens in the oven, but that don't make 'em biscuits." '

Mr. Tait threw back his head and roared with laughter. Abe was tempted into a few short explosions himself by the unaffected heartiness of the preacher's enjoyment.

When Mr. Tait got his breath he said, 'You don't consider yourself a native, then.'

'Me? I've been here five years only. I'm a stranger.'

'You don't mean it's unfriendly,' Tait said, looking at him straight.

'Oh, no,' Abe said. 'I have friends, a good many. It's like I'm a summer person. City people.'

Mr. Tait was smiling, his eyes roaming around the front yard. 'These little New England country villages!' he said. 'No more conservative places on earth, and no better places once you are accepted. Let's hope we can get them to let us in.'

'Sure.' Abe was wondering what the minister had come for, or if he was really making a call. Maybe he had just stopped casually, as he had appeared to.

'Now that you've got your house built,' Mr. Tait said, 'perhaps they'll soften a little. When a man builds a home in a place it means that he intends to stay.'

'I stayed all right when it was a tent,' Abe said with a shrug. 'Winter and summer, I stayed all right.'

'Ah, but now you're really in the village, with a house. And a new wife, I hear. I don't believe I ever met Mrs. Kaplan.'

'I don't suppose,' Abe said. He looked at the minister, and the minister wore an expectant air. 'Well, come in,' Abe said. 'I'll make you acquainted with her. She's from New York.'

'So I understood,' said Mr. Tait, and came along behind Abe into the tailor shop.

Ruth was sweeping the dining room. 'Ruth,' Abe said. 'Come in here. This is Mr. Tait, the minister. He wants to meet somebody from New York.'

'I was just telling your husband,' Mr. Tait said, 'since we're all company, we ought to stick together.'

'Yes,' Ruth said, uncomprehending. 'Well, how do you

do? It's a pleasure to meet you.' Her warm welcoming smile made Abe feel good just to see it.

'Mr. Tait just came a few weeks ago, about when you did. He's going the rounds making calls on everybody. Is that it?'

'That's about it. You can't be a good shepherd unless you know every sheep in your flock.'

Abe exploded in short laughter. 'Sheep! Sheep, that's good.'

'Abe,' Ruth said, 'get Mr. Tait a chair, why don't you?'

He jumped into the dining room and came back with two. That was one thing about having a wife, especially one from New York. She knew how things should be done, even such a thing as this call from the preacher. She knew how to make people feel comfortable, but she didn't fall all over them. She acted like somebody who knew her own value.

'Madame!' he said, and held the chair for her to sit down in. Mr. Tait sat down too then, and Abe kicked the padded stool out from his work bench and perched on it. Balancing there, he reached for the tobacco can and rolled a cigarette, scattering crumbs on the congoleum.

'Maybe Mr. Tait would like to roll himself one,' Ruth said.

The minister said he would not, thank you. Abe licked the edge of the paper and rolled and crushed the cigarette together. 'So you like this village,' he said.

'Very much. Don't you?'

'I like it, yes. But I am not in your business.'

Mr. Tait agreed.

'And in your business you have to deal with people I would not like to deal with.' He lighted the cigarette, ducked from the explosive flame-up, and brought his lips back to puff cautiously at the smoldering stump.

'I haven't found anyone yet that I wouldn't be delighted to deal with,' Mr. Tait said.

'You will meet them,' Abe said, waving his arm. 'Being a preacher, you cannot choose your friends.'

Mr. Tait pondered this, and agreed that in a way it was true, but that being forced to work with all kinds of people made one eventually more tolerant of human frailty and more brotherly toward mankind at large. And after all, we were all God's children.

'Still,' Abe said, 'I would not want to have to do it.' He laughed and made a strong gesture of repudiation and brushed the cigarette against his coat and knocked the stringy coal of burning tobacco off on the floor. It smoldered there until he finally put his shoe on it. Ruth went and got broom and dustpan and swept up, rubbing with her fingers against the little brown mark on the congoleum.

'I could name you names,' Abe said. 'I could give you chapter and verse, but you should find these things out for yourself, who is sheep and who is goats and who is a wolf in sheep's clothing.'

Mr. Tait said with a smile that he hoped there weren't any as bad as all that, and Abe threw his hands outward, giving up the subject. He hunched on the stool and dropped one shoulder and squinted at Mr. Tait, and then pointed a finger.

'You are an intelligent man. You have had an education. I wish you would tell me please how did you happen to get into this preaching business?'

'It seemed the field in which I could do most,' Mr. Tait said. His eyebrows were up slightly, and he looked a little at bay.

'For who? For yourself?'

'Abe, you're getting excited,' Ruth said.

'Of course not,' said Mr. Tait. 'For others.'

'For others,' Abe said. 'So. Always you should think of others first and yourself last.'

'That's the best Christian tradition. Naturally human nature is frail, and falls short.'

Abe was silent for a moment, brooding. Then he chopped out a laugh. 'It fails sometimes, so? I tell you, it fails all over this village. I know all these people. There are good enough people among them, but I don't know any Christians who think of others first and themselves last. Well, one, John Mills maybe. But these others! Who is the worst man in town to owe money to? Who is it fatal if he holds your mortgage? Who will sting you in a trade and think he should be proud of himself for it? You will see them in your congregation — big important people in your congregation.'

'You should keep quiet while you've still got some sense,' Ruth said.

'Why should I shut up speaking the truth? Mr. Tait here is maybe a Christian by his own definition, but except maybe for John Mills there isn't such another Christian in the village. Not even the people who hire him and pay his salary are such Christians. They are the farthest away of all.'

'Abe!' Ruth said, and stood up. But Mr. Tait held up a placating hand.

'No, no. Let him say it out. We're none of us so tender we can't stand open discussion. This is the way to get things out in the open where we can do something. And I assure you,' he said, smiling, 'I want to see them all ironed out, because I hope that before too long we can see you both members of the Christian fellowship of the village.'

Abe looked at him hard, laughed incredulously, batted at the air with one hand.

'Abe gets so excited,' Ruth said. 'He doesn't mean half of what he says.'

'What?' Abe said. 'I beg your pardon. I mean every word I say. I say the Christianity of a lot of these people is bunkum.'

'Naturally you're more critical than I would be,' said Mr. Tait. 'And yet in other ways I wonder if you are? The spiritual state of the village is my personal charge and duty. I like to think of Christianity as simply the real true brotherhood of man, and I hope that through my efforts that brotherhood can be promoted a little bit.'

'Nobody could ask anything fairer than that,' Ruth said. 'Abe gets so excited — he loves to argue.'

'I suppose,' Mr. Tait was going on, 'that the Christian tradition of the brotherhood of all men does clash now and then with the more restricted tribal tradition of Jewish separateness and exclusiveness. But after all, Christian belief is rooted in a reformed Jewish faith, and there's no real reason . . .'

Abe bent his head to glare angrily from the stool. 'You speak to me as if I were a Jew?'

Mr. Tait's eyes, cheeks, and mouth all tightened slightly, and his neck stiffened, but he went on smiling. 'Well, aren't you? You're not a member of the only Christian church in the village. Your name is Kaplan. You don't attend, so far as I know, the Catholic chapel in the Corners. So I assume that you're Jewish. Why not? I have no prejudice against Judaism. I have many Jewish friends, several rabbis, in fact.'

'Listen!' Abe said. He was almost falling off the stool, leaning forward to point a dramatic finger at Mr. Tait's chest. 'Rabbis or Christians, it is all the same to me. I know those rabbis too, inside and outside. I am not talking against Christianity only, that is as good a religion as any. I am talking about hypocrites. I am talking about ways of fooling yourself and putting your brains to sleep. I am talking about living one way and pretending another.

The brotherhood of man, that is fine, those are fine words, but who is a brother? Could I get a room at that inn down on the square except by some accident the way my wife did? You tell me. And all this nonsense of prayers and a God that watches the sparrows fall, and this notion of "I am right and you will go to hell," that is what I am talking about.'

For a while Mr. Tait sat as if musing. Then he shook his head, and twitched the corners of his mouth as if loosening them. Ruth had taken Abe's shoulder and rattled him into silence. The minister rose, still smiling slightly, still shaking his head.

'Well,' he said, 'I see we can agree to disagree. I like people to be honest, as you have been, even when they express sentiments in which I profoundly disbelieve, and by which I must say I am considerably shocked. Some-time let's get together again and try to get to some meeting of minds.'

'Why not?' Abe said. 'I am always willing for an argument, and on this business of religion I will argue anybody. I grew up in a synagogue, I know all that stuff. My eyes are perfectly good to see this Christianity here, too. I'll argue any time, but you will not make a believer of me. I believe in using my brains, not putting them to sleep.'

He hopped off the stool and opened the door for Mr. Tait affably, and on the steps they shook hands. As the minister went out across the plank and into the sunny street Abe was waving and shouting things. 'Come again any time,' he was saying. 'I will have this religion business out with anybody.'

He would have yelled more, might even have walked out on the grass and shouted last words and afterthoughts, if Ruth hadn't pulled him inside and shut both the screen and the door.

'My Lord!' she said. 'You certainly do fine! Why don't you go walking up and down the street shouting "There isn't any God!" '

'You think I am scared to?'

'No. I know you're not scared to. That's just the trouble. We have to *live* in this place.'

'So while we are living here we will let everybody know where we stand,' Abe said. 'I am not one of these who will act worse than he talks. Maybe I will talk worse than I act, how do you know? Did you ever know me to cheat my neighbors or tell lies? We will let people know exactly where to find us. I do not believe in this hypocrisy business.'

9

The Siren

MRS. SOPHUS WELD did not have her own way with many
things in Westwick. Every proposal she had ever made
for putting Westwick on the map and making it a bustling
little summer colony had met the gelid smile, the polite
rebuff. The university people who had been coming to
Westwick for a generation or more did not want it on the
map. They had something quiet, well-bred, pleasant, uncomplicated by any intrusive spirits other than Mrs. Weld,
and they were hanging onto it and fencing it in and keeping it just as long as the world would let them. Many of
them were so far from wanting to be part of a bustling
little summer colony that they left their names off their
mail boxes, allowed weeds to grow in their roadways, and
maintained 'think-houses' off in the deep woods to which
they could retreat at the sound of a motor.

Only one suggestion of Mrs. Weld's, her most grandiose,
had ever borne fruit of any kind, and it hadn't borne the
kind that Mrs. Weld had expected it to. She had offered to
bring up to Westwick a double quartet from the Philadelphia Symphony, of which she was unaccountably one
of the angels, and give the village entirely free a music
festival that would put the place on the map just as surely
as Whatsitsname where the Berkshire Festival was held.
But the Westwick Association did not want Mrs. Weld
promoting and controlling any such cultural enterprise.
It found loopholes and objections, thought that the village
might get caught in obligations it couldn't live up to,

frankly feared the 'distinguished people' that Mrs. Weld prophesied would be lured in. Finally it voted a substitute proposal for lakeshore concerts from records, the record collection to be assembled by popular subscription.

Mrs. Weld, all but frozen out, shouldered her way back in by suggesting that Weld Island offered the best stage from which to broadcast, and the handiest gathering-point for people from every part of the lake — a suggestion so obviously true that no one on the committee could gainsay it. Thereafter, every Sunday evening, Mrs. Weld was, in a way, where she wanted to be — at the center of the cultural life of Westwick.

She was not a woman who could sit still. For the first few concerts her old dock proved ample, but when listeners began to show a tendency to come ashore and listen from the land, she had her dock extended fifteen feet and built a little demountable bleacher at its landward end. As it turned out, few people chose to sit in it, because it offered no chance for a family group to feel private and secluded as it could feel in a boat or under the trees. It was almost certain, moreover, that at some time during the concert some uninitiated helper groping for the switch that controlled the record-changing light would accidentally hit the big switch and turn a half-dozen powerful floodlights into the eyes of the bleacherites.

Later Mrs. Weld set out two large floats, seventy-five feet offshore, to which anchorless boats and canoes could attach themselves during the music. Somehow few did, most of them preferring to drift around. Still later, Mrs. Weld erected a tall flagpole above her boathouse and flew the American flag all day Sunday. At sunset, at about the halfway point in the concert, she would motion one of her henchmen, who would creak from his chair near the

phonograph and tiptoe to the halyards and haul Old Glory
down with a faint ceremonious squeak of pulleys.

She felt her responsibilities, even anticipated them. To
make things easier for landing parties she had in a bull-
dozer that cleared fifty feet of shore and laid down a ramp
for the beaching of canoes. Thereafter the infirm or aged
could come ashore and listen at their ease, and at the
ramp they would be met and flagged into a parking space
by Mrs. Weld's chauffeur or by one of the three or four
myrmidons she hired especially for the evening. After
the concert the same myrmidons would be there with flashlights, darting about and complicating traffic with contradictory signals and making themselves very efficient
and useful. Sometimes Mrs. Weld herself would come out
and stand spraddle-legged baying her helpers on.

She managed the concerts as if she were directing
Yankee Stadium during a world series, but one thing she
couldn't manage. True to its original intention, the Association never gave her a chance to say what should be
played. By fraud or guile or plain stubbornness it persistently managed to avoid playing the numbers that Mrs.
Weld as persistently requested. Almost every Monday,
before the meeting of the program committee, Mrs. Weld
dictated a letter to Miss Barnes requesting specific pieces,
and had her chauffeur deliver it personally. Principally
what she wanted was a change in the theme song. She
was sick of the *Egmont* Overture, and she had never liked
it anyway, and besides it wasn't appropriate. Her own
choice was 'When You Come to the End of a Perfect Day,'
though she had also suggested 'Just a Song at Twilight'
and 'In the Gloaming,' both of them just as appropriate
to the time and occasion. She had also, many times, requested that these heavy classical numbers that all
sounded like finger exercises be omitted, and some good
tuneful pleasant music substituted, things like 'Humor-

esque' or MacDowell's 'To a Wild Rose.' Or why not play some lively things like the *William Tell* Overture? Her letters piled up in the program committee's folder and the committee went on playing Brahms and Bach and Haydn and Mozart and Beethoven and Mahler and Smetana and Stravinski and Sibelius.

Having the upper hand, they left her nothing but the mechanical details, and when she had exhausted all the obvious improvements in these matters she began devising less obvious ones. About the middle of August, on a Thursday evening, she got the notion of making over a stretch of lake shore into a park where people could lounge and listen. Much better than the dock or the grandstand. She put Miss Barnes on it at once, and within an hour she came in to say that she had located four workmen who would be around in the morning.

Andy Mount pulled his boat up on the ramp and came around the edge of the vegetable garden at seven o'clock. Nobody seemed to be up in the three cottages strung out under the cedars, and there was no sign of his Uncle James or of the Shurtleff boys from Sunday Mountain. He walked past the workshop and between two of the cottages. It was dewy and fresh under the trees; the sun coming in flat under the trimmed-up branches glinted on the wet grass and on the wide patch of snow-on-the-mountain before the main house.

He went clear over to the other side of the point, north of the dock, and leaned his double-bitted axe against a tree and sat down on a stump to wait for the others. Woods and lake were utterly breathless. Not a ripple moved against the shore, not a leaf or a needle fell. Back in the island woods a white-throated sparrow was ecstatically pouring out his one liquid song. Andy looked at his big silver Ingersoll. Five past seven. But his watch might be wrong. It seemed awfully early, somehow.

Through the fringe of boughs along the island's edge he could look over at the unpeopled north shore, beyond Turtle Rocks. The rocks themselves were out of sight behind the jut of the point, but he could see the mill-pond water and the steep sun-slanted shore. It seemed to him too that he could hear splashing, and he half rose to peer through the trees. A swimmer came in sight from around the point, as if coming from the rocks; someone darkly tanned, who cracked the mirror-water in a swift strong crawl. Andy watched, admiring the easy power of the swimming, wondering who was man enough to get up and swim when it was as early and as cold as this.

The swimmer came straight on to a point a hundred yards down the shore, the brown arms and shoulders gleaming now in the sun, now passing into the shadow. In the shallow water the swimmer staggered and lurched upright, and Andy froze where he stood when he saw that it was a woman, naked as a fish. Without hurry or appearance of alarm, she splashed up on the bank, pulled herself in by the knee of a cedar, reached a white terrycloth robe off a limb, slid into it, kicked her feet into clogs or sandals, and started up the shore path toward the cottages.

There was nowhere Andy could hide until she had gone by. All he could do was to take advantage of a moment when she was out of sight among the trees, and duck back to his stump, where he sat down and stared fixedly out over the lake. With all his senses focused, as it were, in the back of his neck, he felt the exact moment when she discovered him, felt the slight slurring pause in her stride, and then she went on, twenty yards behind him, to the central cottage.

He bent his neck slightly, getting a sidelong look over his shoulder. The woman — it was Mrs. Weld's secretary, the blonde woman with the short hair — went up the steps, her calves walnut-brown below the white robe. She was the one to be swimming in the cold morning water. There was a story that she had bicycled clear to Mount Washington and back, more than a hundred miles, between dinner and supper. Carefully he withdrew his gaze from the empty screen door and let his neck turn almost imperceptibly toward the front again, moving as slowly as he would have moved if a hummingbird had been in a flower near his face. The image of the brown woman standing upright on the rooty bank with her water-dark hair swung back, her hand reaching for the robe on the limb, was tense and living in his mind. He sat still on the stump and looked out over the lake, and his blood burned with desire and his hands shook with wonder and a bright feverish excitement. He was still sitting there almost an hour later when his Uncle James and the Shurtleff boys came together between the cottages from the direction of the ramp.

The older Shurtleff looked at him sharply, with a shrewd, hanging grin. His face was edged like an axe, and his hair lay every way on his head, a dull black mat, as if it had not seen a comb for so long it had become felted. His eyes pried at Andy's face.

'Well, well,' he said. 'She been in yet?'

Andy went brick-red. 'Who?'

'Who?' Shurtleff said. 'Who? Look at the boy! Danged if he don't look guilty's a burglar. Who'd you think you'd see, comin' down here early?'

'I don't know.'

'Well, who *did* you see?'

'Nobody,' Andy said. 'I've been waiting an hour to get to work.'.

'Don't nobody start at seven on a summer-folks job,' the younger Shurtleff said. He was gopher-toothed like his brother, but less in need of a shave. He looked at James Mount and squinted his eyes. 'What held you up, James? Sh'd think you'd be down to see the sights too.'

'I'm a married man,' James said. He winked at Andy and spat on the ground.

'What are you talking about, anyway?' the boy said.

Young Shurtleff searched in his frock pockets for a cigarette. 'Didn't see nawthin', all the time you was here?'

'What would I see?'

'Folks been sayin' this secretary of Mrs. Weld's takes a swim in her bare skin every mornin'. The Prouty boy was up fishin' t'other mornin', said she swum clean across the channel and back, naked as you please.'

Andy opened empty hands and shrugged. He heard the elder Shurtleff say, 'Won't be a fish in this pond, she keeps that up.'

'How's that?' James said.

Shurtleff made an obscene gesture. 'Stiffen up and drown'd,' he said, and cackled with sudden loud laughter.

His brother was looking speculatively toward the house. 'Wonder if she's married?'

'Why, I hadn't heard so,' James said. 'You gettin' ambitions that way?'

'Wouldn't turn it down,' Shurtleff said. 'She must be married, showin' off that way. Wouldn't any girl be that bold.'

'Well, if she's married, that makes it easy,' James said. 'She'd never miss a slice off a cut loaf.'

Shurtleff senior smacked his seat and laughed again, and then they fell silent suddenly, standing in a quiet little knot on the shore, as the back door opened and the secretary, in a white shirt and gray slacks, came out and started out the path toward them.

Andy moved a little behind the others, knowing that if he looked at her openly he would look at her as if she had no clothes on, and that she would recognize the look. He was hot and embarrassed, and he did not particularly like the cool, arrogant expressionlessness of the secretary. Her hair still showed the marks of the comb. Her voice was crisp, a little loud, and her eyes touched them each briefly, impersonally. Andy could make nothing of the glance she gave him. It simply recognized that he was there, as if counting him, without individualizing him in any way.

She showed them what Mrs. Weld wanted done. From a point a few yards below her boathouse to the first out-curving in the shore, perhaps two hundred feet, she wanted all weeds and bushes cut out and cleaned up. She wanted the cedars thinned, leaving only one tree every fifteen or twenty feet. Where there was grass under the trees, she wanted it scythed and then mown with a lawn-mower until it was as smooth as it could be made. Where there was not grass, she wanted sod laid in. They could cut the sod across in Charbon's meadow, where there was a good deal of clover. There were tools of all kinds, including a grass roller, in the shop.

Walking them down through the cedars, stooping under low branches, talking crisply with her cool eyes touching now one, now the other, allowing them no personalities but only their identity as workmen, she stopped at the bottom end of the projected park, rolling the starched cuffs of her shirt up her brown smooth arms. 'When you get that much done, there's one last job,' she said. 'Mrs. Weld will be particular about it. Maybe she'll want to show you herself how she wants it done. Have any of you ever seen a formal garden, with the bushes and hedges trimmed in ornamental designs?'

'You mean cut out into shapes?' James asked.

'Yes. Would you know how to do it?'

'Reckon a man could figure it out,' James said. 'What kind of shapes does Mrs. Weld want?'

The cool blue eyes came to rest on James, and it seemed to Andy that in her eyes and in the corners of her mouth there was a faint sneer. Whether it was for his uncle, or Mrs. Weld, or this job which she was giving directions for, he couldn't tell. 'What would you suggest?' she said.

James screwed up his face. 'Cows, maybe. Sheep. Could be we could find one spread out, sort of, make a fish or somethin' out of it. Might get a tall one into a long-legged bird, like the kind they have cut out of a board on folks' lawns.'

'Yes,' she said, watching him with that remote, shadowy twist of irony in her face. 'You've got imagination. Give it free rein.'

Ray Shurtleff, silent till now, quelled by the efficiency of the secretary, uneasy under her level eyes, made one desperate attempt to distinguish himself from the other three digits who made up the work gang. 'Mrs. Weld's that fond of livestock, I got eighteen head of caows she can pasture in here. Little more lifelike than cedar ones.'

The eyes barely brushed him. 'I expect you'd better take that up with Mrs. Weld yourself,' she said. With her sleeves rolled neatly to the middle of her round upper arms, she said, 'Mrs. Weld likes things done in a hurry. You can come in for your pay at five o'clock, and the rate will depend on how much of this is done. She pays by the day, and she pays high for good work.'

She left them, swinging with her vigorous free stride down the shore. James Mount looked after her, then looked at Ray Shurtleff. His toothless mouth opened, but he made no sound. When he had closed his mouth again after an absolutely soundless cackle, he said, 'No, Ray. You ain't man enough. Ain't anybody I know round here that *is* man enough.'

All day Andy kept his mouth shut and worked, and when the Shurtleffs pointed out places where a man could sit completely out of sight and command the whole main cove and Turtle Rocks, he made no sign that he heard. It was perfectly clear to him, in spite of the unchecked excitement that still beat in him when he thought of the naked body staggering up out of the shallows, that he would not come down early the next morning and try to catch another look. He knew the Shurtleffs wouldn't either. There was something in the way the woman looked at you, not exactly contemptuously, but with an inhuman impersonality, that discouraged even the determined lewdness of the Shurtleffs. It was a good hour after her departure before they recovered from the confused state of mind she had left them in, and got back into the swing of steady work and an occasional smoke and occasional remark. Andy, swinging a grub-hoe on the roots of little felled cedars, thought with wonder how, desirable, how graceful and warm and living she had been at a distance, and how cold and even repellent she was when you met her face to face.

He nursed the contradictory images in his mind all day, and at five o'clock when they went into the office for their pay he stayed behind his Uncle James. A half hour before, the secretary had walked unhurriedly through the cleared-out area along shore, inspecting the amount of work done. Now, as they came up the steps in a close huddle, Andy darted his eyes around the office in search of her, and was half disappointed, half positively glad to see the room empty. There was a letter in the typewriter, and the breeze from the open window behind riffled the two sheets of paper and the blue carbon between them. From outside came the low sound of women's voices, indistinct and mumbling as the sound of flies on the warm side of a barn.

James leaned out the window, his grinning toothless face turning right and then left. 'Were you looking for me?' the secretary's voice said clearly.

'I understood you to say we got our pay here at five,' James said.

'Just a minute,' the voice said. Then in another tone it said, 'You don't have to go in yet. Wait a minute and I'll run you over in the motorboat. We can tow your skiff.'

Miss Barnes appeared in the doorway. She had glasses in her hand, and slipped them on as she sat down.

From a metal box she took a package of bills, thumbed off four ones and four fives, snapped the box shut, and looked up at James Mount. One by one they stepped forward and took their six dollars. Andy came last. He was weak all over, and it cost him agony to lift his eyes. Even when he managed it, he looked past rather than at the secretary, and on the patch of lawn outside the window he saw Helen Barlow. She lifted a nervously gay hand, and in his surprise at seeing her he forgot himself momentarily. 'Well, hello, Helen,' he said.

He was aware that the secretary had said something. He turned his glazed eyes on her and saw her standing with the new bills in her hand, her eyes impatient and her mouth hard. In the instant when their glances met with a little sparklike shock, he had a feeling that she disliked him intensely.

'Six dollars,' she said.

'Thank you,' Andy said. For very desperation, in his confusion and embarrassment, he craned to make a little gesture of farewell at Helen Barlow outside the window. The secretary stood with her fingers on the desk until he got his feet working and followed the others outside.

That was all, but the contradictory emotions aroused by his brief contact with Flo Barnes bothered him all the way home, all through chores, all through the pork chops and boiled potatoes and rice pudding that old Mrs. Knight came over to set up for him and Allan. It nagged at him, sitting out on the porch after supper, until he got up and walked aimlessly through the square and out the road. No matter how his mind ducked and turned, it kept coming back, slyly, until it caught itself up in the act of gloating over the bare brown body, the smooth perfection of every limb and every movement. He saw her image generally at a distance, but even close-up it had power to shake him — the way the starched cuff of her sleeve turned up along the round arm, the strong throat within the open collar of her shirt, the walnut calves below the terry-cloth robe, mounting the steps and vanishing within the house with a movement of lithe ankles.

He lived with the memory of her bare flesh in orgiastic intimacy, yet through every erotic vision he allowed himself to construct, her icy blue eyes looked at him as they might have looked at a signpost, and the mouth was shadowed by an unspoken but obvious contempt.

When he looked up in the late dusk and found himself opposite the garage and dock that Mrs. Weld maintained on the mainland opposite the south channel, he swore aloud at the thing which was being done to him, and set off at a hard, conscience-smitten run up the road and away from temptation. When he came to the four corners where the lake road turned away toward Sudbury, he slowed to a winded walk, but he kept on going, headed for the lighted kitchen of Donald Swain's place.

The night was overcast, a little breathless, quite warm. From the steps where they sat they could see on the left the faint pale shape of the hydrangea bush, and on the right, lighted by the light from the window, the tall, ever-so-quietly-nodding yellow heads of the goldenglow. At their feet the grass stretched off short-mown into the darkness.

They had exhausted words, and had come to the quiet part, the kissing part. Nancy lay within his shoulder, and their arms were around each other's waists. The girl's pale blonde hair was under his nose, and he sniffed at it, playing.

'Old Blondie,' he said. 'Just the color of a Jersey cow.'

'I wish 'twas,' Nancy said. 'That would be a lovely color of hair.'

'Nicer the way 'tis,' he said, and then added, 'You're the second blonde I've seen today.'

It came out as if it had been hiding there, waiting for a door to open. It slid out like a cat slipping between a walker's feet, and he sat staring hotly down the vanishing apron of lawn. With everything lovely, Nancy sweet as sugaring time, giving him her deliberate, shut-eyed kisses that were like fruits to be picked, one at a time, he had to say that. So far as he knew, the woman hadn't been on his mind for a half hour, but out she popped, just the same.

Nancy turned her face toward his, her eyes faintly shining. 'I bet I know who.'

'Who?'

'Mrs. Weld's secretary, the one with the short hair.'

'What makes you think so?'

'She's the only one around with hair as light's mine, and you were working there today.'

'You ought to be a detective,' he said uneasily, laughing, seeing the brown body in the shallows, the careless, back-thrown hair, the reaching arm.

'She's pretty,' Nancy said. 'She's a knockout.'

'Is she?' he said, shifting his back against the pillar.

'She could be in the movies,' Nancy said. 'For certain kinds of parts she'd be wonderful.'

He bent and kissed her, forcing himself to feel the tenderness of her lips, the softness of her skin. 'I can't imagine her doing that,' he said. 'Movies or otherwise.'

'She's the outdoor type,' Nancy said. 'She'd do better in

Westerns. She'd look wonderful in a black sombrero with a tie-string under the chin.'

She lay comfortably against him, accepting his kisses when he gave them, uncomplicated and affectionate and fifteen. The very thought of what it might be to hold a woman like Flo Barnes in his arms this way made him shake. 'She's got funny eyes,' he said. 'They'd scare a man near out of his mind.'

'They're awful light,' Nancy agreed. 'She must be Swedish, maybe. Lots of Swedes have those light blue eyes.' She lay speculating, her whole mind given over to the problem of who besides Swedish girls had light-blue eyes, and he looked down at her pretty childish face, feeling years older, feeling like her father almost, feeling protective and warmly involved. She was a country girl, maybe, and she still had two years to go in high school, and she didn't know everything a woman from the city knew, and probably never would. But when he bent over her again to rub his nose softly against hers and kiss her he could see, in the dim dusky light from the window, no arrogance in her blue eyes, and no shadow of irony or contempt on her mouth. Danger lay where his mind had been wandering; safety lay here.

10

Circle Four Hands Around

IT WAS A LITTLE like being God, distributing the mail.
From outside, where people waited, the letterboxes were
single, private, impregnable with glass and bronze and
cunning combination locks. The majesty of the law pro-
tected them, as the handbills and reward notices tacked
all over the walls made plain. From the viewpoint of the
waiting box-renter the mailbox was a privacy as sanctified
as any he could command. But from Helen Barlow's point
of view, from back of the box wall, the whole honeycomb
was open and available. From where she worked it was
possible to see into anyone's affairs, read his postcards,
estimate his bills. With a little malice she could have
wrecked lives; with a will to snoop she could have known
secrets of everyone in the village.

A little like being God. Gaylord Brown, behind her,
finished sorting first-class mail into the star route sacks
and handed the packet of letters over his shoulder. Helen
turned to take them, bringing the smeared front window
into her vision, and just as she turned she saw Flo Barnes
cross the pane, turning her head to look in.

The feeling of having impregnable barricades between
herself and the village vanished between two breaths.
The post office became not a fortress but a trap. She was
not like God now, but something on which God looked
down, knowing every thought and act, and it did no good
to pretend that the letterbox was private because it was
bound in metal and locked with a two-dialed lock to

which no one else had the combination. God didn't need the combination. Secrets could be kept from the front, but from the rear they were wide open.

Her hands still automatically slid letters edgewise into the narrow pigeonholes, but there was a heavy thudding in her chest, and her mind fluttered like a bird caught in a room. If the whole village could walk around behind the wall and look and see it all, the way God saw it, every act and every thought. If Mrs. Bentham knew everything, and old Mrs. Budd knew, and Mr. Tait and Mrs. Tait and Mrs. Thatcher and lewd old James Mount. If Vina Mount knew, and could stand insolent and with curling lip, and talk about it with her drunken boy friends down on the river.

The door of the Weld box — she knew it, out of all that battery of boxes — swung open, and Flo's straight brows and blue eyes and the evenly-tanned upper part of her face were there. Helen flashed a tight smile and moved sideward, religiously reaching and stooping. But when she had to cross the open box again Flo's eyes were still there. The brows frowned a peremptory summons, but Helen did not heed it. She formed a word with her lips, 'Later!' and escaped to other boxes. The thudding of her heart filled her whole head. After a moment the box door slammed.

Until all the mail was sorted, Gaylord kept the stamp window down, and there was no communication between outside and inside. Henry Ball came in the side door and got the sealed sack for Sudbury, came back and gathered up the star route sacks. When the door had closed behind him there was only the little job of stuffing newspapers and catalogues into the boxes. Box doors began to swing open and click shut again, feet shuffled outside as people made up their minds they had all the mail that was coming.

Helen stayed till the last, through the little clean-up jobs, but when Gaylord looked at her and wrinkled his long lip and said, 'Well, reckon we can sell a few stamps,' she smiled a sick smile and said, 'I'll be running along, then,' and slipped out the door that let her into the alley.

For a second she hesitated. Someone crossed the narrow opening between the post office and the firehouse, and her heart stopped, but the walker went on. She turned and ran down the alley into the sloping back-yard strewn with rusty cans and old square blocks of cement buried in the long grass. Straight ahead the lot angled between the back sheds of the Pugh place and lost itself in woods. To her left the cross alley, unused except by children cutting through the back lots, opened onto the Corners road above the feed store.

There was a chance that she might fly out the feed store alley and come around through the square and home before Flo saw her. But it was too risky. Flo had probably already discovered her escape from the post office. She fled down the lot, through a boggy spot into open woods, across a fence and down the steep wooded hillside until she reached the brook, which fell through a gravelly chute into the old millpond above the road. From there it went underground through a culvert into the mill.

Helen stopped by the pond and got her breath, looking back up along the wooded slope in fear that Flo's figure might appear in pursuit of her. The last of the day was stretched from the hills above Broken-Musket Brook clear across to the slopes of Sunday. The woods behind her were very still, with only the chuckle of water and the abrupt sweet tune of a peabody bird in the quiet. Not a leaf moved on the late goldenrod and joe pye weed at the roadside. The mill was deserted; there was not a car on the road.

She felt how the quiet threatened her, how lonely it

was and how soon the dark would come on, and suddenly the village seemed a friendly and protecting place full of light and the sounds of life. She wanted to start straight up the road and go to her house and feel the warmth of the big range and smell the smells of supper, and see her father settling to his evening reading. But there was too much danger that Flo would be waiting for her. The only chance she had of escaping was by walking clear around the village and coming in like a sneak thief from back of the hill.

As she started up the edge of Livesy's meadow and crossed into the rough golf course she said to herself, quite simply — or to God, she wasn't sure which — the thing that was overpoweringly on her mind. 'Please,' she said, 'let me keep out of her way! Just let me get in without her seeing me. She'll be gone in a few more days. Please let me keep out of her way till she goes and everything will be all right.'

It was at least two miles around by the elaborately safe way she had chosen to go. In the rough the stubble snagged her stockings and pricked her ankles, and in boggy spots she sank over her shoetops in squelching grassy mud. Once, at the edge of a wide sand trap, she stopped to get her breath and look back. The valley was bleak with the oncoming dark. The evening star was pale above the cemetery hill.

By the time she had picked her way the length of the golf course and come over the hill to where she could see the wink of lighted windows in the village through the trees, it was almost fully dark. She had to feel with her feet through the pasture back of the clubhouse. The sky was filling with stars.

Across the half-cleared patch that Daniel Pratt had been clearing for as long as she could remember she had to move with great care, for the caves left by uprooted stumps were treacherous in the dark, and there were exposed roots and snags of old cedars to bump into. She was tired and close to tears when she made the fence, parted the wires, and got through onto the county road.

For a moment she was tempted to turn straight down the road and home. That way it would be less than half a mile of easy walking. But she would have to go down almost to the square, turn up the hill with the arc light shining on her. The very thought terrified her.

By now, across the arch from east to west, crossing Cassiopeia and the Dipper, a shimmering band of light began to play, delusive and fleeting, at one moment looking like a luminous wisp of cloud, at another moment gone. The girl hugged her arms across her chest and hurried into the straggling timber beyond the road. The wind had a bite like winter.

The Northern Lights shed a vague sort of moonlight through the air, but she had to walk stooping, her hands before her to ward off branches. She knew that her mother would be worried. The mail had been an hour late to begin with. It must be eight o'clock now. It was comforting to know that in a few minutes she would slip in from the back shed, muddy-footed and breathless and with her hair snagged with twigs, but safe. She would tell her mother she had gone for a walk and forgotten to pay attention to the time. She would say she was tired and not feeling well, and go up to her room, and if anyone telephoned, or knocked on the door, she could tell her mother to say she wasn't well enough to see anyone.

It might even be possible — and she stopped in the dark among the spruces, thinking of it — to go to bed and play sick for all of the next week, just lie in her bed as her father sat in his chair, pull her privacy in around her like curtains around a four-poster, and be safe, and snug, and by herself. . . . She wouldn't have to come out until Flo Barnes was gone, and the whole dreadful thing was finished and over. She could go to bed and almost dream it away, as simply as lying down to sleep. Somehow she felt that her father would approve such action. Somehow she felt that he knew her fear, and was himself terrified of Flo. She even thought of talking to him about it.

The woods thinned, and off to her left she saw a farm. Channing's. The meadow that lay between woods and house was fenced away from her by a three-wire fence, but rather than walk any longer through the woods she fought through the prickly tangle of wild-apple trees along the fence, climbed carefully over the wires, and got out into the smooth grass. In a few minutes, following along the barbed wire, she came to the fringe of woods along the east side of her father's hayfield.

Here too the tangle was thick along the old crumbling snake fence, and she snagged her hair getting through and over. But on the other side she saw, just a skip and a hop across the hilltop field, the barn roof sagging like the back of a tired old horse, the lower line of connecting sheds, the square calm yellow pane of the kitchen window. Beyond the vague cluster of buildings the slim dark spire of the church pinned the sky up and back. She kicked one foot against the other, staring out of her covert into the empty field. She was wet halfway to the knees, and chattering with cold, but the kitchen window was as inviting and heartening as the smiling face of a friend.

She ran out across the lot to the back wall of the barn, and came around it to the unused milkroom door. And at the milkroom door someone stepped from the shadow of the building, and she knew it was Flo Barnes.

11

Pale of Settlement

No SINGLE THING brought her to it. Abe kept saying at first that it was the newness, that she was strange yet, that it took time to get acquainted and get the feel of a new place. But she knew he was wrong, for the feeling grew worse with every day and week. And after she got sick, Abe said of course it was the illness. Coming on for some time, that had made her unhappy and spoiled things for her. As soon as she was up and around things would look different.

But Abe was talking to reassure himself. Ruth knew that what ailed her was not the strangeness and not really the sickness, but the village itself, the people in it, the things they said and the way they acted. It was Mrs. Boyce, giving a fancy la-de-da luncheon in the church, imitating the ways of city women, and asking every married village woman, every mortal one, except Ruth. Abe was furious when he heard about that, but within five minutes he was acting apologetic, saying, of course Mrs. Boyce didn't ask any city women, just village women, and maybe she still thought of Ruth as a city person, coming from New York and staying at the inn and all that.

'Which I'm not,' Ruth said, 'and she knows it perfectly well.'

'Yes,' Abe said. 'Yes. Well — do you care?'

'Do I care about missing her hayseed luncheon, do you mean?'

'Yes.'

'No,' Ruth said. 'But I care about not being asked, and so would you.' She went upstairs to the bedroom. It wasn't even not being asked that bothered her. It was the deliberateness with which she had been left out. She thought that anyone with any kindness or hospitality or simple humanity would have asked a newcomer, even if she was a dubious guest.

As it turned out, she couldn't have gone anyway, because the day before the luncheon was to be given she came down sick, and there she lay.

Occasionally a customer of Abe's, generally a summer person, would come up the ladderlike stair and sit a few minutes and talk. She always brightened at those casual unpremeditated visits, and felt better. Once Mary Dow came with some dahlias from her garden, and once old Mr. Dow left a couple of books. But apart from those, no one called. For days on end she had lain expecting Helen Barlow, who liked to talk about plays and music and books, and who worked just down in the square and had whole afternoons of free time, but not once did Helen appear, and in her illness she grew bitter, blaming even Abe, thinking that the way he acted about her sickness was enough to scare anybody away.

Her ailment embarrassed and flustered and dismayed him. It was a feminine business, mysterious and alarming, and she could hear him down below, whispering loudly, whenever anyone asked about her. 'She's in bed,' he would say. 'She isn't feeling so well.' If they persisted, saying with solicitude, 'Cold?' or 'This sorethroat that's going around?' he would speak in that tone that always meant he was making jerky motions with his arms. 'Oh, you know,' he would say. 'Some of this business of the insides. I don't understand it.' Everything he said sounded to her straining ears like an attempt to discourage people's solicitude.

But after she had lain there a week, with headaches for company and a perspective of isolated years to look into, she did not blame Abe. He was gentle and helpful and alarmed, and if he tiptoed too much he did it out of consideration for her, and if he dropped his voice when people asked about her sickness, and evaded their direct questions, it was because he was self-accusing and afraid, feeling that he was responsible, that it was marrying him which had got her into this.

She couldn't really blame Abe, but she could lie there long hot afternoons under the roof and grow bitter about the village, and lonely for New York and her friends and her job. She heard from Harold Swett, who repeated it as a good joke, that Mr. Tait had mentioned in a sermon the unbelievers in the village and had made it pretty plain he was talking about Abe. She could lie there and sort through their faces and feel that there wasn't a one, not a single one, who in two months had given her any reason for liking or affection. Most of all she could hate the Boyces, not only because of that luncheon snub but because of the chickens.

There was a good deal of weakness with her sickness, so much so that sometimes she lay for an hour crying weakly, her eyes running over and wetting her pillow, and sometimes her head ached so that in spite of her weakness she could not rest. Her body found every button in the mattress, every unbound wire in the springs, and many nights she lay burning-eyed until dawn or after, waiting for sleep that did not come, thinking over her life with a scrupulous attention to every slightest detail, looking into the future through speculations as ornate as the plots of novels, and wondering what this sickness might mean. Who in this hick town would know what ailed her? She doubted if the doctor Abe brought in knew enough to wash his hands; he didn't smell aseptic the way a doctor should, but reeked of pipe smoke.

Oh Lord, she would say, and turn her pillow and ease her aching hips and listen forlornly to Abe's light snoring beside her. He was sweet, and he tried to help, but how could he know that the thing she would have appreciated most was that he should stay sleepless with her through the long night hours?

About daylight she would find the sleep she had been hunting for, but it would be broken, haunted by strange cries that no amount of burrowing into the pillow 'could shut out. After a half hour of trying she would be awake again, angry and ready to cry, and would recognize the sounds which had awakened her as the crowing of roosters over in Boyce's chicken yard back of the Richie place.

'Well, but what do you expect?' Abe said when she complained to him. 'Roosters crow, that's all. You get used to it. I never hear them at all.'

'I do, though,' she said. 'There's one that sounds exactly as if he were having his throat cut. He gives me the most horrible nightmares, hearing this gurgling and screaming and being half asleep so I don't realize what it is. I wish you could speak to Mr. Boyce and see if he could do something.'

He stared at the floor and pulled his nose and puckered his lips. 'I don't see what he could do. You can't stop a rooster from crowing.'

'You can cut his head off.'

'Off two hundred roosters? He cuts the heads off five or six every day, selling them to people. But two hundred, that's impossible.'

'He could find that one that gurgles and chokes, and sell him to the first customer.'

She saw him framing answers to her in his mind, trying out explanations and soothing words as one would try them out for a petulant.child, and it infuriated her. She saw his hesitation, his will to humor her, and she would

not be humored and put aside. 'These roosters, you understand,' he said, 'they are young roosters, just learning
how to crow. That is what makes the gurgles.'

'I don't care what makes it!' she cried. 'You've got a
sick wife here, and if old Boyce had any consideration
he'd do something about his roosters. And if you had any
consideration you'd go and tell him so.'

He was silent for quite a long while, shrugging to himself, puckering his lips at thoughts that occurred to him.
He lifted his eyes and essayed a smile, a pleading, listen-
to-reason look. 'It doesn't last,' he said. 'Look at it. He
starts with two hundred young roosters, he sells a half
dozen a day, and he has been selling them for broilers
and fryers for a month. Even if he doesn't sell any on
Sunday, that is maybe a hundred and fifty he has sold.
There are only fifty, maybe, making this noise . . .'

'Only fifty,' she said, and turned her back on him.
'That sure makes it a lot nicer, to know there are only
fifty. And one that gargles.'

She lay with her back to him, yielding not an inch to
his words or his hands or his silences, hating herself for
being sick, for breaking down, for being hysterical and
unreasonable; hating the village for its barriers and its
roosters. Finally Abe tiptoed out and went away.

Later, when he brought up her dinner, he told her that
he had been to see Boyce. 'There is nothing he can do,'
he said. 'I told him about this rooster which gargles and
he looked at me as if he thought I should be put in some
asylum. That will be a joke all over this village.'

Helplessly she felt the ill-temper rise in her, the shrew-
ishness that was unlike her, that was unworthy of her, but
that she couldn't help. 'All right,' she said. 'It's a joke.
It's a great big joke, and I should laugh like anything because I haven't had any sleep for four nights. Why can't
he keep his roosters inside the chicken house, at least

while people are sick? If he'd shut them indoors they could crow all they wanted and never disturb anybody.'

'Well, maybe,' he said. With a flash of his old argumentative spirit he said, 'Have they put rubber tires on the elevated now? How can you sleep in New York with all that banging going past? This is the same kind of a thing.'

'No, it isn't anything of the kind,' Ruth said. 'You know when the elevated comes, for one thing. And it isn't alive, for another, it's just noise. And there's nothing you can do about it. That's the difference. There's something old Boyce could do about his roosters, if he wanted to.'

In the end she drove him out again, threatening to go herself, weak as she was, if he wouldn't. He came back muttering and exclamatory, rigid with anger. He wouldn't tell her what had passed between him and Mr. Boyce except that they had quarreled, and that he had threatened to shoot any rooster of Boyce's that was loose out in the yard at dawn and jumping on fences and crowing. 'And now I am going down to Bentham's and buy the gun.'

'Oh, Abe,' she said, 'you shouldn't have threatened anything like that!'

'Listen! Do these roosters bother you or don't they?'

'Yes, but not . . .'

'So if they bother you, and you are sick, not just some woman making a fuss, then Boyce should try to do something. And when I come twice to ask him, friendly as you please, if he can't do something, and he pays no attention and looks at me as if I am crazy, then I will shoot his roosters next time they crow.'

Ruth caught his hand and pulled him down on the bed. 'I wouldn't let you do that. They'd put you in jail.' What had been unbearable to her before seemed bearable enough now, and she was ashamed of having been so unreasonably irritated. She soothed Abe down, pleased that he could get so angry for her sake, and they had a kind of reconciliation and a long talk, and afterward she had a nap and awoke feeling better.

But even when she was well enough to walk as far as the post office or the library, she felt as if her illness marked a boundary, that since her spell in bed she could never be deceived again about her position in the village. People spoke to her, women inquired how she was feeling, old Allan Richie commented, 'Well, looks if you were up and about again,' but she was not fooled, and neither she nor Abe would speak to Sam Boyce or his wife. Roundabout, it came back to them that some people in the village thought Mrs. Kaplan was consumptive — a communication that made Ruth so angry she cried, and went up to the bedroom to look at her face in the mirror, noting its thinness and the shadowed eyes.

It was only the summer people who made her life bearable at all, and she was obsessed with the fear of what the village would be like after they went home. The only cultural institution in the village proper, the library, was made almost impossible by old Mrs. Emma Budd, sitting in the room like a skeleton on wires. Every time she went in for a book Ruth came out feeling bitter and somehow degraded, though not a word might have been said on either side. And now the summer people were already beginning to leave. Abe's racks were less crowded, the half-completed suits no longer lay around on his bench. Within a few days it would be Labor Day, and by then there would hardly be a soul left in Westwick except these dour and unyielding villagers, the acid women and the silent men, the people with whom she had no means of communication, and could have none.

And on the day before Labor Day would be the last concert of the year. After that there would be no music except what her little radio would bring her — a radio too weak to pick up anything but Montreal and St. Johnsbury, Vermont, and too likely, in the midst of any program worth listening to, to give way to uncontrollable and hysterical static. The static Ruth blamed on the Pratts, down below Harold Swett's. There were radio sermons on at the same hour as Ruth's favorite symphonic program, and Evelyn Pratt, very religious but not rigidly denominational in her tastes, dialed back and forth among three stations. Every time she turned the dial of her old superheterodyne Ruth's loudspeaker made a noise like a falling tin roof.

'This place is going to be like a tomb,' she said to Mary Dow one afternoon in the tailor shop. 'With everybody interesting gone, and no concerts, no good conversation, no nothing.' She turned her eyes on her visitor and unaccountably felt the smarting of almost-tears. 'When I think of how many things you can do in the winter in New York,' she said. 'All for nothing, too, you don't need any more than bus fare. All the museums, and the galleries along 57th Street. You can get yourself a real art education, just going to shows in those galleries. And all the free concerts, and WQXR . . . For that matter, just walking along any street in New York is as good as a show.' She sighed, dimpling at Mary Dow and turning her nostalgia into a laugh. 'But I guess I'd give the whole business if I could only get some good music on the radio up here. They could take away my breakfast and lunch if they'd leave me some music.'

Mary Dow's lively face, the eyes constantly round and the mouth ready to smile, as if she had just been startled by the most unexpected and happiest of surprises, and in an instant would be running wildly like a delighted child to welcome something — this friendly face rounded still more, and the brows frowned quickly at some thought.

'Oh, why didn't I think of it yesterday!' she said. 'I wonder if it's too late now?'

Abe wandered in from the dining room, mussed from his afternoon nap on the couch there. 'What is this?' he said. 'Think of what yesterday?'

'The program committee for the music met yesterday to make arrangements for the storage of the machine and records. Last winter we left them in Mrs. Weld's cottage, and the cold did something to the machine — it had to be fixed this spring. What we want is some place that's warm and dry, that's all, and where the people will be careful of the records. But they could play them, all they wanted. Oh, why didn't I think of you last night? But it might not be settled yet. I doubt if it is. Would you like to keep them if I can fix it?'

'Would I?' Ruth said. 'Oh, would I!'

'Say,' Abe said, talking so fast the words tripped and tangled. 'Say, that would be nice if you could. You never saw — she likes music like nobody ever did. You never saw anybody so crazy over music.'

'You wait right here,' Mary Dow said. 'I'll go see Molly Porter this minute. She was going to look into some other possibilities, but I'll bet she hasn't done a thing yet.'

She went out, running lightly as a child across the patch of lawn Abe had created from the former rank grass. 'Well, Madame,' Abe said, and stopped. 'What, you are crying?' he said softly.

'Oh, Abe,' she said. 'All that *beautiful* record collection! And that machine! Think of having that any time you want it. When you feel like Beethoven, put it on. When you want to skip and dance, out comes Mozart. If you feel like sitting and grumping, here's old Sibelius. I can't imagine anything so wonderful!'

Her eyes wandered away from his face, the tears that had jumped in them already forgotten, and went speculatively around the walls. 'Where could we put it?' she said. 'It's pretty big, and it shouldn't be too near the stove, because heat might blister it, or warp the records. It shouldn't be up against an outside wall, either, if it's as cold up here as you say it is. Where would you think, Abe? In here or in the dining room?'

'How about this,' Abe said. 'How about moving my bench down, against the wall, like this. Then you've got maybe five feet clear, all inside wall, eight or ten feet from the stove. Eh? It would be handy and out of the way both.'

He was pushing against the heavy bench, sliding it across the congoleum, when Ruth cried that Mrs. Dow was back. They were both at the door at once, opening it for her. But when Mary Dow came in they both stepped back, seeing her face.

'I'm so *dread*fully sorry,' she said. 'If I'd had the slightest bit of brains in my head I'd have thought of you last night, and then it could have been all fixed by now. But Molly Porter's already talked with Mrs. Tait, and I guess it's all settled. Next year I'll have some sense, and speak up in . . .'

'Mrs. Tait?' Ruth said. 'Oh, Lord, she doesn't even *like* music. She hasn't gone to a concert this summer. It'll just sit there and gather dust!' Tears of weakness and disappointment were in her eyes; she turned her head.

'Oh, well now, look,' Abe said. 'Maybe we can get one of these machines, a little one. Sears Roebuck sells records. We can order some from there.'

'We can't order anything like what that collection's got,' Ruth said. She stood quietly, her hands back of her against the bench. 'We haven't got money enough, anyway.'

Abruptly she ran past them, touching Mary Dow's arm fleetingly and saying as she ran up the stairs, 'I'm sorry, I can't help it! It was the one thing that might have . . . I can't help it!'

Abe gnawed his lip and looked at Mary Dow with sick eyes. He sighed, a windy, defeated sound. 'You know how it is,' he said apologetically. 'She hasn't been well, she doesn't feel good yet. And this is a disappointment, you can't deny that. Yes, it is a disappointment.'

12

The Craftsman

INDIFFERENTLY, doing a routine job for the millionth time, going about it as if sullen at the tedium of old chores, the clouds about noon gathered back of Sunday Mountain. For a while the peak's bald crown and timbered slopes were visible, but then the clouds slipped around the flanks until only the granite profile showed, and then the gray poured over, with thunder rumbling under it and lightning whipping it along, and came over Canadian Notch in a douche of cold rain.

At a little after one Baptiste Charbon, trying to get a second cutting from his lower meadow, gave up and put his team into a run for the barn with only a half-load on, and behind him the rain came, not in gusts or with any particular fury, but with a businesslike thoroughness, wetting down the tumbles, soaking into the matted stems and stubble. Along the county road the ditches began to trickle thin streams of brown mud, and the brook that came down below the Dow place sounded louder through its culvert. Beyond the tip of Weld Island three boys in a sailboat drove for shore in a gray squall.

At the town dock the waves began to dance and slap and spank restlessly under the hemlock planks, and though there did not yet seem to be any wind, the boats moored there jerked at their painters and bumped their noses softly against the dock. Rain roughed the water out in the lake, and all around the dock there were sudden little popping noises like the gasping of fish, as drops hit the surface. The gray planks were freckled, then streaked, then dark, and the rain passed on toward the village.

It put the inn guests up on the verandah and routed three old gentlemen playing darts against a maple. The little after-lunch scattering of people before the store was driven to shelter. Parley Pugh, stretched out under the creamery truck working on a loose spring shackle, poked his squinting greasy face out, got a drop in his eye, and lay for a minute with his face under the runningboard as if calculating probabilities. By the time he had his mind made up, the square of dry ground on which he lay was outlined with drip-holes from the streaming running-boards, and he dug out and ran stooping through the hard rain across the street and up the drive to John Mills' shop.

Andy Mount, working on a batch of chairs with old John Mills, watched through the window as the rain closed in upon the town. The shop was snug, with a little fire going, for old John was eighty, and needed warmth. The air was sweet with the smell of planed pine, the vinegar smell of oak, the richness of linseed oil. There was something, too, as perceptible as an odor, that em-anated from the old man, a tincture, a quintessence ex-pressed most by his face and his hands. He had a face as gentle as a blind child's, and great knobby lobster-claw hands that looked as clumsy as fire-tongs and were actual-ly precision instruments. Andy had been working for the old man only three days, but he had seen already how ,men dribbled in and sat and passed the time of day, sit-ting on nail kegs and talking or not talking as they pleased. He had been trying to phrase in his own mind why they came, but it was difficult to say. All he knew was that they took something away from those visits, they went away as if they had refreshed themselves at a spring, they were reassured.

When Parley Pugh thudded in with his denim frock

rain-streaked and water running on his face, Andy nodded as John Mills did, and moved down the bench to turn on the motor and begin ripping out slats for chairbacks on the bandsaw, feeding the thin boards into the saw and thinking that in a few more days now Peter Dow would be going down to Dryden, and that Andy Mount would not be going with him.

He knew he had not made a decision. He had simply tightened his hands around something, and shut his mind to the lure of the other complex and dangerous possibility. In his present mood, it suited him exactly to be here in John Mills' warm shop. As much as anyone in the village he needed reassurance, he needed to listen and watch men who had perhaps made his choice before him, and to see what they had made of that choosing. There was comfort in old John's smooth-worn bench, in his reverend age, in his clumsy-looking old blotched hands, and the skill in them. To work with good, familiar tools was better for him than any amount of talk would have been.

The rain was a steady gravelly patter on the steel roof, and it streamed on the windows. The woodpile outside was sooty black in the wet. Back of him in the room the easy voices came out tentatively, retired again. On the bench the stack of identical slats grew, and he pushed it away and started another. The pulsating strip of light where the saw hummed was slight, almost unnoticeable, yet it was full of purpose, even danger; it demanded the undivided attention of its master. It was a force that did not shift or wander, but it cut clean everything held against it, an edge against which lives could be shaped as he was shaping slats. He laid the movable against the fixed and watched the penciled pattern line become a thin gap, the board become a shaped and meaningful thing. And he watched his own hands, round-nailed, brown, yellow in the palms with clear callous. In a certain number of years — fifteen, twenty, thirty, fifty — they might look like the hands of John Mills, with thick ridged nails and thickened joints and mottled skin.

The rain outside was obviously going to last. Andy gathered some scraps from the box and threw them into the ashy coals in the stove. Pugh, sitting on a keg with his gumboots muddying the floor, was making idle talk for an idle hour. Andy listened just as idly, bellying up to the bench.

'They can get somebody else, far as I'm concerned,' Parley was saying. 'Or just let them folks be.'

'Thought you'd got all around last week,' John Mills said.

'Did. I was lucky to get off that rud alive. First door I stopped at, that was Graham. The old lady opens — you know how she is, face like a drag saw, all teeth — and I says, "Come to administer the freeman's oath to your boy John." "He ain't aimin' to vote," she says, and shuts the door. Next place I stop, that's White's. Two kids without clothes on sittin' with their feet in the spring tub. Says I, "Where's your big brother?" They just giggle. Thinks I, I might's well find out, and I paound on the door. Nobody comes, Pa, Ma, or brother. Nobody on the whole place but them two naked young ones, and neither of them fully witted. Caows still in the stanchions at nine, stable so dirty you wanted stilts to walk through it. Next place I come to, that's Beatty, you know, that moved in here from Maine way ten-twelve years ago. Never quite right in the head, shell-shocked in the war or something. His daughter's come of age, might be wantin' to vote. But I knock ten minutes before I start anybody, and then Beatty opens the door a crack and I see he's got it chained inside, and he's got a shotgun. I'm abashed, but I tell him I'm come to administer the freeman's oath. He ain't interested, not a mite. When I see 'twasn't any use standin' there havin' a stare-fight with him, I come away. Same way clear around that rud, clean through to the highway.'

'Did you see Leila Pruett?' Andy asked. He knew that road; his family's old farm had been just off it, on Pickerel Pond.

'Be funny if I didn't,' Parley said. 'Out drivin' a tedder in a bathing suit. See her five miles away, like a red posy.' He felt his thigh and lifted one side of his face in a grin. 'Old iron seat'd be a mite hot, I sh'd think.'

They all laughed. Andy shut off the saw and hunted in the parts box for the right sandwheel. 'She used to scare me to death,' he said. 'She'd meet everything that came down that road, never missed. Once I was bringing down a load of potatoes.' He stopped, looking at John Mills and then at Parley Pugh to see if he was over-stepping himself. They were listening. 'You know how she sails out into the road as if she was going to send you about your business and no nonsense? And how she talks sometimes — half in poetry? She stopped me in the road and looked in at the sacks of spuds and says, "What is in the sack, a lifeless form? You will be left all forlorn." Then she came around to the wheel and looked me right in the eyes, just like that, a foot away. She never has to hunt around for words, you know. They just bubble out of her. "The French will show no mercy," she says. "I can point out whole hillsides," she says, "whole hillsides polluted with innocent blood!"'

He laughed a little lamely. 'I got so I'd whip up old Baldy half a mile from there and go by like a runaway.'

Parley's lip pulled up on one side in his devilish grin. He needed a shave and his denim cap was grease-stained. 'She's a queer one,' he said, 'but she ain't any queerer than the rest on that rud. Seems if everybody up that way, his brains is all toggled up with baling wire.'

Old John said softly, talking to the shaped chair seat in his hands, 'I remember when Leila was a pretty little girl. Then she went down country and worked a while in a hospital for crippled children. Seemed like seeing all those game-legged little ones set her off, somehow. Folks said she did all sorts of wild things, tried to burn the hospital down, and turned in one of the doctors to the police, said he'd got after her, you know. But when she was right there wasn't a nicer girl than Leila.'

Andy put the sandwheel on the chuck, ashamed that he had started this and appeared to make fun of Leila Pruett's askew mind. Who was he to gossip? His own family had lived on that road of defeated and queer farmers, and though neither of his parents had been raddled like Mrs. Graham or gone and strange like Leila, his mother *had* married Branch Willard, as worthless a good-for-nothing as the town had produced in two generations. And they had had that fire. Some people made one sort of shift and some made another against the stony acres and the mortgage and the loneliness and the endless labor without profit. His own mother needed a good word said for her, as surely as Leila Pruett did, and he knew, gratefully, that old John would have said it. He would say the best he could of anyone.

There was a stamping on the porch, and James Mount put his head in. He never did come through a door like other people, but always stuck his head around it first, as if he expected something to be thrown at him. First the tobacco-stained toothless grin would appear, and then the whole man, walking spryly, shaking his shoulders.

'Anybody workin' in here?' he said.

'Not enough to hurt,' old John said mildly. 'Come in, James. You look a mite wet.'

'Only down to the hide,' James said. He held his hands to the fire, and his merry little eyes touched Parley and

Andy, letting them in on the joke. 'Takes a hard rain to
wet me any deeper.'

Parley grunted. 'Can't get through that layer of hard-
pan.'

'Oh, there's drainage,' James said. 'There's drainage.'
He kicked a nail keg closer to the fire and sat down, and
the room was as it had been before, no more changed
than if one more child had entered a full classroom.
James was absorbed, and his voice became part of the
general voice, his key the company key. Andy lost the
thread of the talk, concentrating on the mechanical routine of smoothing the slats against the sandwheel, hypno-
tizing himself with the hot angry *sizzzzzz* and the floating powdery dust. John Mills was mixing up a batch of
glue, and its smell went through the room like another
voice. The rain beat steadily on the roof.

Finally Parley said, 'You won't be startin' school after
Labor Day this year, Andrew.'

'Graduated last June,' Andy said. The question took
him off guard, and he kept his head down.

'Be workin' out?'

'Soon as we're through here I told Pliny Hall I'd do
some road work.'

Parley leaned to light a long shaving in the stove, got
his pipe going, and teetered his keg back. 'Heard some
talk about you goin' daown country.'

'I thought some of it,' Andy said. 'I decided not to.' His
face was hot; he did not want to talk about this, and for
some reason the presence of John Mills made the whole
thing worse.

'Some business about college, wa'n't it?'

'E-yeah.'

'Ain't but one college person in the village, as I recall,'
Parley said, tipped back comfortably.

'Two,' Andy said. 'Helen Barlow and Alex Thompson.
But . . .'

'Never saw that college made Alex any better,' Parley said. 'Runs that turkey farm, might've been postmaster if he'd been willin' to turn Democrat. Nawthin' he couldn't have done without college. Don't see how he's been helped at all, except he gets to play the head Wise Man at the Christmas pageant down to the school, with his head wrapped up in a velveteen cushion cover.' He moved his gumboots gently, spreading around the half-dried mud and water he had left on the floor. 'Head always was wrapped up in somethin', seems like.'

'Well,' Andy said, 'I wasn't going, so . . .'

'Or Helen Barlow. Helen's a nice enough girl, but notional. Family always thought she was too good for the village boys after she went to college. Should have been raisin' a family for the last four years.'

Mr. Mills' voice, gentle as his face, said, 'Andy's a smart boy, Parley. 'Tisn't as if he had all the education he could hold.'

'Passed the high school, ain't he?' Parley said.

'Speakin' of education,' James Mount said, 'summer folks gettin' scarcer. Came across the square just now and didn't stumble over one.'

Parley rose and looked out the window. Standing, he exposed the long scar that ran down the side of his face and into his neck. A falling tree had caught him years ago and he had smiled off center ever since. His lip lifted as if a string were pulling it straight up. 'Too early in the day,' he said. 'Give you till tonight you'll be stumblin' fine.'

He went out. Within three minutes the door opened again and Allan Richie came in, his white eyebrows moving all over his face. Andy felt his entrance like an intrusion. Even James, thriftless as he was, fitted easily into the atmosphere of John's shop, but Allan Richie brought something sharp and foreign.

'Get that box done, John?' he said.

'Right here.' With his lobster-claw hands old John pulled out a clean pine chest from under the bench. A fresher smell of pine came out when he opened the lid to show it. Allan looked it over, reaching under his oilskins to bring out a snap purse ten inches long.

'How much?'

The old man hesitated. 'Well, the lumber cost about three and a half, and there's the hardware. I shouldn't think I could take less than about five dollars.'

'Pay him less than ten and you're a bandit,' James said from his keg.

Allan's face thrust in James's direction and his eyebrows twitched. 'You the new manager?'

'Just been appointed,' James said.

Andy was at the bench, wondering if he should speak up. Then without having made up his mind whether he should or not, he heard himself saying, 'I kept a time-card on that job, Mr. Mills. You paid three-sixty for lumber and sixty cents for hardware and you put in four hours' time.'

The embarrassed blood pounded up into his face, and knowing himself too brash for his years, he said to Allan Richie, 'He doesn't ever figure his time is worth anything. I think he ought to figure it at a dollar an hour.'

'Oh, you do,' Allan said. He held a five-dollar bill between his fingers, his eyes as bright as a weasel's. 'Goes up pretty fast,' he said. 'Jumps five to eight like scat.'

'Eight-twenty, if you figure it the way I did,' Andy said, and got redder than ever.

'Ten,' said James Mount.

John Mills was smiling, shaking his head. 'Oh, now boys, I can't ask any such price as that for a little pine box.'

For a minute Allan looked at Andy and James alternately. Then he fished deep in the purse and got out a wad of one-dollar bills, smoothed off three, and laid them with the five in John's hand. 'I'm payin' you eight,' he said. 'You can take the twenty cents out of Andrew's wages.'

He went to the door and looked out. 'Get all spattered up if I took it now,' he said. 'Andrew, you can bring it home when you come, if 'tain't rainin'.'

'All right,' Andy said.

John Mills was still protesting, but James tipped his keg over and the protests were lost as Allan went out into the drizzle.

'Thunderation,' James said. 'Allan got a bargain, and he knows it. I can remember a lot of other bargains, too. Remember those wagons you and Henry used to make in your old carriage works? Remember when you used to pay up to three hundred dollars a thousand just for the right kind of lumber to put in them wagons? I saw one yesterday that was built in 1906, and still solid.' He stood looking at old John with his toothless mouth half open, his eyes squinting. 'Remember why you and Henry quit makin' wagons?'

'There wasn't any reason to any more,' John said. 'Sears Roebuck would sell a good wagon for a hundred and forty dollars.'

'Not a *really* good wagon,' James said. 'There ain't been any since you quit makin' 'em. I recall you'd put a hundred and fifty dollars' worth of lumber and iron into a wagon, and work three weeks makin' it, and then you'd sell it for two hundred dollars, apologizin' all the time. Yon remember now why you quit makin' wagons?'

Mills smiled. 'I guess so, James.'

'Best wagons in the world,' James said, 'and you gave 'em away. What would Allan Richie have sold wagons like that for, you think?'

'I don't know,' the old man said. 'Folks've said we made good wagons. I guess we did. But what I'm doing now, it don't amount to enough to charge folks for. I just putter around.'

He went into the house to put his bills away, and James sat on the keg shaking his head, grinning strangely at Andy. 'There was three of 'em in this village once,' he said. 'Old John and his brother Henry and old Cass Casswell. Any one of 'em could make you anything, and make it better'n you'd get it anywheres else. And not a one had a kid's notion how to charge for his work.' Pushing back his hat, he exposed his gray disordered hair. Lacking teeth to chew tobacco properly, he tucked a wad of snuff into the pouch of his cheek and gummed it around. 'When I was your age,' he said, 'I used to think old Cass Casswell was just abaout God, just the way you do old John now.'

It came to Andy strangely, like something out of an old book. He had heard his mother talk about James when he was young, how everyone had thought he would be somebody. He could play any kind of musical instrument, just pick it up and in a week or so he could play anything on it. Then he got married while he was still in high school, and children kept piling up on him, and he couldn't hold his farm, so that he had to hire out, skidding logs or working on the roads, and playing for dances in the Corners or the village. Somewhere, back in those years that were so alike and so telescoped, the talent he had started with had gone little by little, as his teeth had gone, and he sat there now a toothless and disreputable and drunken man, old at fifty. Here was another outcome of the choice Andy was making, another way he could end up. His hands might acquire all the skill and the horny stiff-jointed precision of John Mills', but he might lose his teeth and his talent fighting a losing fight, as James had.

His uncle's speckled eyes were unwaveringly on his face, and his hanging grin never changed. 'I guess you feel that way about old John, don't you, kid?'

'You couldn't help it,' Andy said.

'No,' James said. 'And don't you never forget to. But ain't one in a million can be like John. Probably couldn't anybody be like him any more. Times change, and people with 'em.'

The old man came back from the house, smiling his vague sweet smile. 'John,' James Mount said, 'if you was advisin' a young man with brains, what would you say? Get out and get a good schooling so's he could do somethin', or hang around this village and try to keep it from fallin' apart?'

'I take it you mean Andrew,' John Mills said.

'I don't see anybody else around here with either the brains or the chance to do anythin',' James said, and winked at his nephew. But Andy was watching old John. In the old cabinet-maker was somehow concentrated everything that was best in the village, the integrity and the honesty and the kindness, the artisan's skills and the artisan's bone-deep satisfaction in his work. Peter Dow had once said to him that old John was a twelfth-century guild worker lost in the twentieth century. It was true, as James said, that there were no more like him; perhaps the world had lost the knack of producing them. He listened for what the old man would say, because what he said would matter.

'I'd go, Andrew,' John said. 'There isn't much else we can teach you around here. You'd stay the same size all your life.'

Speaking out of the confusion and the doubts that had eaten at him for weeks, out of the arguments of Peter Dow and the moral resistance of Allan Richie, out of his dreams of knowledge and power and triumphs in the world where the monumental granite of Dryden showed between the noble elms, out of the fears and withdrawals and shames, his memory of his sad, weak mother, his groping for security and stability and his itch for new things, Andy said, 'But Mr. Mills . . . Uncle James . . . what if I didn't make it? What if I went down there and it was too much for me? Wouldn't it be better if I'd stayed right on here? Or what if I stick it out down there and do get to be a doctor or something, I couldn't live anywhere but around here, I know I couldn't. I wake up in the nights sometimes just thinking about it, so homesick I . . .'

He stopped, because there was no way of telling them the deeper reasons, the obscure intangible fear he had of losing himself. He didn't want to be like Helen Barlow, lost between two worlds. And he feared the complexity, the indescribably mixed and tangled and contradictory vision of the world that books had brought him. Somehow, at the center of that fear, he always managed to find the image of Mrs. Weld's secretary. The whole prospect of going down to school was like that woman, like a basilisk that he feared and despised but could not keep himself from looking at.

'I'd go,' John Mills said again. 'Isn't much of anything around here for a young fellow any more.'

He turned to the bench, snapped on the saw switch, and reached over a glued but unshaped chair seat. Andy moved to clear away the slats he had left on the bench. The old man bent to shift the pine box he had made for Allan Richie. He shoved it under the bench and straightened up. A surprised, breathless grunt came out of his half-opened mouth. His face purpled with a rush of blood, his eyes bulged, his left hand stabbed down, groping for the bench, to steady himself.

'What?' Andy said stupidly.

The old man gurgled, a wet sound in his throat. Braced

on one stiff arm, he leaned on the bench, his face and neck distended with dark blood. The hand on which he leaned slid six inches, caught, slid another inch or two.

Andy shouted and leaped at the same instant, just as John Mills collapsed. The boy's driving body met the slipping weight, and his desperately grabbing hand caught the old man's wrist. He never could sort out afterward, from the swift and violent sensations of that instant, exactly what he remembered and what he simply inferred must have happened. But he knew that there was a moment of toppling effort to keep the dead weight of the old man's body from driving him against the bench. He remembered, or supposed, a sensation as if a stiff charge of electricity had gone up his arm; the echo of a scream, perhaps his own; and then he was leaning, half supporting with his right arm the fallen body of Mr. Mills. He saw the bright blood on the white overalls, and then he found his own left hand curled against his chest, its third and fourth fingers and the corner of the palm gone as neatly as a slice is taken from a loaf of bread. The motor was still humming softly, and there was still light on the singing line of the saw.

James was at his side, helping to let the body of John Mills down to the floor. Andy let go with his right arm and stood up, tightening the fingers of his right hand around his left wrist. He felt no pain, but the furious pumping of blood from his hand made him light-headed and sick. Still holding his wrist tightly, he raised his foot and kicked the switch, quieting the deadly saw. His two fingers lay on the metal plate through which the saw pierced the bench, things as natural to see there as the feet of chickens cut off by the butcher.

His uncle, kneeling by old John, had his eyes on Andy. His voice came from far off. 'Can you hang on?'

Andy nodded, and James was gone. The boy sat down on a keg, his head down. The blood fell in quick drops now, not in streams, and formed a small puddle between his feet. While he sat there, hanging to his pale consciousness by an effort of pure will, he thought for the first time how it had happened, and looked at John Mills. The old man lay with suffused face, breathing harshly and rapidly. His white hair was in a puddle of blood and sawdust.

Andy looked at the blood soiling Mr. Mills' hair, then at his own hand clenched around the maimed thing on his knees. He couldn't let go without freeing that terrible pumping jet again, but he didn't like to see the thin white hair in the bloody sawdust. He stood up and put his shoe gently against the white head and tried to shove it over, but he couldn't. He was sitting with his head down, his mutilated hand between his knees and his fingers clenched in a fierce tourniquet around his wrist, when Florence Pugh came running with a clean-laundered sheet, a pillow, and a bucket of warm water.

Parley was right behind her. He knelt by Andy. 'James is callin' Stafford for the doctor. I dunno as there's anythin' we'd dare do about that hand till he comes.'

'Take a strip of sheet and tie it around his wrist,' his wife said. 'And take him where he can lay down, poor boy.'

'No,' Andy said. 'No, thanks. I can hold it with my hand.'

It seemed to him that he was the calmest person there, that the thing to do was to sit quietly and eventually the proper help would come and he would be taken care of. He heard Parley arguing with his wife about something, and was vaguely irritated at their excitability, but he did not listen to what they said. The puddle of blood between his feet kept slipping away, receding so that he looked at it from a great height as one might look at a lake over a cliff.

In the distance there was a vague, diffused roar like blasting, and he wondered stupidly if it came from the quarry at the Corners. Then he was aware of people around him, Marjorie Bentham and Mrs. Tait and two or three others. The roar came again, and he realized that it came from the slamming of the door as people entered. Somebody said, 'Hadn't we better get them both into bed?' and somebody else said, 'He won't go,' and several said at once, 'How did it happen? Did anybody see it?'

He heard Florence Pugh telling someone to get a strip of sheet tied around that poor boy's wrist and get him lying down, he'd fall off that keg in a faint, at least get him a chair. . . .

Sometime later the door blasted again, and the voices, far away and jumbled, said, 'Here he is! Here's the doctor.' Andy fought off the darkness that kept sifting down on him. He tried to sit up straight as the doctor stooped beside him, and he heard the stammering voice of Arlene Knight: 'I cleaned off the bench, I thought you mmmmm-m-m-m-ight want it for an o-o-o-operating table. But his f-f-f-ingers were there, they're right there now, maybe you can s-s-s-s-ew them back on.'

The doctor's voice was rough as a file. 'Nothing to that notion. Let's get him up here now. How you feeling, boy?'

'All right,' Andy said, and stood up. He got his feet under him, but consciousness went out in a shower of darkness. From a great distance he heard someone say 'Easy, easy!', and he put out his hands to catch himself. But his hands were tied. He fell twisting, trying to light on his shoulder, but never alighted. He thought, 'I couldn't save him after all, he fell before I got to him,' and still falling, still with his hands tied, he went to sleep. When he awoke he was in his own bed in the gable, his left hand an unfamiliar bandaged lump across his chest and Norma Pratt and Mrs. Barlow sitting by his bed. 'Well, now,' Mrs. Barlow said encouragingly as he opened his eyes. 'Well, now, that's better!'

13

Last Concert

THEY HAD EATEN late and had walked for more than an hour up above the cemetery. Already, at the brink of September, there were premonitions of winter. They passed patches of bracken withered and brown as if fire had seared them. The only flowers they saw were closed gentians and a luxuriant late crop of fireweed in the cellar of a burned house.

'Let's go back,' Ruth said abruptly, and they turned and came back down the hill to the cemetery road, past the inn and through the crowded square and home. 'I think I'll lie down a while,' she said, and went up to the bedroom.

Abe sat unhappily on his front steps, looking down the street, watching two cars, loaded to the roofs with bundles and bags and children, start out on the road toward Stafford and the down-country. A day or two, and there would be nobody left. His mind, turning delicately to Ruth upstairs, tired, maybe sick, with this blight on her and her unhappiness growing with her dislike of the village, veered away because he knew that once the street became empty of cars and summer people it would be thirty times worse for her.

In summer it was possible to feel that Westwick was part of the United States, an accessible part of the continent. People came in from Boston or New Haven or New York, the store handled Pepperidge Farm bread at thirty cents a loaf, the afternoon mail brought the *Times*

and the *Tribune.* But at the end of summer the whole
fiction was exposed. After Labor Day the *Times* and
Tribune would disappear from Bentham's counter. Along
the lake, the cottages, showing more and more as the
leaves thinned, would turn black shuttered windows on
the road. As the maples burned down the hills Mose
Thatcher would skid his ice-shanty down onto the shore
opposite the island to have it ready for February and
March.

Within a week now one would rarely hear the words
Boston and New Haven and Providence. Once the summer intrusion was over, people's minds would venture no
farther than Lancaster or Woodsville or Laconia. In the
fall it was as if a large room were suddenly emptied of
people, and those who were left hitched their chairs in a
closer, more intimate, more self-sufficient circle around
the fire.

Then there would be no one to give her what she
craved, books and music and talk. There would only be
Pratt with his hairy peasant hands hanging down before
him, and his sheeplike face and his closed peasant mind.
There would only be Sam Boyce, skinny and miserly with
words. There would only be a lot of people who, seen
from her eyes, looked now as lumpish and taciturn as
Neanderthal villagers might have been.

Down in the square, Stephen Dow's tall figure came
out of the crowd and started up the street. Abe got up
and met him at the foot of the church drive. He felt blue
and depressed, knowing that Mr. Dow was making a
round of farewell calls. 'I don't like to see you go,' Abe
said. 'Somehow this year it is different, with a wife who
isn't well. I hate to see people leaving here.'

'Cheer up,' Mr. Dow said. 'It will only be a few months
until half the people in Massachusetts and Connecticut
are back up here crowding you off the road.'

Abe shrugged. 'I don't know. It's different this year. Spring is a long way off. I don't know.'

'Is Mrs. Kaplan around?' Mr. Dow said. 'I'd like to say good-bye to her.'

'She is lying down. She doesn't feel so well. Maybe it is better if you don't. Things like that depress her.'

'Give her my best then,' Mr. Dow said. He shook Abe's hand, looking down with a half smile. 'Tell her we all hope she feels better soon.' He put a hand on Abe's shoulder. 'Good-bye,' he said. 'We'll see you in June. Take care of yourselves.'

'Yes,' Abe said. 'Well, good-bye.'

He stood at the foot of the drive and watched Mr. Dow climb slowly upward. At the top, where the road curved out onto the level, the old man stopped and waved once, and then he went out of sight. Abe looked at his watch. It was almost six. Wincing a little, he went inside and climbed the stairs into the bedroom. Ruth was lying with her face to the wall.

'How is it?' he said. 'Are you feeling all right, eh?'

An indistinguishable sound came from the pillow.

'What?' Abe said anxiously, and bent over her.

'I'm all right!' she said, so sharply that he straightened up. He rubbed his neck, staring at her.

'I was just thinking, maybe we should have a snack before we go to the concert.'

Ruth rolled over on her back. She did not look at Abe, but lay watching the roof. 'I don't know whether I want to go or not.'

'Ah, now,' he said. '*You* miss this Moussorgsky business?'

'It'll be cold.'

'Since when have you started caring whether it was cold or not? It has been cold other nights. This is the last concert, you wouldn't want to miss it.'

'I could miss it easy as pie,' Ruth said wearily. He sat down on the edge of the bed, intent on kidding her out of this, but she turned to the wall again.

'Say now, listen,' he said. 'You aren't sick any more, you are getting well. This is the way a sick woman acts.'

'It's the way I act,' she said.

Abe sighed. For a while he sat wondering how he could make it easier for her, but by an unnoticeable transition the train of his thought turned to how long September was after the summer people went, and how October lingered and smoldered and burned away through Indian summer and into the November rains. How November was endless gray wet days whipped by the wind out of Canada, with storms that tightened abruptly into snow, and with long periods of soggy thaw. December, too, snow and white woods and blocked roads, and around Christmas always the rain again, the moist warm air of delusive thaw before the world hardened into January and winter began in earnest. Two feet, three feet, four feet of snow, until the drifts pushed back by the plows were eight-foot banks on either side of the roads. Then the cold, unrelaxing, sometimes with bitter wind and sometimes deep and still and burning in the lungs, when thermometers hit thirty and thirty-five and forty below and every chimney in town wore a straight feather of white woodsmoke. It was a long way to think ahead, clear up to those days in April when, with the snow still deep in the woods, the sap began to run in the maples and the farmers waded waist-deep with their sap buckets and the fires burned all night in draughty sugarhouses. In April, finally, you could smell spring coming, in spite of the snow. You could feel it coming like a promise of wonder, until you went wild with it as dogs and children do, and once you sniffed that promise on the wet wind you could stand any delay or setback, because you knew that the season was coming on

into mudtime, and that mudtime would open into summer
for three brief months again.

But it was a long time to wait, until April. Eight months.
He sat on the bed in the house he had built against those
months of winter and could think of nothing to say.

Ruth said it. 'Abe,' she said, rolling over to face him,
'why can't we go away for the winter?'

When he heard it, he knew he had been expecting it.
Ever since the sickness and the trouble with Boyce, and
especially since the disappointment about the records, he
had known it must come. It did not shock or dismay him;
it merely saddened him, because he felt that somehow he
had failed. To stay through the winter, to stay all the
rest of their lives in the good new house, had been such
an idea once.

'I don't see how,' he said.

'How much money have we got?'

'Not much. Not enough to go away.'

'Haven't we got enough to get us south, maybe to
Florida? You said you made your expenses the winter
you went down there.'

'For one person only,' he said. 'And then I didn't have
payments on a house.'

'Well, New York then,' she said. 'That would be better
yet. I could get my old job back, and you could get a job
too. You're a good tailor, there'd be dozens of jobs you
could get.'

'I had that kind of a job once,' he said after a pause.
'That was what sent me up here with tuberculosis.'

Ruth rolled over again, and for several minutes Abe sat
looking out the window. Finally he said, 'You can't stand
it here, is that it?'

'I hate it. I'd die, Abe. I really would.'

He sighed and rose. 'Well, we can think about it. But
I think now we should go to the concert. You think you

don't care, but I have seen you when music comes on. You feel better right away.'

'All right,' she said apathetically, and sat up, feeling for hairpins.

'I remember that first time,' he said. 'You remember? That was the Tchaikowsky thing, the *Pathétique*.'

Her eyes were large and dark and sober, her mouth like the mouth of a child who has been crying a long time. 'Lord,' she said, 'that seems like ten years ago.'

Late in the afternoon John Mills's bedroom was full of greenish twilight. It was a plain room, almost bare. The flowers on the bedtable next to the mounded shape of the old man under the quilt were like flowers at the head of a grave.

Stephen Dow was thinking that they might as well be at the head of a grave. From where he sat, old John's face looked gentle and peaceful, but from the other side, he knew, it was twisted in a fixed grimace, and all up and down that side, foot and leg and shoulder and gnarled skillful hand, John Mills was dead.

Mr. Dow sighed. One trouble with being a historian was that you got into the habit of thinking in centuries, of leaping decades as a child would pass a summer day. And then one day your own life came and touched you on the shoulder, telling you that time was not forever. His own hair was as white as the hair of old John, and if his face was still straight and his right side still flexible, those were accidents of history.

It was very late in the afternoon. Mr. Dow stood up and reached his hat from the dresser, noticing in the watery dusk the simple clean lines of the piece. It was one of old John's making, and love as much as linseed oil and rubbing had given the cherry wood its finish.

'Good-bye, John,' Mr. Dow said, and let himself out.

As he passed through the kitchen Mrs. Pugh stood up.
'Is he all right?'

'He's all right,' Mr. Dow said.

When he stood outside it was nearly time for Henry
Ball to come through with the Sunday papers. There was
an inordinate Labor Day week-end jam in the square,
twenty or thirty cars and two dozen people crowding the
little crossroads. It was a good deal different from the
time, forty or more years ago, when he had come through
in a one-horse buggy searching out places both beautiful
and isolated for summer retreats. Since then Westwick
had had to learn to deal with every sort of down-country
strangers from historians and professors of Greek to
people like Mrs. Sophus Weld. That was the trouble, he
thought ruefully, about trying to take refuge in simplicity.
The lovers of the simple were too inevitably complex.

The place had changed; something fine had gone out of
it, or was going. Something that had been peculiarly and
wonderfully native lay now like old John Mills with half
its face pulled into a stiff grimace and one side gone dead.
Looking out into the square full of the invaders and con-
templating how the whole life of the village had altered
so that now it existed mainly to supply the campers, and
lived only during the summer months, Mr. Dow felt a
twinge of guilt. He had been the very first, and his re-
sponsibility was that much greater. If he had not been
able to believe that out of the confusion of two ways of
life there would come not only destruction but some survival, and not only survival but perhaps eventual enrich-
ment, he would have gone away from John Mills's door
feeling that his last visit had been less a farewell than
an act of expiation.

He had other visits to make, bills to settle, books to
return, before he went down for the winter. He dropped
two books through the slot in the locked door of the library,

went past the post office to mail some letters, worked his way out of the crowd and up the street, where he met Abe Kaplan and talked with him for a minute or two.

Abe's air of sad patience was like the autumnal feeling that Mr. Dow had had ever since his visit to John Mills, and he climbed the hill slowly, ruminating on decay and change. His legs were tired from the climb, and he felt the remoteness of being seventy-two as he mounted the Barlow porch. Only an impulse had turned him up the hill. He had no particular reason to call on the Barlows, except that the obscure notion of doing penance before all the village lingered in his mind. Something was passing; he might as well say good-bye to all of it.

He knocked at the door, and looking in the door pane he saw Mrs. Barlow reach quickly to the sink and take her teeth out of a cup there. She came across the kitchen wiping her hands on her apron, smiling her teeth into place. She was a woman whom Mr. Dow had known for forty years, and who had never been anything very real to him. There had never been any cause to dislike her or to like her; nothing could be said against her habits or her housekeeping, and she even maintained a kind of social superiority in the village on the strength of George Barlow's three rented farms. Yet she seemed to him somehow large and doughy as a personality, as if she could assume any shape she was punched into, and would assume it without complaint other than a few yeasty sighs.

'Good evening,' he said as the door opened. He stepped in and shook her moist hand. She was flustered.

'Oh, Mr. Dow,' she said. 'Come in. My goodness, I'm in such a mess, been makin' piccalilli, but come in.'

'Smells wonderful,' Mr. Dow said. He sniffed at the rich sharp smell that cut back through decades, as much a part of New Hampshire for him as the delicate uncoiling of roadside ferns in mudtime, or the worms of sawdust that a crosscut chewed out of a maple log. He had smelled piccalilli in dozens of farm and village kitchens, and he knew the look of windowsills where green tomatoes sat at the end of summer, hopefully exposed to the daytime sun. They had always had trouble ripening tomatoes in this part of the state, and had always had to save them in relish. But they always tried to ripen them anyway, even artificially.

He hung his hat on the back of a chair and went into the dining room. George Barlow shaved only once a week, and Mr. Dow was a little startled to see his face without the grizzly bristles that usually covered it. It was a sagging, secretive, petulant, pouty face, full of invalid irritabilities. The eyes reminded the old man of the eyes of a porcupine trapped in a flashlight beam, eyes that stared glassily and yet seemed constantly to swim in every direction at once, looking for an escape.

'Well, George,' Mr. Dow said, and shook Barlow's hand. 'Almost ready for another winter?'

The shaven, unfairly-exposed lips said the proper thing, but the eyes still looked furtive and trapped. 'Winter don't make no difference to me, long as I can get somebody to put me up a woodpile,' Barlow said, and flattened the paper in his lap. Mrs. Barlow brought a straight chair.

'Set down, Mr. Dow. I'll just have to run and keep my eye on that kettle for a minute.'

'I can only stay a second,' Mr. Dow said. 'Just a round of good-bye calls before I go down. I've just been down seeing John Mills.'

The furtive little eyes jumped and wavered. 'Tell me he's paralyzed all daown one side.'

'It's too bad,' Mr. Dow said. 'John's a fine man.'

'Some folks figure he's a mite soft-headed,' Barlow said. 'Wouldn't hurt a fly, though.'

It occurred to Stephen Dow that he didn't like discussing old John with this invalid, and it seemed to him a kind of outrage that John should finally be brought down by the same slow sclerosis that had held Barlow in his chair for four years. Looking at Barlow's exposed face and at his eyes that hid something, he was reminded of the daughter, Helen. There was something of the same look in her face when she talked to you, as if behind her desperately-smiling mask she was crouched down hoping no one saw her.

'Helen down at the post office?' he said.

'Eh?' The paper rattled in the invalid's lap, and his heels shifted rapidly, in a curious tattoo, against the footstool. His attempt to hide whatever thought had frightened him was almost ghastly, and Mr. Dow found himself thinking, the man should grow a real beard, it would be a cunning thing to do, to hide that mouth.

'Helen's upstairs lying down,' Mrs. Barlow said. 'She ain't been well at all last few days. But she'd like to say hello, I know. I'll call her, just a minute.'

'Oh, don't bother her,' the old man said. 'If she isn't well, let her rest. All I wanted was to wish her luck with the school.'

'She'd want to say good-bye to you,' Mrs. Barlow said. With the big pewter stirring spoon in her hand she went to the stair door and called. A voice answered faintly, through a couple of doors, from up above. 'Mr. Dow's down here,' Mrs. Barlow said. 'Come on down and say hello, do.'

Helen's voice said something else, but Mrs. Barlow paid no attention. She moved away from the stair and said, 'She's deserved the village school a long time, but up to now she couldn't get anything but little one-room standard schools, and she wouldn't take any of those. George and me made sacrifices to send her to Durham. She did real well there.'

'I'm sure she did,' Mr. Dow said. He would have liked to say his good-byes and go, but in uncertainty whether the girl was or was not coming down, he lingered. George Barlow's hands rustled like mice in the newspaper. An uncomfortable silence fell on the three, as if there was nothing whatever to talk about. Mrs. Barlow moved to the stair door again and called. 'Helen, are you coming down? Mr. Dow'll think you don't care whether he calls or not.'

'I'm coming,' the light hurried voice said, and in a moment there were feet on the stairs.

The girl appeared in the stairway, smiling at the room as if a light were glaring in her eyes. Mr. Dow made the note that she was really quite pretty in a frail sort of way, but that she was certainly almost as jumpy as her father.

'Hello, Mr. Dow,' she said. 'I'm sorry I was slow getting down.'

'Not at all,' he said. 'I'm sorry you haven't been feeling well.'

'It isn't anything. I've just been . . . sort of . . . upset.' She gave him the strained smile again, and he found himself wondering if she really was agitated and trying to act calmly or if she was putting on an obviously brave front about nothing.

'Can't be anything serious,' he said playfully. 'You look almost as tanned and healthy as your friend from out on the island.'

The girl's eyes were suddenly immense and startled, and every line in her face tightened. She looked as if she had been hit by a sudden pain. Possibly she had, Mr. Dow thought. One thing you learned was that reading people's faces was an extremely dubious pastime. So often you found that the guilty look you detected in your neighbor's eye was nothing more than dyspepsia. To ease the awkwardness Mr. Dow went on talking.

'That's an amazing girl. Is it true she rode a bicycle clear over to Mount Washington and back in an afternoon?'

'I . . . think so.'

'And has she really swum all the way across the lake and back out beyond the island?'

'I . . . guess so,' Helen said. 'She's very good at sports.'

'She hasn't quite got you riding a hundred miles in an afternoon, or swimming three miles, has she?'

As if with enormous effort, the girl's unwilling face lifted. Her head shook, the lips made the difficult smile. 'No,' she said.

'I've seen you with her a good deal,' he said, 'but I hadn't ever thought of you as the New Woman in quite that way.'

It was then that the absolute terror in the girl's face finally made itself clear. She was not simply suffering from pain or nausea. She was frightened to death, and everything he said about the Weld secretary brought the terror more unmistakably into her eyes. Very carefully, cursing his own stupidity, he acknowledged the suspicion and put it aside. He did not want to pry.

'Well,' he said, and smiled at her, wanting to thaw that frozen terrified look. 'So now it's almost Labor Day, and there'll be no more swimming and bicycling for a long while. We can all put the summer away in mothballs. You're about ready for school, I imagine.'

The strained mask did not relax. 'I guess,' she half whispered.

'Good luck with it,' he said, still trying to reassure her, and took her hand. 'The village is lucky.'

Her eyes searched his face, and she smiled as if smiling were anguish. Her hand was clammy and apparently without bones.

With his hat in his hand, Mr. Dow stood in the kitchen

talking to Mrs. Barlow for a moment. When he leaned
into the dining room again to say a last good-bye, Helen
had disappeared up the stairs, and her father was sitting
bolt upright in his chair, almost supporting himself on
his hands, glaring after her, his face convulsed as if at
some tremendous physical effort, and his mouth working.

' 'Night, George,' Mr. Dow said. The paralytic jumped
and jerked around, at the same time letting himself go so
that he slid down in the chair. The chairback bent his
head forward, pressing his chin into his chest.

'Be seein' you, Mr. Dow,' he said, and his cheeks
twitched.

Stephen Dow took hold of the doorknob. On the win-
dowsill beside the door was a row of green tomatoes. He
touched one with his fingers. It was almost rock-hard.

'Good night,' he said softly, and let himself out.

It was quite dark when the last amplified raspings of
the turntable ground into silence. Glimmers of light shook
along the water to show the abrupt side of a boat, the
roundness of a canoe, and dark shapes began to move off
over the lake. Someone switched on the floodlights on
the Weld dock, showing people clambering down from
the bleachers, moving in toward the path, walking among
the balloony shapes of the pruned cedars in the new lake-
side park. Ruth held the flashlight on the bow while Abe
pulled on the braided clothesline anchor rope. The line
swayed and stretched oblique and white in the green
water, and the boat moved under them, going to meet the
anchor, until the line straightened and hung heavy and
the big angular rock rose out of the depths and was pulled
dripping inboard.

'Well,' Abe said, scrambling onto the rowing thwart.
'How was it? Pretty good?'

'It was all right. It was fine.'

They rowed away, leaving the lighted boathouses like Venetian houses at the end of a canal, and Abe said, 'Try the light up ahead sometimes. There's a big rock here that comes out at low water.'

She blinked the flash three times, letting it finger the wind-roughed surface. 'There it is, off to the left, closer to shore. You're all right.'

Abe rowed steadily, putting muscle behind the oars, but by the time they cleared the point and felt the fresh breeze from the open lake the lighter canoes and kayaks and sailboats were all gone in the dark. There was not a star showing; only in the west a little watery light was left on the sky from the sunset. In the boat it was difficult to see from one thwart to the next.

'Don't work so hard, Abe,' Ruth said. 'What's the hurry?'

'I thought maybe you are cold.'

'I'm all right.'

'You want to take a row, maybe?'

'All right.'

'Now you are talking,' he said. 'Now you are making sense.' He swung away from the white-bouldered, dark-rooted island that Ruth was following with her flashlight, and turned out into midlake. In the dense moving darkness the breeze freshened; there was a chop under the bow. In the stern Ruth was silent, her flashlight dark. Hesitantly Abe reached for her with his voice.

'This is like that first night, eh? That was a black one too.'

'It's windier tonight,' she said. 'That night it was perfectly still.'

'Yes,' he said. 'I guess it is windier.'

Some time later, drifting with trailing oars, they swung around slowly before the wind and saw down the lake the sparse lights of the village appearing and disappearing through the wind-moved shore trees. Around the whole periphery of shore were cottage lights like low stars. The sky was lighter than the shore, but not light enough now, even in the west, to pick up a glimmer from the water or show an object in the boat more than a few feet away.

'I wish there was some way, Ruth,' Abe said.

He waited for an answer, but she said nothing. In the almost-absolute dark, between dark water and dark sky, between village lights and cottage lights, they swung as if suspended, and he had a curious dizzying moment of upside-downness.

'If we had not built the house,' he said awkwardly. 'I am the one to blame for that. I thought it would be better than a wedding trip. That was a bad mistake.'

'Don't feel bad about it,' she said. 'You're not to blame for anything. I'm sorry I said anything. It'll be all right.'

'But you don't feel at home,' he said. 'You feel lonesome and shut out.'

'Maybe we can do something about the radio, put on an aerial or something. The Philharmonic broadcasts will be starting, and there's the opera on Saturday.'

'Say, that's an idea,' Abe said. 'I will get Anson, he is an electrical fellow. He will put us up an aerial that will shut out that Pratt sermon-static.'

'Sure,' she said, comforting him. 'That's all it needs, probably.'

'And there is this business of records. When we get home we will look in the Sears Roebuck catalog and see what such a phonograph, a little one, will cost.'

'Sure,' her disembodied voice said.

They drifted on little rocking waves before the wind toward the distant village. The wind was fresh, with just an edge of chill in it, but it was not really cold.

Over an hour later they were still drifting. Ruth hadn't

said anything for a long time, but Abe had a feeling that
she liked this, that it would be a mistake to say anything
or try to plan anything or cheer her up. Sometimes she
got frightened of the quiet and the dark, but this was a
good healing quiet, and there was no fear in this dark.

The windows of the village were folded into the blackness by now, and there was no sign of light or life along
the impenetrable wall of black where the dock should
be. Once, a few minutes back, he had thought he heard
the rattle of oars, but now he heard nothing except the
chuckle of water under the drifting boat and the distant
sound, so indistinct and fitful that it might have been
imaginary like the rowing noises, of wind in the shore
trees.

He was about to lean forward and ask Ruth for the
flashlight so that he could locate the dock when the other
sound came: the hard, near clatter of loose oars, the little
fluty sound as if someone had sucked in his breath suddenly, and the wallowing splash.

It was very near, perfectly distinct and quite loud, and
it shocked Abe so that he fell on his knees in the boat,
groping frantically. 'The light!' he said. 'Give me the
flashlight!'

The smooth barrel touched his wrist and fell. He
grabbed it up, fought the switch button for a moment,
snapped it on backwards so that the hot light blazed in
his own eyes, reversed it and shot the beam out over the
lake. In his momentary dazzlement he could see at first
only the wrinkled water. Then the swinging light
brought out, staring white, the shape of a rowboat fifty
feet away. One oar hung in the rowlock by its worn
leather collar. There was no one in the boat.

Abe shouted. The noise left his lips and winged away
like a rock thrown to arouse the village. Ruth shouted
too, and he had a momentary glimpse of her scared face

as he slid into the rowing thwart. While he rowed, she flashed the light on the empty boat, and they both watched for any sign of life near it. There was none. Abe shouted again, and as they swung up beside the empty boat he leaped up, rocking their own boat wildly, and let the anchor rock down. The rope hissed through his hands and then went slack with ten feet to spare. 'Hang onto this, tie it up!' he said to Ruth, and struggled out of his coat.

Ruth was crying, 'Abe, what are you going to do? Abe, you can't swim very well. Don't jump in, Abe, please!'

'Tie up that other boat too,' he said. 'And keep yelling.' He crawled up in the bow and let himself over the side. The water grabbed his legs with chilling cold, stopping his breath and plastering his pants to his legs. 'Turn the light straight down in the water,' he said to Ruth. 'Keep it there. I will be all right. I can hang onto the anchor rope if I get tired.' He put his face in the water, took it out to take a deep breath, and dove under, kicking and swimming and pulling his way down, his eyes glaring around into the murky darkness for a sign of something, anything, and the pressure closing in around him terrifyingly as he fought his way down.

Andy was in bed when he heard the furious iron clangor of the firebell. He swung his feet out of bed and went to the window, gritting his teeth at the instant swelling pain that throbbed up from his injured hand. Holding the hand close against his chest, he stared out into the street.

Down in front of the firehouse old man Pratt was standing with only trousers on over his long underwear. The lights of a car backing to swing into the street picked him out sharply and then left him. The fire truck rolled out of the firehouse, bumped into the street with Donald

Swain running to grab the endgate and Herbert Pratt picking it up from the other side on the run, and roared into the square. Because of the intervening houses Andy couldn't see where it went, but he heard it slow as if turning, and then roar again. Norma Pratt ran down the street and grabbed the rope of the now-silent firebell and yanked at it. In the high single light at the peak of the firehouse gable Andy saw the shadowy bell swing in its iron frame, and heard the wild iron outcry begin again. Harold Swett ran down the outside stairway and disappeared down the street at a hard run. Downstairs the door slammed, and Andy knew that Mr. Richie was on his way. The lights flashed up on the inn's porches.

Clumsily, in one-handed haste, hating the pain and the helplessness of his crippling, Andy got into pants and socks and shoes. He had never realized until the accident how many things a man did left-handed — like button his pants, for instance. Right-handed, the buttons were backwards, the buttonholes elusive, everything so clumsy and slow that he broke into a sweat. He hurt himself again getting a sweater over his right arm and buttoned down across his sling, and he was still fumbling awkwardly at the last sweater buttons as he went downstairs and outside.

He could not run without starting the pounding pain, and so he was alone when he reached the street. From over toward the dock he heard the noise of shouting, and saw a glow on the low clouds. As he turned into the dock road he saw many headlights, and figures black against them, and the running shapes of men, women, and children.

But he saw no fire. He walked along the rutted road holding himself back from running. The firebell stopped, and in a few minutes Norma Pratt's cocker spaniel pounded by him. He could see that the crowd was concentrated on the dock, and out on the lake were moving lights. It was no fire, then, but an accident or a drowning.

Cars were backing and jockeying at the end of the dock as Donald Swain maneuvered them into a half circle so that their headlights would focus on the boats that moved like light-trapped insects a hundred and fifty yards out in the water. In the center of the semicircle of lights was the firetruck, its spotlight glaring out over the heads of the crowd.

The firetruck's motor was talking quietly to itself. Andy moved up close to where Donald straddled the hood, shouting directions. The crowd shifted and moved restlessly. There was shouting from out at the boats, and a dozen people shushed the crowd, but when the feet and voices were still the shouting had died. Donald stood on the hood holding onto the top of the cab and peering out into the web of lightbeams. On the other side Allan Richie cocked his sharp face upward. 'Who was it?' he said. 'Somebody drown? Who?'

Donald continued to stare out over the lake. 'I don't know, Allan.'

'Who started all this fire alarm?'

'I did. We were over at Martin's, and just as we were startin' home we heard yellin' and screamin' down here. Martin and John La Pere run down, and I grabbed the bell rope.'

'What're they doin' out there?'

'I don't know,' Donald said. 'They took grapnels.'

'How do they know where to drag?'

'I don't know.'

'Seems like a funny time of night for a boatride,' Allan said. 'Suppose it was some camper kids spoonin'?'

'If I knew I could tell you,' Donald said. 'There was two boats out there.'

'Two!' Allan said. He disappeared into the jam on the

dock again, and Donald shouted at the crowd, 'Keep off to the side. Stay back so the headlights can shine on 'em.'

Four boys, all summer folks, pounded up the road and onto the hollow planks. 'What's happened?' they said. They pushed to the edge of the watching crowd, standing on tiptoe and asking questions of everybody around them.

'Let's get a boat and go out there,' one said.

'Eaton's,' said another. 'It was still out this afternoon.'

'You better stay out of their road,' Donald said. 'They'll holler if they need more boats.'

The four looked blankly up for a moment. Then one broke, and in a moment they were all off up the shore.

A ring of canoes and skiffs was already beginning to form around the two white rowboats and the two green ones that moved misty and light-netted just beyond clear visibility. Somebody shouted, and while the dock buzzed a rowboat came in from the outer ring and moved up close to one of the green boats. Andy looked up. 'Can you see what they're doing?'

'Looks like they're puttin' somebody in the boat,' Donald said. 'Dang if it doesn't.' He reached down a hand, and Andy took it and climbed the fender to the hood. The ring of boats did not appear to move; their flashlights and lanterns were like the eyes of watching foxes. Then a boat pulled from the central cluster, fuzzy and melting in the almost-dissipated light, and the word started around, 'They're bringin' somebody in! They must have got him, whoever it was. They're comin' in with him!'

'They're still grappling,' somebody else said. 'Look, they're starting back and forth again. They can't have found anybody.'

'Or else there was more than one,' the crowd voice said. 'There was two boats.'

'Get blankets ready!' some woman said. But the crowd

voice said, 'They'd be dead, it's been thirty-forty minutes since the alarm first went out.'

'Well, get blankets anyway,' the woman voice said triumphantly. 'Whoever's in that boat is all huddled up!'

As the boat came down the lightpath and individual figures could be easily picked out, Donald said, 'That's Raoul La Pere rowin'. Can't see who he's got with him.'

'One's a woman,' Andy said. He could see the light dress and the bare arms. The word went around the crowd. 'One's a woman, no coat on. Must have been neckers. Can you see who? Who's the other one?'

Two women came running with robes from automobiles. They stood ready at the dock as Raoul La Pere angled in. Flashlights jumped on the occupants of the boat. One was a woman, sure enough. The other was all huddled up in the stern with a coat around him, and as a more powerful spot touched his hair they could see it was tangled and wet. 'It's somebody they got out, all right. He's alive, too. Get those blankets ready, he'll be froze stiff . . .'

'By golly,' Andy said to Donald, 'it's the Kaplans.'

They stood up in the boat, wobbling, and a dozen hands reached down to help them onto the dock. In the shifting light of the torches Abe's face was blue. His hair was pasted to his big domed head, and his eyes glared and his teeth chattered. Ruth clung to his arm, and the voices beat at them, 'What happened, Abe? Anybody else out there? Was it you that yelled? What are they still doing out there?'

The women threw blankets over Abe's whole head and shoulders, leading him up the dock. Ruth was trying to answer questions and at the same time get Abe loose. 'He didn't fall in, it was somebody else. We were coming in and heard a big splash. Abe tried to rescue them, but he can't swim very well . . . was hanging onto the anchor

rope, we let that down right by the boat, so we wouldn't
drift and lose the place . . . '

Standing on the hood clinging with his good hand to
the top of the cab, watching the seethe of heads and
bodies below him, straining his eyes out into the diffused
light-beams, Andy had a sense of unreality so strong that
for a moment he was positive this whole clamor of bells
and stabs of ineffective glaring light and weave of crowd-
figures and mutter of the crowd-voice was a confused
dream, and the people who milled below him were the
heterogeneous scourings of a consciousness unwilling to
woo sleep. They stood on the dock in ignorance, asking
questions of people as ignorant as themselves, and somebody was drowned but no one knew who, or even, really
definitely, *if*. Out on the water other men dragged the
lake bottom for something they were afraid to find. Someone was dead, but who? said the voice which spoke over
and through this dream. Someone had left in the darkness and was not yet missed, but only searched for.

The crowd was shifting, buzzing. The whole group
moved up and down, floating and dreamlike, when the
weight shifted on the buoyed dock. Andy looked down
over them and saw the blonde woman shouldering her
way through the press. Her open shirt collar looked
dazzlingly white between her brown throat and the blue
blazer she wore. She came close to the fender, looking
restlessly around. Her eyes noted Andy above her, and
dismissed him. She stood on tiptoe, hunting for someone
in the crowd, impatient and arrogant, a frown between
her eyes. Andy watched her.

The two remaining fingers of his left hand, poking
through the bulky mass of bandage, were going numb
in the night air, and with his eyes on Flo Barnes he
massaged them back to life with his right.

Then he saw Flo's head twist around, and he realized

that the talk, the hum, the scuffling, the confusion of
sound and movement, had stopped. He could distinctly
hear the voices of the men out in the boats. It was as
quiet as if they were all grouped around Weld's dock
waiting for a concert to begin. Andy glanced back, over
toward where the women were helping Abe Kaplan into
a car. Everyone was looking back that way; even the
efficient figure of Florence Pugh, glorified in the past few
days by more first-aid work than had been necessary in
years before, stopped half-bent at the waist after closing
the door on Abe, and stared incredulously at the end of
the dock, where the parked cars made a semicircle of
fierce footlights round a patch of trampled and almost
bare ground.

George Barlow, the paralytic, stood there. He held a
blanket bathrobe clenched shut against his chest, and his
clean-shaven face was like a dead man's. As they
watched, he took three tottering steps forward, leaning
and dragging his slippered feet.

'Where is she?' he said. His voice was hoarse, hardly
more than a croak. In the silence that followed his words
Andy heard the wind swoop and sigh in the trees further
up the shore.

'She's done it!' the croaking voice said. 'I knew she'd
do it. I knew the minute I saw her face tonight!'

There was a sound like a hiccough from below. The
boy looked down. Flo Barnes had one fist against her
mouth. It looked as if she were biting the knuckles. In
the light raveling off from the hot beam of the spot he
saw the sweat come up on her forehead as if she had been
spattered with water.

14

Toonerville Down

NINE O'CLOCK on a September morning. The kind of day,
Laura Bentham was thinking, when you never could tell
what it would do. If you went out without a wrap of some
kind, it would be sure to rain, and if you got all done up
in a raincoat and rubbers it would blow off clear and be
sunshiny as you please.

She got into her raincoat in order to tempt the sun,
picked up the baskets by their heavy twisted handles and
leaning against the weight went down the stairs and
through the back room and into the store.

There was no one around except her husband, showing
work gloves to Howard Pembrook. 'You goin' out some-
wheres?' Martin asked over Pembrook's shoulder.

She lifted the baskets, pointing up in the direction of
the church.

Martin nodded, and she went out. As she stepped
down from the sidewalk the sun swam out of a cloud and
sent her long shadow back almost to the creamery. A tall
thin woman on an errand, the shadow followed her across
the square past the corner of the inn, carrying its elon-
gated baskets on its arms. It went up the street with the
real woman walking in its tracks. When the real woman
turned up the church drive the shadow woman turned
too, and together they climbed the hill and walked past
manse and church. But when Mrs. Bentham started in
the driveway of the Barlow place the cloud had moved
across the sun again and she went the last fifty feet alone.

225

Mrs. Barlow let her in. She looked tired around the eyes,
and her mouth drooped, but she was neat and tidy even
at this time in the morning, and she looked moderately
cheerful, considering. She had always been a tidy woman,
almost nasty-neat about herself and her house. When
she did up a wash it looked as fresh and lovely in its
basket as if it had been done up by a laundry in the city.
But whatever Alice did, she thought as she put the heavy
baskets down and opened the hot raincoat, you'd have a
hard time finding anything to say bad about her. She was
a good housewife and a good neighbor and one of the
strongest church women in the village.

From force of habit she turned her head, looking into
the dining room, and her hurrying mind stopped short,
shocked. George Barlow sat in his usual place in the wide
chair, but there was nothing restful or easy about the way
he sat. His face was gaunt, so gaunt he seemed to have
lost twenty pounds in the past week, and his eyes glared
out of dark holes. His mouth twisted meanly, and he
pounded on the chair arm, looking through Laura Bentham as if she had been made of cellophane.

'Alice!' his wire-edged voice said. '*Alice!*'

Alice Barlow stepped into the dining-room and closed
the door behind her. Mrs. Bentham stayed stock-still and
listened, but all she could hear was the mumble of voices
and the sound of a shade being pulled down. Then Mrs.
Barlow came out again, pulling the door shut so quickly
that Mrs. Bentham couldn't get a peep inside.

'He's so upset,' Mrs. Barlow said. 'He can't bear to see
anybody, or be seen. If there's a step on the porch he's
shouting straight off to have the door closed.'

'He takes it hard,' Mrs. Bentham said with sympathy.
''Twon't be easy for him to get over, or you either.'

'He's always took things hard,' Mrs. Barlow said, and
wiped a tear away from each eye with her knuckle. She

reached out and got a kitchen chair and moved it out from the table, saying, 'Here, set down, take off your coat. I declare, I forget everything.'

'Don't you worry about me a mite,' Mrs. Bentham said.

The fat woman cried quietly, without sobbing and apparently without effort, her hands in her lap. 'He's always took things hard,' she said. 'Seems if sometimes he just couldn't *bear* to have things happen the way they happened. Time and again I've seen him set near crazy at some little thing.'

Mrs. Bentham made a sound of sympathy.

'Seems if he just never could *accept* things like he ought,' Mrs. Barlow said.

'It's hard,' Mrs. Bentham said. 'It's terrible hard.'

In the silence that fell upon them Mrs. Bentham was acutely aware of the closed door to the dining room and the man who sat on the other side glaring in unrelieved, palsied terror at the blank wall. In Mrs. Barlow's clean, well-kept, decent house where the familiar frail ghost of the daughter lingered, and where the unquiet living ghost of George Barlow crouched behind a wall of immobility and silence, she could think of nothing to say. She ached to talk to Alice Barlow about her husband's walking, that night. To wonder aloud with her if he'd had a premonition, or if Helen might have said something to him that frightened him. To ask if he'd shown any signs since of being able to walk, or if all was as it had been. But she knew she would not discuss these things in this house.

'Well, we bear up somehow,' Mrs. Barlow's flat voice said at last. 'I don't know why the Lord should have visited us, or why she should be taken just when she was goin' to start teachin' and take her proper place in the village. But it don't do to kick against things the way George does. What the Lord sends, we've got to make up our minds to bear.'

'Isn't that the truth?' the visitor said. 'There's no way a person can set themselves up to unravel God's reasons. We'll know them on the other side, but not here.'

'Helen was like George,' the fat woman said. 'She couldn't stand things as they were, either. Seems if she was always readin' books that set her further off. She just couldn't accept things, always wantin' somethin' else.'

The storekeeper's wife turned her plain gold wedding ring around her finger, wondering whether the Barlows knew what the village was saying — that the girl must have jumped. Abe Kaplan had neither seen nor heard signs of any struggle after the splash. And yet what on earth would lead a girl like Helen . . .

She sighed and stood up, lifting the basket up onto the drainboard of the sink. 'I brought you and George a sick-basket,' she said. 'Seems if the least the womenfolks could do was put you up a mite of somethin' to make things easier.'

'Now that's nice as it can be,' Mrs. Barlow said. She lifted the towel and looked in. 'Some of Florence Pugh's strawberry preserve,' she said, and lifted, peering further. 'Looks like one of Sue Brown's cakes, ain't it?'

She let the towel fall again, her eyes full of weak tears, and said once more, 'This is nice as it can be. It's a pity George's appetite's no better.' Then, 'But you don't have to go,' she said. 'Just set and I'll make up a cup of coffee.'

'I wish I could,' Mrs. Bentham said. 'But I've got to take another basket to Mrs. Kaplan. You know he's still in the hospital over to Stafford. She takes the bus over every morning, and I'd miss her if I stopped.'

'I ought to go see her,' Mrs. Barlow said. 'Even if he is an unbeliever, as Mr. Tait says, he did try hard to do something that night. I ought to tell her how we're obliged.'

'I'll tell her,' Mrs. Bentham said. 'I'm sure she'd like to know.'

'I'd appreciate it,' Mrs. Barlow said. 'I'm sure she must be all right when you get to know her. Helen thought she was nice.'

'There's good in everybody, if you look,' Mrs. Bentham said.

She opened the door and went out onto the porch. In the few minutes she had been inside the sky had almost wholly cleared, and only tail-ends of cloud were scudding eastward before a brisk wind. The maple in front of the house bowed its top branches where the wind got at it over the roof.

'Clearin' weather,' Mrs. Bentham said. She smiled at Alice Barlow, a quick, encouraging smile. 'I hope George is better. I hope you're both better.'

'We bear it however we can,' Mrs. Barlow said. 'There are things you think you couldn't bear, but when they come you bear them somehow. There ain't a thing you can do by resistin'.'

'Alice!' the edged invalid voice was calling from the dining room. 'Alice! Is she gone?'

Ten o'clock on a September morning. At this hour the creamery gave to the village an almost-urban noisiness and bustle. Coming down past the post office carrying the heavy basket that Mrs. Bentham had given her, Ruth turned an appreciative ear to the rattle and clang and the busy motor sound, and an appreciative eye on the truck and the bending overalled figure of Parley Pugh unloading milk cans. It was like coming down some street in New York and seeing men working at the open wings of sidewalk elevators, with vans backed angling in to the curb and traffic snarling up behind, while people streamed past on their way to work.

Well, not quite like New York. But she watched Parley Pugh put the cans, each with its red number, onto the

belt that carried them through the creamery wall into
the steam washer. Through the high windows she could
see where the track turned, and where the cans tipped
down and the arm came up and knocked their caps off.
Beyond where she could see, she knew there was another
stretch of open belt where the cans came out dripping
and steaming, and where another little Rube Goldberg
arm slapped their hats back on. Then they went stiffly
out along the belt in single file like lead soldiers duly
slain and carried off the field. The whole business of
washing milk cans that came at this hour was like a slap-
stick comedy routine. She would have gone across the
street to watch it except that the strong creamy buttery
smell of the place, a smell that seemed to congeal like
little globules of fat on the hosed-down concrete, always
made her a little sick. Besides, it was almost bus time.

Like a tempted and reluctant child she went past,
stooping to the heavy basket. She noticed that the overcast morning was giving way to bright sun, and that the
streaked and threatening clouds she had risen to had all
blown away eastward. Now round white cumuli lay
puffily around the horizon as if the whole ball of the
world had been packed like an Easter egg in clean cotton. The dome overhead was scoured clear.

The bus came, and she found a seat by the window,
watching the steaming roadside. At one farm a group of
men were threshing oats, and she saw them briefly like
a painting in strong primary colors, red of threshing engine and blue of overalls and gold of grain, and above all
the golden dust rising from the blower. She found herself pleased to recognize an ensilage machine and to know
what the farmer was doing with it. When she got off before the hotel in Stafford and started up the hill with
her basket she whistled softly and breathily, the whistle
getting jerky as the hill got steep, but lasting until she

stood on the lawn before the hospital. Quite casually it
occurred to her that she felt good. There wasn't any
dragged-out feeling, even after a stiff climb. It was a nice
day, too. She changed the basket to the other hand and
went in.

The hospital was an old white frame house made over.
Downstairs there was a waiting room, a nurse's room, a
kitchen, and one private bedroom, all more or less visible
from the hall. Upstairs were the operating room and two
wards, one for men, one for women. Something was going on in the operating room. The door into the hall was
shut, and the ether-smell was strong.

She turned up the linoleum hall and looked into the
men's ward. Abe, in the bed nearest the window, was
alone in the room. He was propped up a little, looking
out the window, and his face in profile looked white and
thin. She tiptoed in.

'Hello!' she said, at the side of his bed. 'Have they
turned this into a private room for you?'

He jumped, and his head turned, and it did her good
to see how life and warmth flooded into his face. 'Ah,
Ruth!' he said. 'I was just lying here expecting you.'

'Well, here I am. How do you feel?'

'Oh, feel! I feel fine. This business here now, this since
the oxygen tent, this is pie. Pneumonia is a cinch once
it is over. Now it is just lying around getting fattened
up.'

She took off her hat and jacket and laid them on the
next empty bed and bent down and kissed him. 'Where
is everybody? Have they all got well?'

'That farmer, Paul Root, has gone home on a crutch.
The other one, Will Page, is in the operating room now.
You can smell the ether.'

'Are they going to put him back in here with you?'

'I suppose so, sure.'

'I hope not. He struck me as an old crab.'

Abe laughed and shifted in the bed, making room. 'Come here, sit down where I can get at you.' He pulled her down beside him and held her hand, laughing at something he was thinking of.

'Maybe if you had a rupture you would be a crab too. But listen, there was a joke this morning. Will was mad, he has been here two days waiting for the surgeon to get up from Concord, and he was crabbing at the nurse when the doctor looked around the edge of the door. You know this Will Page is a hairy man, oh, he's hairy! All over him, even on his shoulders and back, he has this black hair. So the doctor interrupts him when he is crabbing and says, "Well, Will, I was aiming to keep you here till your pelt got prime, but if you keep squawking I guess we'll have to shave you off and get you operated on." They have got him in there now.'

He laughed very hard and wiped his eyes. Ruth laughed too, though she didn't think it was very funny. She supposed that when you lay around in a hospital bed for a few days anything in the least funny sounded like Olson and Johnson.

The nurse came in, a chunky woman with braids around her head. She smiled at Ruth, and said to Abe, 'Well, Abie, anything you're needing?'

'I am needing nothing, Emmy,' Abe said. 'Say, how are they coming on Will?'

'They're just about sewing the sponges up in him,' the nurse said. 'I've got to get his bed ready.' She yanked off the sheets and tucked a wide rubber sheet underneath, made the bed again, folded the covers well back, got out a couple of white enamel pans from the bed-table cupboard, and pulled the curtains between the beds. When she went out, rubbersoled and quick on her feet, Ruth said, 'It looks as if you had a playmate, all this Abie and Emmy stuff.'

Waving his hand as if brushing something away, his eyes peering up at her, Abe said, 'That makes you jealous, eh? Well, I'll tell you. In this hospital everybody is by his first name. There are no misters around here.'

He lay smiling, moving his thumb on the back of her hand. 'When you get sick you are like a member of a club,' he said. He looked out the window at the framed view of a steep unmown field of browning grass and tall clumps of late goldenrod, the whole field liquid with movement under the urging of the wind. 'It looks like good weather,' Abe said. 'Such a day as is good for walks. Is it as good as it looks?'

'It's a nice day,' she said. 'But you haven't asked me what I brought you.'

'Well, what did you bring me?'

'It isn't me, really. Look.'

She lifted the heavy basket and uncovered it for him to see. 'Everything you can imagine,' she said. 'I left some of the jars of things at home, because they were heavy and you couldn't have used them, but here's a cake, and a whole swarm of doughnuts, and jam, and a loaf of fresh bread. Just look.'

'I am looking,' Abe said. 'Where does all this come from, tell me that?'

'Mrs. Bentham brought it up, but it's from all the women in town. They make up a basket like this when someone gets sick, apparently. Everybody puts something in and sends it on, like a chain letter.'

'So this time they let you in,' Abe said.

Her eyes jumped down to meet his warm brown ones. 'Oh, it wasn't me. It was you. You're the sick one.'

'For me, eh? How should I use cake and doughnuts in a hospital?'

Reaching down to straighten his wild hair, she said, 'Well, I don't care who they meant it for. It was nice of them.'

'Sure,' Abe said, still rubbing her hand. 'There are some good people in the village, high-grade people.'

'It could be that it's only a kind of routine when somebody's sick,' she said, thinking aloud. 'I'm not assuming because they send us this basket that we're being taken into the bosom of every family in the place.'

'No,' he said. 'That would be a pretty foolish thing to assume. But it is possible to live here, eh?'

'Of course,' she said. 'I'm over all that.'

'We are very funny,' Abe said after a pause. 'Two Jews who are not really Jews, we live here all alone, as you might say, just as if we were in a play and were supposed to represent the homelessness of the children of Israel, eh? All around us are these strangers, and wherever we go we are separate, we do not get invited in like other people. This is a funny thing for us to come to, me born in Russia and you born in Hungary, and both of us orphans. We should set up a wailing wall, eh?'

'I guess we'll get along,' Ruth said.

Bright noon on a September day. Fat white clouds bumping across the sky before a wind that blew clean off the timber and stone of the main range. An effervescence in the air, no dust, no dampness, the sort of air that makes colts throw up heads and tails and run through pastures, the very bite and wine of life that searched the lungs and cleared the head.

At the same time, under and through and surrounded by this windy sparkle that invited all sorts of wild outbursts, there were all the prosaic activities of nearly-noon: a remote metallic hammering where Harold Swett worked on a truck, the rattle of chains and the ground-shaking rumble of logs rolling down at the mill, the knock of Norma Pratt's dust mop against the porch rail, the slam of Bentham's screen, the sad slow whistling of old Allan

Youngberg puttering in Pratt's shed. Steep light and sound of chores, the smell and taste and feel of everyday under the sky which said that no day was everyday, that each day held impossibly lovely ˙promises, that the horizons could be leaped like crumbling fences, and that beyond the horizons the wonderful was as commonplace as the common was here.

Andy came out into it, into the mixed excitement and monotony of noonday, and heard the sounds and smelled the smells of all his life, and smelled the quickening wind. He had said his good-byes. He had shaken Allan Richie's hand, he had slapped the horses for the last time on their dusty haunches. All last evening he had spent in Donald Swain's kitchen, with doughnuts and pickles and maple syrup poured boiling on cracked ice, as in sugaring time. When Donald and Mrs. Swain went to bed, he and Nancy had sat a long time over their good-byes.

He stood in the bright vertical light with his suitcase in his hand, looking over the roof of the inn to the school-house and thinking of Nancy in class there, just about ready now to go out with the Home Economics class and start the hot lunch for the primary pupils. He remembered her tears falling on the back of his hand as they sat in the kitchen with her head against his chest, and in his suitcase was the decorated leather book-cover she had given him for a keepsake.

But the wind that blew over Sunday Mountain blew his mind clean away, blew it like a paper loose in the street, scaled it far ahead in one long planing flight, and let it down, and skidded it, and lifted it again; and when he saw Henry Ball's black Ford roll into the square and park before the post office he went down the street into the heart of the village on legs that seemed stilt-long, carrying his suitcase in his right hand and holding his left, out of the sling now but still mummied in bandages, with his thumb hooked carefully in his belt. In the middle of the road a bird had been knocked down by a car and flattened into the gravel. The wind blew its stiff wing upright and flapped it, let it down and blew it up again, as if trying to revive even the dead.

Andy put his face in the window of Henry Ball's car. 'Still got room for me?'

'Seems if I ought to,' Henry said. 'Wait till I see Gaylord a minute.'

He tucked some papers into the glove compartment and went into the post office. Andy slid into the car and lifted his suitcase on end into the seat beside him. Now he was charioted, now he was wheeled. Yet it was as if something in him held its breath, waiting for a door to open somewhere, a voice to call out, a figure to come running, shouting, 'Wait a minute! You can't go! You'll have to come back!' Something, he felt, waited to catch him up; he was starting with a loose rope around his feet that would trip him as soon as he moved. It couldn't be possible that this was the morning, that on this day in this sun and wind he would jump this horizon and be loose in the half-terrifying freedom of another world.

But Henry Ball came out, started the car, put it in reverse and backed it up, shifted and rolled out around the corner of the square, and no one called out, no door opened, no rope snapped tight around his ankles. The wheels rolled on down past the mill, past the stacked lumber and the long piles of slabwood and the heap of sawdust where old Johnny Miner was shoveling a cart full for his ice-house. The wheels rolled, and the road bent down around the lake past the piped spring and across Broken-Musket Brook, and still no one called, no messenger came flying after.

Henry Ball drove fast, as he always did. When they crossed the Corners bridge and turned into the long single street he let the Ford roll, and it rolled to a stop just short of the tracks, next to the powdered egg plant. Andy opened the door and slid out, pulling his suitcase after.

'Well, kid,' Henry said. 'You're on your way.'

'Guess so.' The boy shook his head and grinned. The same wind that had blown through Westwick Village blew through the Corners, and his mind was up aloft, tugging like a kite.

'Guess we'll see you, come vacation time.'

'Don't see why not,' Andy said. 'Thanks for the ride, Henry.'

Ball lifted his hand from the wheel. 'Take it easy, boy.'

He pulled away, and Andy crossed the tracks and walked up the platform by the freight scales. There he went carefully through his pockets, checking the ticket, the wallet, the address book and telephone numbers for when he got to Dryden. He wondered a little anxiously if he should have brought his high-school diploma. But Mr. Dow would have said something, if it was necessary to get him in. For an instant that impressive pile of monumental granite that was his first imaginative vision of Dryden showed through its arch of elms; but he corrected the picture immediately into the ivied brick with white cornices and window frames that the booklet showed. He took the booklet from his pocket and sat on his suitcase studying it for the twentieth time, memorizing the map of the campus. It would be a fine thing to go down there like a hick and get lost.

The train whistled for the crossing down the valley, and Andy stood up, shoving the booklet back into his pocket. He felt carefully of his bandaged hand, the emptiness where his fingers had been, the deep bone-ache and the strange futile pulling of nerves and muscles when he flexed the tendons that had once controlled the fingers. If he trusted the sensations of his left hand, the fingers were still there, but his right felt only the soft bandage and the acutely narrow palm.

The wind blew his hair, and he let go his crippled hand to scoop the forelock out of his eyes just as the train, looking surprised as if not able to explain how it had got there, came around the bend with its nose to the rails like a beagle with his nose to a rabbit track. The Toonerville had always had that hound look; it seemed to smell its way rather than run on any surveyed route.

The engine pulled past him and lay down and panted quietly. Mr. Quillen, the station agent, came out and passed some papers up to the engineer in the cab. Two men in the mail half of the combination car eased down two cartons to Mr. Quillen, and accepted the handful of letters he passed up. A woman with a big black purse under one arm and a child in the other came hurrying and climbed up onto the back platform and into the passenger half of the car. The one o'clock whistle at the Corners mill let loose with a long hoarse toot, and the engineer answered it with two perky toots on his own whistle. Like the toy train in the children's story, like a Little Engine That Could, the engine puffed and dug in and started its three cars. Andy shoved his suitcase onto the platform and swung aboard. At a pace that a jog-trotting boy could have kept up with, the train snuffed its way out past the potato warehouse siding and out along the hill to the rocky corner that gave the town its name. Then it seemed to smell something off in the woods, and with a suddenness that lurched Andy off balance it ducked into the untrodden timber.

Looking back from the platform Andy saw the right of way narrow to a mere slit as the woods converged. The fences on either side had been swarmed under and obliterated by the riotous growth of choke-cherry, hazel, elm, maple, squaw maple, spruce, hemlock, cedar, hackmatack, fir, white pine, birch, beech, and butternut. Trees reached in and fingered the sides of the train as it followed a blind contour along the hillside.

Nothing was visible backward except the narrow green slot lined by the parallel rails as in a perspective exercise. The village, the Corners, the sounds of noon, even the gusty scented wind, were all gone. The boy craned to look forward up along the cars. The swaying gray-green cars filled the slot almost to the trees, and on the curves he saw the engine, bowling along now at thirty miles an hour, running like a hound on a hot trail.

He let his eyes drop to the trackside. They were running through an incredible blackberry patch, a stretch of many rods overgrown with vines, and every vine drooping to the ground with red and black berries. The instant longing for the cool familiar taste, the juicy soft bulbs and the harder cores against the roof of the mouth, filled him with a nostalgia that was almost panic. The taste of blackberries had always been associated with woodcutting, with the fall woods and the turning maples and the long days on a crosscut. The taste of wedge-shaped beechnuts was in those days too, and the color of wintergreen berries bright among the litter and the frosted ferns.

The patch was gone before he could feel half the things that were crowding his mind. He tried to look ahead, but could see nothing beyond the nearest car. The train rocked and bounced along the rough tracks on a blind impetuous course.

There was no point in looking backward, either. The trees closed softly around the backward tracks like snow over footprints. Ahead was Woodsville, and the Boston and Maine, no toy train but a mainliner that poured passengers and freight into Boston. Ahead, around the curving, opening aisles, was a world so much bigger that he could not visualize it except in terms of maps. At Wells River they would run out of yellow New Hampshire and into green Vermont, and away down along the Connecticut River they would run out of green Vermont into red Massachusetts. The world went on, incomprehensibly huge, and there were a thousand frontiers to be crossed. He went willingly, even eagerly, but he went with the spectral taste of ripe blackberries on his lips and with his eyes already homesick for the autumn woods and the mown meadows and the tarnished silver farms, for the limited responsibilities and the worn-out obligations and the narrow security that it would be fatal to accept.

THE END